INNOVATION'S MUSE

USA TODAY BESTSELLING AUTHOR

ALLYSON LINDT

For my eternal dragon

CHAPTER ONE

Lexi thought she knew ambivalence. The events that had occurred in the labyrinth, in the underworld, and with Cerberus had turned her emotions into chopped salad.

And none of that compared to what raged inside when Actaeon stepped between her and the woman who'd erased her mother from existence.

A light breeze whipped around them, pushing Lexi's hair in her face and kicking up the sand of the beach around them.

Actaeon's face was twisted in an expression that matched Lexi's inner turmoil, but he'd stopped her from lunging at Cassandra.

Not that Lexi would have. Probably not.

"You would have." Cerberus spoke in her head.

She needed to practice which thoughts he heard and which she kept to herself. *"Busted."*

"What are you doing here?" Actaeon asked Cassandra.

She shook her head. "I don't know where *here* is, besides on a beach."

A stunning one, on a Greek island. A beach with an empty stretch of sand that led to an ocean of blue, blending into an orange sunset.

All of it ruined by Cassandra.

"Different question. How did you get here?" Actaeon's voice was stern but not rude.

Lexi hated that. She shouldn't be jealous, but knowing that didn't stop the envy that sliced through her. It didn't matter that fate insisted she was meant for Actaeon, or that she'd felt an undeniable pull since the first time she met him. It had been less than a week since their first encounter, and he'd gone to the underworld and back for Cassandra.

Not the second time. That time he did it for me. The thought should have soothed Lexi. It didn't. She didn't know Actaeon as well as she did Cerberus, but she felt *something* for him. A something that was rapidly diminishing the longer he took his ex-girlfriend's side.

Cassandra's gaze never left Actaeon. Her expression was flat, but intensity burned in her dark eyes. "I've never been anywhere else," she said. "Or rather, this place, about two minutes before I heard all of you talking, is the only thing I remember. I didn't really kill anyone, did I?"

You destroyed Persephone's soul. Became Hades vessel because you couldn't have the man you love. And now you have the nerve to show up here, in said man's backyard, and pretend none of that ever happened?

Lexi didn't say any of it, because above all else, Cassandra looked sincere. Honest. Like she believed the bullshit coming out of her own mouth. And she did. Something for Lexi to dislike about her ability to see when people were lying—it told her this woman wasn't.

That didn't mean Lexi wanted to listen to her anymore. She stood and brushed the sand from her jeans. "I'll be inside. Enjoy your conversation."

Yeah, okay, Actaeon didn't technically owe Lexi anything. He'd stuck by her with no obligation, never requesting anything in return—that alone was the opposite of her encounters with other immortals.

And then he'd invited her and Cerberus to live in his house. Still without a request for remuneration. She didn't want to play the angsty teenager, but she'd thought when he talked about them discovering what their future held, he was speaking romantically. Not just about her being a warm spot in his bed until the next trauma-ridden individual came along.

"Lex." Actaeon's call hit her back. He didn't chase her, though.

It would have hurt more if Cerberus didn't stay by her side.

"Unless you're only doing it because you have to," she thought.

"I don't have to do anything you don't command me to." Cerberus jogged forward a few

steps, to slide the back door open for her. "I don't want to see her any more than you do. She locked me in a binding circle. She destroyed my queen," he said aloud.

Lexi leaned against a nearby wall and let her head *thunk* against the plaster. "Have you ever seen this before?"

"Someone come back from the dead, wind up at their ex's house, and not have a single memory of their past? No. And If I haven't seen something when it comes to death, it doesn't happen."

Because only her birth father, Hades, knew more about the topic than Cerberus—the hellhound shifter who had guarded the gates of underworld for millennia.

Lexi scrubbed her face. "Why isn't that reassuring?"

Her entire life she'd been told the gods were here to be worshiped. That they'd earned the people's love and adoration.

She knew better. Her stepfather—the man she called *Dad*—taught her the gods were petty and loathsome. Meant to be feared and avoided at all costs, lest their egos destroy her.

Then she tumbled headfirst into their world. Falling for a servant, falling for a hero, unsure whether she should hide from the gods or cooperate with them.

The back door slid open and shut again, and she knew without looking that Actaeon and Cassandra had joined them. Actaeon radiated a silver aura that encased Lexi in ice and comfort whenever he was around.

Right now, she resented that soothing feeling as much as she did the rest of the situation. She kicked away from the wall, never turning in their direction.

"Lexi," Actaeon said. "Hear me out."

She wanted to say *no*, but it was his home. She looked at him. "What?"

"She told me I'd see her again. Her returning to earth was always a possibility." Actaeon spoke softly, as if reminding himself more than telling them. "That she'd die, and I'd come for her, but that she couldn't see beyond that."

Cassandra stood next to him, eyes wide and mouth clamped shut. Her silence made her even more infuriating. If she were the insane woman Lexi had encountered in the underworld, Lexi wouldn't be questioning if her hate was justified.

"Your point is?" Cerberus' irritation crackled under Lexi's skin, tightening in her neck and back.

"If she really doesn't know who she is—"

"Excuse me. *If*?" Cassandra cut Actaeon off. "Whoever you think I am, I'm sorry this woman has all of you so worked up, but that's not me."

Actaeon shrugged. "That's my point. Am I supposed to turn my back and tell her to go to the next house?"

"What would you do instead? Let her stay here?" The edge in Cerberus' voice hinted at his opinion on the matter.

Actaeon raised an eyebrow and squared his shoulders at the implied threat of *don't you dare.* "I'm thinking about it."

The words cut Lexi deep. She didn't care about Actaeon because fate said they'd fall in love. Fuck fate. But she liked him. Enjoyed his company.

Or was she just grateful to him for rescuing her?

This situation was more surreal than stepping through a gate created by a siren, into a separate plane of existence, to walk through a maze that only existed in people's heads. That was something Lexi had been raised to expect.

Sitting in the middle of an open floor plan, on marble that gleamed despite the fact that Actaeon probably hadn't been home in months—years?—in a multi-million-dollar home, on a private island in Greece? Nothing in her lifetime had prepared her for this.

Oh, and the whole *psycho bitch who killed her mother returning from the dead* thing was a bit overwhelming too.

"If you're that concerned about her welfare, you could give her hotel money." Cerberus had been so kind and understanding about Lexi's complicated potential relationships. He wanted her to be happy. To explore. And to be by his side at the same time. A spiteful part of her was grateful he didn't have the same generosity when it came to Cassandra. "We all remember she killed Persephone and willingly freed Hades, don't we?" he said.

Cassandra held up her hands. "I did what? Hades is dead. That's what they teach in school, right?"

That was another thing bothering Lexi, though she hadn't been able to put her finger on it. Cassandra seemed to have the knowledge she needed to live in this world—a solid understanding of current history and slang—but she didn't know her own past?

Actaeon looked at Lexi. "What do you think?"

She didn't care for being asked to break a tie. Especially not one like this. "She murdered my mother."

Cerberus was smug. She felt it flowing through the new bond they shared. The one created when he became her servant, sworn to serve only her—to do what she wished, when she commanded it. A connection only gods were supposed to be able to form but that Lexi had managed without realizing it.

Actaeon clenched his jaw. "She doesn't remember doing that."

"That doesn't mean she'll never remember. Lexi had a siren put a block on her memory, and it came back," Cerberus straightened up, making it obvious he was taller and broader shouldered than Actaeon.

"And what if Cassandra's doesn't?" Actaeon's aura surged brighter. "You're going to punish her for something she hasn't done?"

"Punish her? By making her live a life similar to what I've done for the last four decades?" Lexi was tired of the posturing. Did Actaeon hear himself? "And she's done plenty already. She killed Persephone. Because she was a jealous you didn't love her anymore. Her crimes don't vanish because she can't remember them."

"If I put her in a hotel and walk away, and someone comes looking for her, she's defenseless without her past." Actaeon stepped closer. It was a subtle shift, but it placed him between Cerberus and Cassandra.

Lexi's fury surged, smothering her hurt. She clenched her jaw at the protective stance.

"If she's really her, she should see it coming." Cerberus was as much poking at Actaeon as amusing himself at this point.

I miss you. The words echoed in Lexi's skull.

"What?" She looked at Cerberus.

"What, what?"

"I don't have to."

The voice wasn't his, but it was definitely in her head. "Is that you?" She knew better but didn't have another answer.

Cerberus frowned. "Is what me?"

She listened. Nothing. *"Hello?"* she asked, tentatively.

"Hi." Cerberus's reply was audible. "What's going on?"

She furrowed her brow and turned her thoughts inward. Whatever she'd heard was silent now. Or she'd imagined it. "Nothing. I think our mystery guest's insanity is contagious."

Cerberus tugged Lexi close and wrapped his arms around her. It pulled her away from Actaeon at the same time. "I can't imagine why the situation might be upsetting you." Sarcasm dripped form his words

Lexi rested her head against his shoulder. Despite the fact that both men had said they were okay with Lexi being involved with them at the same time, there was a petty part of her that wanted Actaeon to be jealous. To feel even a hint of what Lexi was experiencing.

Actaeon's expression was stone, but his aura flickered.

Finally, a reaction directed toward Lexi.

"I miss you."

The phrase sent a chill down her spine, and she closed her eyes, willing the odd voice away.

Actaeon had invited Lexi and Cerberus to stay here because he wanted them to make it their home. The idea of sharing this place was foreign but comforting. The thought of getting to know Lexi

better—seeing if this was more than a passing infatuation—sang to him.

Now he was half a breath from reminding them this was his house, and refusing to throw Cassandra out on the street. He believed her memory was gone, but it was her. Her scent. The way she held herself…

He wasn't defending Cassandra because he wanted her back, or because he felt she should be forgiven for her crimes. Actaeon was responsible for driving her to this, and in this state, she was helpless.

Then Lexi started talking in sentence fragments. And the air changed.

The weight pressed in on Actaeon, and the scent of sunshine filled his nostrils. He knew who was at the door before he heard the knock.

This was the last thing he wanted to deal with tonight. *Fuck*, his uncle was high on his list of gods he never wanted to deal with, and that was a difficult list to top.

Before he could stop Cassandra, she answered the door.

Irritation surged through Actaeon at her presumption. He met Apollo's gaze, said, "Nope," and slammed the door shut.

"How does anyone know we're here?" Lexi sounded frustrated.

"Zeus sent us. Who knows whom he told?" Actaeon looped his thumb under the leather cord that hung around his neck, to expose a black stone. "Plus, the magic on this broke during the fight with Hades."

The piece of onyx had been imbued with siren magic that kept Actaeon's true self masked behind an illusion.

He didn't plan on getting it replaced. He was no longer willing to pay the siren's price. But that meant he was the aural equivalent of a homing beacon now. Every god and servant could find him without much effort. Which made him like any other powerful hero.

Apollo hammered on the door. "Two minutes," he shouted. "My knocking is only a courtesy."

Actaeon rolled his eyes and opened the door again.

"My favorite nephew." Apollo's greeting lacked sincerity.

"*Only,*" Actaeon corrected him.

"And yet you make it such a difficult choice."

Splendid. First Cassandra-blank, and now this. "What do you want?"

"I heard you have a guest." Apollo was using his power to make himself look more imposing. It was a neat trick for someone who was less two meters tall and with a wiry build. His loose clothing, meant to let in the sun, exaggerated his thin frame.

Actaeon gestured at Lexi. "Apollo, Lexi. Lexi, my mother's asshole brother."

"Right. The brat." Apollo didn't sound impressed.

Cerberus growled and stepped forward, but Actaeon was faster and looking for an outlet for his frustration.

Actaeon summoned a hunting dagger without effort, and pressed the tip to Apollo's throat. Actaeon could kill a weaker god without breaking a sweat. Apollo didn't meet that definition, but he'd suffer a bit. "It's been a long week, and I don't usually need an excuse. Why. Are you. Here?"

Apollo held up his hands. "Cassandra. That's the guest I meant."

"Me?" She stepped forward. "Do I know you? Or rather, do you know me? Because these people don't seem to like me very much."

"They don't like anyone." Apollo smoothed out his baggy tank top when Actaeon stepped away. "And yes, I know you. I felt you the moment you returned to this plane. Don't you recognize me?"

"I don't remember anything." Cassandra shook her head.

Apollo looked at Actaeon. "Are you keeping her for a reason?"

"Haven't decided yet." Which wasn't quite true. It was a question of convincing Lexi to agree with his decision.

Apollo stepped around him and reached a hand toward Cassandra. "You can stay with me."

"Just like that?" Cassandra seemed to be taking all of this in stride. No protests. A handful of questions. She was the most even-keel amnesiac ever.

One more thing to set Actaeon's teeth on edge. The Cassandra he'd known was energetic and passionate. This woman was very much a blank slate.

"I owe you," Apollo said to Cassandra.

Actaeon shook his head. "This is a bad idea."

"I'm talking to her, not you."

"Shut up, shut up, *shut up!*" Lexi's shout startled him.

He whirled to see her drop to her knees on the tile, cradling her head in her hands.

Cerberus knelt next to her. "Talk to me out loud. Don't stay in your head."

"It won't stop." She sounded as though it took immense effort to breathe. "He's in my thoughts. He keeps saying he misses me."

"Who?" Actaeon's concern spiked.

"I don't know." She clenched her fists in her hair and tugged. "It's so loud. I need it to stop."

"Look at me." Cerberus placed a finger under her chin and lifted her face.

She focused on him for a second, before curling her head into her hands again. "I need it to go away. I can't think. It won't shut up."

Apollo stepped toward her. "I can make it stop."

"How?" Cerberus asked.

"I can make her sleep."

That hardly sounded like a solution.

Lexi shook her head. "And what happens when I wake up?"

"You hope the voices have stopped." Apollo made it sound like the only obvious answer.

She scooted away from him, sliding her butt on the tile. "I'll cope."

Actaeon moved in front of her, and locked his gaze on Apollo. He might feel responsible for a Cassandra who didn't remember her past, but he'd never forgive himself if something happened to Lexi.

The scream that ripped from her throat next sent chills down his spine. If this was coping, he didn't want to see her losing it.

Lexi fought to think through the shouting in her skull. She heard one distinct voice, but swore there were others underneath. It didn't cause her physical pain, and the words weren't scary or maddening on their own. Things like *we miss you* and *join us* were simple thoughts.

But shouted by dozens—hundreds? Thousands?—in her head, where no one else could hear, made them terrifying.

She felt like something in her mind had cracked, and she was struggling to keep the contents from spilling out. Fear nudged her toward an edge she swore might be insanity. So many sounds. Voices. Begging her to listen. Hammering against her skull.

"What can I do?" Cerberus' question was another voice in a sea of strain.

She looked at him. "Don't add to the chaos." The words came out more harshly than she intended, and the frown that flashed across his face matched what bounced in her head.

Great. Because she needed to deal with his pouting, on top of this.

"You need to get it under control," he said aloud.

Not helpful. "Because I'm not trying?"

"Lexi." The voice was Actaeon's. He rested a hand on her cheek and forced her gaze to his.

The touch chased away the chaos. No. That wasn't right. It blanketed it.

She stumbled in a suddenly empty mind. For several seconds, she didn't dare speak. What if words triggered another avalanche? A switch had been flipped in her head and the looming madness had been amputated.

"I think it stopped." She tested the syllables, not wanting to taunt whatever just happened. For all she knew, it was some god's servant who she'd never learned about in school, fucking with her because of… reasons.

She looked at Cerberus. "I'm sorry for snapping."

"What was that?" He leaned closer, edging Actaeon aside, and studying her with concern. Understanding flowed through their bond.

She tested out a smile. "I was hoping one of you could tell me. It was like someone played hundreds of sound files all at the same time in my head. All of them slightly out of sync with each other."

They all shook their heads.

"It could have been…" Apollo trailed off when she whipped her head in his direction. She'd forgotten he was there. "No. Never mind," he said.

Lexi glared. She climbed to her feet, so she could face him on equal ground. The less time she spent looking up to gods—literally or otherwise, the better she felt. "Uh… wrong. Could have been what?"

Apollo held his hand out to Cassandra. "Are you ready, my dear?"

Cassandra looked between him and everyone else, then grasped his fingers.

"Wait." Lexi's shout greeted empty air, as the two vanished. Frustration surged inside. She summoned the illusion of an arrow, and let it fly through the spot where Apollo had just stood. It vanished before it hit the far wall.

Completely ineffective, just like him. Go figure.

She scrubbed her face, still wary of her own thoughts. The noise might be gone, but it left her mentally exhausted.

The gods were supposed to be the answers to humanity's problems. It was propaganda—one of the many ways they gathered the faith that gave them their power—but until recently, she'd never realized how just useless they were.

"Any clue what he was going to say?" she asked Cerberus and Actaeon.

Actaeon shook his head.

"I don't know, but I can tell you what I do." Cerberus' still radiated concern. "What you and I share? The connection? A god with multiple servants experiences that with all of them."

Actaeon gave a strained laugh. She wanted to feel something from him, too. A flicker of desperation needed to know he was worried. They didn't have that kind of connection though. "Minus the intense sex," he said. "There might be fucking, but none of them actually love those they claim."

Claim. The word tasted odd to Lexi. "But I'm not connected to anyone else."

Cerberus pulled her close. "That's why I don't have an answer for you."

"So do I sit and wait to see if it happens again?" She wasn't fond of that plan.

Actaeon crossed his arms. Though he only stood a few feet away, it felt like miles. "Unless you have any idea at all what triggered it, and want to make it come back."

No. Definitely not. For all she knew, it was Cassandra's fault, and she'd be pleased as could be if she never saw that bitch again. "I guess I wait."

CHAPTER TWO

Icarus crossed his fingers and held his breath, as he hooked power to his latest creation. If this were some classic movie and he were the scientist or the magician, he'd end up with a soot-covered face and his dark hair sticking up on end.

Funny how the two characters were always portrayed in similar ways, both when they failed and when they succeeded.

He didn't even have the satisfaction of a spectacular, movie-magic explosion. The box sat there, mocking him with its lack of doing anything.

His father, Daedalus, was known as one of the greatest inventors in immortal history. And sure, the old man came up with some decent concepts, but he wasn't so much an innovator as he was acceptable at breathing life into other people's ideas.

Icarus had more failures to his name than Daedalus did. Centuries of trying had that impact. Some were intentional—faking his own death as a young man, was the first of those. He'd built glorious wings, and flown too high… Too far… Plummeted into the ocean. All to escape the shadow of being born just another hero in a line of half-mortals, half-gods.

But his successes… Those were incredible.

He scrubbed his face as he dragged out a long groan. This experiment was landing itself squarely in the *failure* column. Was the break-down in a broken solder point? A miscalculation on which parts needed how much electricity?

Icarus snapped his fingers, and showers of sparks exploded through every crease and crack in the black plastic box. Flame caught on the wires and roared up from the useless device. The sinus-tingling scent of burning synthetics filled the air.

It made him smile. With a wave of his fingers over the smoldering pile, he extinguished the flames. He was going to get this. It didn't matter how many years it took; he'd figure out how to imbue this router with his magic so that he didn't need code to access the data running through it.

He whirled in his work room, looking past the open shelves of appliances in different states of disrepair, and grabbed another router from the stack two rows back and one aisle over.

His phone rang. Whoever it was could go to voicemail. With his current luck, it would be that asshole Zeus again. Last time he did the guy a favor, Icarus had built him a fucking maze. Better than

Daedalus ever fathomed. Hades' prison was one of Icarus' finest accomplishments.

Until some uppity brat came along and destroyed it all, by sticking her nose into things she didn't understand.

He'd never met the girl, but Aphrodite had built a trap into the maze for her, and he'd seen the hero's face plastered all over TV when Hades broke free. That was enough information for Icarus.

He tore into the router packaging, shoved everything else aside in his workspace—to make room—and dove back into the task at hand.

Everything faded into the background. The acres of workshop that stretched around him… The endless tables and shelves, with a variety of inventions and experiments… Thoughts of post-enlightenment heroes who couldn't leave well enough alone…

Four hours and two more destroyed devices later, and his eyes burned from the strain. Or from the smoke produced each time he burned another box in frustration. Immortality didn't grant him a reprieve from pain and physical irritation, it just meant he recovered more quickly than mortals.

He needed to clear his head and the air in the room. He opened the windows lining the wall at the far end of his basement workshop. The temperate night drifted in, car exhaust mingling with ozone.

That wasn't a whole lot better, but it was different, and he needed a new perspective.

The tiny blinking light on his phone caught his attention, and he grabbed it and swiped. When he saw the name *George* and both a missed call and a voicemail, he frowned. Concern nudged him. He pulled up the message.

"Hey. It's George. This is going to sound odd, but I've been talking to Ralph, and— On second thought, it does sound nuts. I'm calling to say hi.*"*

A disconcerting sliver of fear grew inside. Icarus had known George since the other man was a teenager. Had been his confidant through The Enlightenment, through his finding love, building a family, and most recently losing the man he'd been with more than half his life.

George and Ralph were together for more than three decades, when Ralph was diagnosed with pancreatic cancer. He'd passed away several years ago.

Icarus dialed George, and drummed his fingers on the workbench while he listened to the ringing. There was no answer, and he hung up before he was asked to leave a message.

It might be a fluke. A bad dream. Early signs of dementia—though George was only sixty-five. No assurance calmed Icarus. He climbed the steps to the main floor of his second-hand shop and looked out the far picture window at the street. It was after ten at night. Too late for a house call, but he didn't care. Instinct told him to look into this, and he didn't like to ignore his gut.

He grabbed a hat from the hook by the back entrance, raked his fingers through his hair, and tugged the cap into place. He was halfway down the alley leading to the main road, when he remembered his shoes and keys.

Missing items fetched, he jogged the couple of blocks to George's. In this town, most places were only a couple of blocks away. In one direction, that distance led to Main Street. Century-old, single story buildings mixed with newer commercial properties that reached up five or ten floors, falling short of touching the sky.

In another direction, brick apartments dotted the street. Shops like Icarus' junk and electronics store broke up the landscape.

And in George's part of town, narrow two-story townhouses were pressed side-by-side. The street had been part of a developer's effort fifty years ago to make this place look more like the bigger cities.

The Enlightenment changed those plans. The place had tried a few times since to grow, but never managed.

Georgie's townhouse was like the others that lined the street, narrow facings climbing to stop far short of reaching the sky.

Icarus pounded on the door and tried to quell his rising worry. Seconds ticked away too slowly for his liking. George was most likely sleeping, but that vague message—

The door swung open, and George stood on the other side. His eyes were wide and bloodshot, and gray stubble covered his chin. He focused on Icarus and smiled. "Hey. Come on in. I just made a fresh pot of coffee."

"This late?" Icarus followed him into the kitchen and sat at the round table near the window.

George had always been an early-to-bed, early-to-rise kind of guy. "It sounded good." Was he slurring his words?

"It does. I'll take a cup of that."

George didn't speak as he grabbed mugs, filled them, and poured a generous helping of milk and sugar into Icarus'.

Icarus didn't press for more information. He wanted his friend to open up naturally, not be led to a part of the conversation that wasn't relevant. Once Icarus had a better grasp on the situation, he could steer the discussion.

George turned from the counter, mugs in hand, and stumbled. One drink slipped, and he lunged for it, dropping the other. Twin crashes echoed through the room, as coffee and ceramic spilled everywhere.

"Damn it," George muttered and knelt in the middle of the mess, reaching for broken pieces of mug.

Icarus pulled him to his feet. "I'll take care of this." He frowned at the tiny shards in his friend's knees, and brushed them away. A series of red dots appeared in the fresh wounds. They were tiny cuts, but there were several. Icarus had a lot of friends in this neighborhood, and George was one of his closest. He didn't like to see the man suffer, even from something like cuts. "Go clean up. Take care of your legs. I've got this."

George looked at him blankly, then nodded. "Thank you. I'll be right back." He hobbled from the room.

Icarus had spent a lot of time here over the years and had a good idea where everything was kept. He threw away the larger pieces of broken mug, mopped, swept, and mopped again.

The floor shone when he was done. But George hadn't returned.

Icarus wandered from the room. Where to look? A glow emanating from the living room gave him a direction. He found George on the couch, watching an infomercial for a signal blocker.

The boast was that it would keep the gods from watching over a buyer's every activity.

"You think something like that works?" George asked.

Icarus sat next to him. "I think it wouldn't be advertised on cable TV if it did." That was the barrier Icarus couldn't breach, and he doubted anyone else had either. The electronics could be blocked. The gods could be hidden from. But hiding from both godly and electronic surveillance at the same time was impossible.

"I've been talking to Ralph," George said. There it was again. The same thing he'd said in his message.

Concern clenched in Icarus' chest. "In your sleep?"

George gave a bitter laugh. "I haven't slept in days. I needed to know it was real. That it wasn't Morpheus."

Probably not. Morpheus didn't care about a random guy in suburbia. He might care about George's adopted daughter—

"It's Ralph." Sadness and surrender filled George's voice.

Icarus wished he could heal that pain. That anyone could. "How is he?" It wasn't Ralph—the dead didn't talk to the living—but this didn't seem like the best time to argue.

"He wants me to join him."

Icarus' heart stalled at the thought of losing this friend. Death wasn't the end for most people, but it did put a damper on potential. He hated to see wasted potential, especially from someone as good as George. The man had made huge innovations in medicine. Discovered chemical compounds that surpassed anything the gods could do.

"You'll find him when your time here is done," Icarus said.

George nodded. "I think that time is now."

"I know how desperately you miss him." Icarus measured his words. He wasn't great at this kind of comfort. Being a more than three-thousand-year-old immortal, and having seen the afterlife, meant death didn't impact him the way it had George. He still cared, though. "Your time here is limited as it is. Once you move on, you'll have eternity with Ralph."

"You don't have any idea how much I miss him. I didn't realize myself until I saw him again." Sorrow bled into George's voice.

Icarus grasped for anything. "You want to see Esper finish college, don't you? You only get one shot at that. She wants you there when she accepts her diploma."

"That's true. Maybe I should call her. Make sure she's all right."

Maybe not at one in the morning. Then again, anything that kept George alive sounded reasonable. "She always loves hearing from you," Icarus said.

"I don't want to wake her." George stood. "And I shouldn't have kept you."

"I was awake anyway. I'll stay as long as you need. Do you want to watch movies? *The Black Swan?*" That had been a favorite of Ralph's. Not the best suggestion Icarus could have made. "*Toy Story 5?* Esper's favorite."

"I know what you're trying to do, and I appreciate it, but I'm doing better now." The sleep and wistfulness cleared from George's voice.

Icarus didn't buy the one-eighty. "It's not a problem. If you're not sleeping anyway…"

George yawned, opening his mouth so wide, Icarus was surprised his jaw didn't split. "I think sleep is a good idea."

"I'll stick around and keep you company regardless." Doubt clawed inside Icarus. This wasn't right. None of this situation was. And he didn't want to leave George alone.

George smiled, shuffled to the front door, and held it open. "I'm fine." His tone was firm. "Get back to your work. I'll give you a call in the morning."

Icarus stayed seated.

"Please, leave. I don't want to get rude."

"All right." Icarus joined his friend at the door. "But I want you to call me the moment you wake up. I'll drop everything to answer. I'm worried about you."

George squeezed his arm. "I'll be fine. I promise."

Icarus was reluctant to return home, but he respected George's request. His focus was shot for the night, though.

He sat behind the counter in his repair shop, poking at another router and waiting for his phone to ring.

The black sky shifted to gray, and then paled further as the sun crept over the horizon.

When the sirens screamed through the neighborhood, sorrow surged inside Icarus, stealing his breath and sending tears to prick his eyelids. He'd failed.

What was he supposed to do? Call George. That was a good idea. The emergency vehicles could be for someone else.

He wasn't surprised when he got George's voicemail. "Give me a call. Worried about you." Icarus tried not to clip off the words. His stomach dropped into his shoes. He'd never get a call back.

An hour later, he was still stuck in mental limbo. The ring of his phone startled him, and he grabbed it. Esper's laughing photo stared at him, and grief and guilt rocked inside.

He hit *Answer*. "Hello."

"Uncle Russ?" Her voice was broken.

"What's up, kiddo?"

"Daddy George is dead. I'm at his house. I don't know what to do. They're asking questions about the body. About him. About this empty pill bottle by his bedside..." Her words vanished in a sob.

Icarus' heart broke for her. "What empty pill bottle?" He didn't want to ask, but he had to know.

"It's not a prescription bottle. It's got vines and thorns on it."

"Okay. I'll talk to whoever you need me to. All right?"

"All right." It was difficult to make out her words through her crying.

"Sit tight. I'll be there in a few minutes."

Icarus' guilt grew as he disconnected. Not only had he failed to talk his friend out of killing himself, but George had also used the pills Icarus gave him, to help with sleep.

Creation, he mentally swore. Mortality sucked.

CHAPTER THREE

Lexi had never been a fan of crowded places. It wasn't just the large swaths of people. The scattered auras clogged her senses. And then there were the cameras to worry about.

This place was more crowded than most. Awnings stretched over stone walkways, protecting the goods in the flea market, but not shielding most of the shoppers from the sun. The spices, meat, flowers, and body odor mingled together, making her stomach churn, and lingering on her tongue.

Cerberus wrapped an arm around her waist and pulled her closer. The contact flowed over and through her, feeling pleasant, but not chasing away her discomfort. They sidestepped two men haggling with a street vendor over a pair of wooden chairs and a matching table.

So many voices ran together, making it difficult to make out which conversations were in Greek and which were English.

"—Alexand—"

Lexi's heart leaped into her throat, and she whirled toward the voice. Her full name? She couldn't have heard that right. Did someone recognize her? She wore an illusion to hide her face, but after Hades' outing her to the entire world, she didn't know which would be worse—an unhappy god looking for vengeance, or family members of someone Hades had killed.

"*Alexander.* You can't go running off like that." A woman brushed past her and grabbed the arm of a young boy a few feet away.

Lexi tried to calm her racing pulse, but it hammered in her ears, mingling with the noise pollution.

"*Zeus promised we were under his protection,*" Cerberus' voice was in her head, rather than out loud.

"*Because I trust Zeus to tell me what time it is without strings attached. And I didn't say anything.*" She hadn't even sent him the thought. It seemed foolish to be out in public, not knowing who might have an issue with her. But she couldn't hide forever. As much as her instinct told her to do exactly that.

Besides, she wasn't safe anywhere. Given Actaeon, Cerberus', and her recognizable auras, they weren't even hidden in his house.

It had been a few days since Cassandra showed up and was almost as quickly whisked away by Apollo. The voices that haunted Lexi that day hadn't come back, and neither had Actaeon's ex, but both were constant thoughts in the back of her mind.

Cerberus had done a decent job of distracting her, though, testing the limits of their new bond. A large part of that involved discovering how much more intense the sex was when they could feel each other's pleasure.

"You didn't have to say it." Cerberus spoke aloud this time. "You reek of anxiety." Being a hellhound shifter gave him an enhanced sense of smell.

That didn't mean she wanted to hear about it. "*Reek* is a strong word."

He nipped the edge of her ear playfully, drawing a sigh. "It's accurate. Come on. I want to show you something. It'll make you feel better. I promise."

That was a big promise to make, but she let him lead her through the streets of the Monastiraki shops anyway. There was so much to take in here. Actaeon told them it was an antique flea market of sorts. He'd wanted to come with them, to show them around, but he was checking on Cassandra.

Lexi was trying to pretend he could do what he wanted. He hadn't made a commitment to her, beyond *hey, you can stay in my house. It's nice having you around.* But anger and hurt surged inside, knowing he hadn't cut ties with *that woman.*

"It's a shitty thing for him to do, even as a friend," Cerberus said.

She was grateful he understood. Actaeon's excuse had been *I owe her.* It sounded a lot like what

Apollo said. What did Cassandra hold over these people that put them in her debt?

Lexi wasn't dwelling on that. She wanted to enjoy her afternoon with Cerberus.

The stalls here had everything. Furniture, books, something Cerberus said were records—she didn't get the appeal of black platters of grooved vinyl, but he'd spent half an hour sifting through the crates.

Lexi had thought she was going stir crazy, sitting around the house, waiting for something bad to happen. Being out in the open was worse. She expected someone to recognize her. Hades declared open season on her before he was banished. And told the world she was his daughter, after he killed thousands. There had to be at least a couple people who wouldn't be happy to meet her.

She wore an illusion now, but mirrors and cameras saw through the disguise. Lexi was used to looking over her shoulder, but this took mandatory paranoia to a whole new level. *You're not safe anywhere. Enjoy this.*

Yeah, that wasn't reassuring.

"Hey. Space cadet." Cerberus' teasing drew her attention.

When she saw where they were, glee raced through her. "No way."

"Didn't I promise?"

He had. Several rows of wooden bookshelves stretched back into a recessed cove, all lined with hardback books that were covered with stunning fantasy artwork.

She traced her fingers along one near her. *Monster Compendium Edition 1.0.* The same version of the monster guide from the roleplaying games she used to play with Dad.

"Take your time," Cerberus said in her head again. *"We've got all afternoon."*

She was grateful he didn't speak out loud. A place like this demanded reverence. *"If I vanish into the stacks, don't send help."*

He laughed and squeezed her hand, before letting go.

She meandered down the aisle, admiring the artwork on the books. Some of the titles were familiar, and others begged for her to discover the new worlds and rules that lay within their pages. The smell of old pages filled her nostrils and mingled with memories from her childhood.

She wanted to grab any volume, curl up in the corner, and lose herself in a universe where gods and monsters could be defeated by a lucky roll of the dice.

She could forget that Actaeon's past had come back to life. That she'd lost her mother for a second time. Forget that Hades would be back sooner, rather than later.

Next time, he'd probably make them miss the days when his worst offense was slaughtering thousands of innocent people.

"I know you." The sharp voice startled her, and a man grabbed her wrist. "You're not welcome in my shop." He gripped hard enough that white marks spread out on her skin, from his fingers. She had a high tolerance for pain, but a hint of it spread up her arm.

Lexi had let her illusion slip while she was distracted. Fuck.

Cerberus stepped between them, breaking the man's grip and shoving him back. "She's not doing anything wrong."

"My daughter is dead because of her old man." Venom dripped from the stranger's voice.

Acid burned up Lexi's throat. "It's okay." She tugged at Cerberus' hand. "Let's go."

"No. You're enjoying yourself."

She clenched her jaw. "Not anymore. Let's go."

He growled, but fell into step beside her as she hurried back onto the street.

Once again the shop owner grabbed her tight and spun her back around. "We're not done talking." He dug his fingers in, hitting nerves and tense muscle, but his gaze bored deeper, as if he was searching her soul.

A low, threatening sound rumbled from Cerberus' chest.

"Don't hurt him," Lexi commanded.

"I don't know why Hades wanted you, but life was fine before he showed up." When the shopkeeper spoke through clenched teeth, spittle hit

Lexi's face. "He's gone. You're here. Someone has to answer."

"Let. Her. Go." Cerberus clenched the man's wrist, eliciting a yelp.

"Stop." Lexi could barely hear over the hammering of her pulse in her ears. *"He's grieving. He's got a right."*

"Not to take it out on you." Cerberus let go anyway.

The shopkeeper pulled a dagger from where it hung at his hip, and pressed the tip to Lexi's throat. "We served Poseidon, and we were happy with the arrangement. If I sacrifice you in his name, will it undo what's happened?"

Carrying out the threat wouldn't fix things any more than his blade would cut her skin. The engravings on it looked ceremonial, but it was just steel. Maybe it had been blessed by Poseidon once upon a time, but it wasn't now.

Lexi struggled for the kindest words she could find, to tell him that. The man's anger was terrifying, but she understood his grief. The gods stole her mother from her twice.

"If you're not going to do anything, let's go." Cerberus was insistent.

She should do that. She yanked free from the man's grip and turned to stride away.

"Stop her," the guy shouted. "She's the reason our families are dead.

Several people in the crowds swiveled in her direction.

Well, fuck.

The shouting started. So many voices overlapping. Not as many as there'd been in her head the other day, but far more threatening.

Hands grabbed at her, some gouging her skin—there was a weak hero or two in the pack—and others ripping at her clothes and hair.

"Let me help you." Cerberus' mental voice added to the chaos, and she worked to process that on top of being shoved against a nearby wall and pinned in place, for the man with the dagger to approach her.

Another noise mingled with his thoughts and their shouts. A strain of music, faint but dark and ugly.

She struggled against the people holding her. Super strength wasn't one of her gifts. Helplessness surged inside. She could let Cerberus help, but she didn't want anyone hurt.

"You're getting hurt. I don't give a fuck about them."

That was part of the problem. She'd seen what his jaws could do to a harpy. If things got any more out of hand here, what could he do to these people? The decision whether or not to let him intervene warred in her head, as the growing anger in the crowd drew more attention. Now people in the middle were being shoved and falling down. This was too much for Cerberus to handle even if she did let him. Would an illusion help? A full-sized projection of Poseidon as if he were still alive?

The panic and indecision that gripped her made it difficult to focus enough to summon such a thing.

She looked over the mob, as if their angry faces would offer a solution. The strange music grew louder, gnawing at her core and leaving a pit in its wake. Her gaze fell on a new face. Beautiful, like a doll's. Lorelei?

Lexi tried to tear her arm away, to turn off her ear cuff. The siren's gift that kept her from seeing through illusions. Why had she left it on in the first place?

And then their surroundings vanished. An office replaced everything. Floor-to-ceiling glass windows looked out over a city below. A black leather couch sat at the far end, a dark-stained table next to it. Chairs that matched the couch were on either end.

Lexi recognized the aura before she saw the god. She turned, to find Zeus standing next to a desk that filled the room behind them. Photos in digital frames decorated the shelves, showing a laughing couple with three younger children.

They were all blond, blue eyed, and pale, unlike the dark-haired, olive-skinned Zeus.

"You're supposed to take the sample photos out before you display the frames," Lexi said.

Zeus' smile was thin. "Charming, as anticipated. And painfully predictable. If you're going to cover your anxiety with something, pick a path no one else takes. Dramatic re-enactments of Shakespeare, perhaps."

She didn't have a comeback. The new environment wasn't as chaotic as what he'd rescued them from, but it felt far more threatening. Still, if he expected abrasion, she'd disappoint. "Lovely to see you again. How may I help you?" she said.

"You could thank me for pulling you out of there. You could ask the guard dog to stand down."

"She's done enough of that." Irritation filled Cerberus' voice.

She hid a wince at the bite in his words. "Thank you," she said to Zeus, trying to sound sincere.

"Better. And they're not my family. In the photos, that is."

"Gee. You think?" Lexi's tension was slowly cooling. Not evaporating so much, as solidifying into a more manageable form. One she could think through and direct.

The blank wall Cerberus projected gnawed at her gut, though.

Zeus gestured to two chairs across from the desk. "Have a seat, please. Can I have anything brought in for you? Water? Coffee?"

"Explanations," Cerberus said. "Starting with where we are."

Lexi didn't sit, and neither did he.

"San Jose. Oxford Data International. This is the CEO's office. He's a good friend, so he's letting me use the place."

Lexi knew the company name. They were one of the larger corporations who gathered and collated behavioral data, for market and faith analysis. Or—in more simple terms—they acted as the long arm of Big Brother and helped the gods figure out what behavior would earn them the most worship. "Very kind of the man. He sounds generous. And his family is lovely."

"They are, aren't they?" Zeus settled into the office chair behind the desk and leaned back. "And I hate to cut the small-talk short, but he's going to want his office back sooner, rather than later."

"Seems fair. Some people in this world work." Cerberus turned toward the door. "Will you tell us where the nearest ley line is, so we can take siren gate out of here, or do I need to look it up?"

"You, of all people, should know we don't work that way, hellhound." The pleasantness slipped from Zeus' voice.

Lexi clenched her jaw, to keep her tension from showing. "What do you mean?" She was surprised she kept her tone even.

"I did something for you—pulled you out of that situation in Greece. I'd like you to do something for me in return."

"Fucking asshole." Cerberus was letting her in his head again.

Lexi wasn't comforted. "We didn't ask for you to pull us out."

"And I'm sure you were doing fine. But what I'd like from you is *actually* not a big deal. Then we can call it even." The phone on the desk chirped, and Zeus flicked out his hand to silence it before the first ring finished.

Lexi might still be feeling her way around this side of the gods' world, but she recognized when she'd been set up. "How convenient that you just happened to see we needed help. Have you been watching and waiting for an opportunity for me to owe you?"

"I may have had the face recognition algorithms tweaked to search for your face. I assure you, it's strictly to provide the safety I promised. I can't be everywhere."

"Safety. Right." Cerberus sounded as unconvinced as Lexi was.

She didn't want to be here any longer than she had to be. "What do we owe you as thanks?"

"It's a simple request and mutually beneficial. There's not much time before Hades regains his strength. It's best to cage him now, rather than waiting to see what happens when he's back to full power."

"Why don't we simply kill him?" Lexi understood why they hadn't before. He was more powerful than any other god, and it took both Actaeon and Heracles to banish him. But they'd weakened him, so striking before he regained his strength made sense.

Zeus' smile implied she was being naive. "As much as I appreciate your bloodlust, how easy do you think it is to kill a god of death? He exists in that state already."

"There has to be a way to destroy his soul. Like what happened to Persephone." Saying the words sent an unexpected surge of grief through Lexi and reminded her why Actaeon wasn't with them right now.

"Persephone was mortal, despite Hades' energy running through her." Hades power had granted her immortality through him. Usually when two gods had a child, their offspring was also a god. Sometimes though, as in Persephone's case, the baby was mortal. "Hades is unique among all of us, and it takes a lot for me to admit when someone is more powerful than I am. Hades can't be killed." Zeus wavered on the last word.

Even without the tell, Lexi felt the lie slide through her like slime. But the knowledge didn't do her any good if she couldn't determine the truth. "So… if you want us to go capture him, that hardly seems like a fair trade for your noble rescue today."

"The person who built the labyrinth—I'd like you to talk to him and get him to build another prison. A more secure one."

Cerberus snorted. "You asked him last time. Do it again."

"It's not that simple." Condescension leaked into Zeus' reply. "Icarus refuses to work with me since this incident with Hades."

"Imagine that. They call him a genius for a reason." Cerberus' smug irritation drifted from him in waves, making Lexi squirm in discomfort.

Being trapped between Zeus' manipulation and Cerberus' annoyance moved to the top ten on her list of least favorite things. "How does sending us to talk to him make things go any more smoothly?" She looked at Cerberus. "Do you know him? Is this something he'll do because you ask?"

"I know *of* him. We've met a couple of times throughout history. We're on neither good nor bad terms." That wasn't helpful. Lexi turned back to Zeus. "I'll ask again. How does sending me make a difference? Eventually, it will come out that we're there at your request. And even if I leave that part out, he'll guess when I tell him I want another prison for Hades."

Zeus' twitched again, and that whiff of dishonesty drifted from him. "You're going to apologize for breaking his maze. Beg forgiveness, tell him the details about how it happened, and then ask him to make a new one."

"What if he tells us *no*?" Cerberus asked.

"Then at least you tried."

All of this for an *oh well*? Lexi wasn't buying it, but she didn't expect Zeus would give them the truth. "What if *I* tell you *no*?"

"I can send you back to that mob in Greece. I've asked Eirene to step in and bring things to a peaceful end, but you could give it a shot instead. You have talents you've yet to discover."

Lexi would much rather let a goddess of peace deal with that crowd. "How do I find Icarus?"

"I'll send you to him." Zeus leaned forward in his seat and extended his hand, fist closed and fingers down.

Lexi hesitated, then stepped closer.

He dropped a pearl into her palm. "This is a single-use portal back to Greece—to Actaeon's home—when you're done," Zeus said.

"Just like that?" It was too easy. All of this. The build-up. The smooth talk. The bullshit. What wasn't he saying?

"Just like that. Ask Icarus to build a new prison for Hades. Be convincing, don't phone it in, and then we're even."

"Regardless of his answer," Cerberus said.

"*Cronus*, yes." Zeus' mask slipped. "Regardless of what he says. Do you want me to draw up a contract?"

"No. This is enough."

"It is?" Lexi didn't understand where Cerberus' sudden acceptance came from.

"Will you fucking trust me for five minutes?"

She recoiled at the frustration in his thought. "When?" she said aloud.

"Now." As Zeus spoke, the room vanished and was replaced by a sidewalk lined with shops. The awnings over most of them were faded, and the windows were aluminum trimmed. Nothing here looked newer than a century old.

Lex and Cerberus stood in front of a junk shop.

Lexi wanted to pull her hair out at the conversation and its unsatisfying conclusion, but she wanted to make things right with Cerberus more. "Can we talk before we go in there?" She searched his face, leaving herself open so he could feel the sincerity.

He opened his mouth, and his phone rang.

She bit back the desire to tell him to ignore it. She'd made enough demands for one day.

Cerberus glanced at the screen, then back at her. "I need to take this. Talk to Icarus, get Zeus' stupid errand done, and then we'll go home." His voice was curt, and he was still walling off his emotions. "Hello," he said into the phone.

"I'm sorry." She sent him the thought, then pushed into the shop.

He didn't reply.

The sooner she got this over with, the better.

CHAPTER FOUR

Actaeon wished he could ignore this sense of responsibility. That he could *actually* be the guy who didn't care. The hurt on Lexi's face when he'd told her his plans for the afternoon, it devoured him. Hours later, it still gnawed at him.

He didn't know how to make her understand. It didn't matter that he fell out of love with Cassandra decades ago. Going toe-to-toe with Zeus and Heracles cost her life. Sent her to whatever sort of hell twisted her mind, until she was willing to let Hades use her as a vessel. Brought her here, with no memory.

He'd done that to her.

This was a kind gesture. Both the most and the least he could offer. He'd invited her to dinner because he wanted to make sure she was adjusting all right and that things were going well with Apollo.

Now Actaeon and Cassandra sat at an outdoor café, surrounded by people and making some of the most banal conversation he remembered ever having.

Every question he asked her was met with a variation of, *Whatever you think is best.*

She was apparently as mundane as mundane got, unless she was the best actress ever. And if that was the case, he'd have a lot bigger problems than whether or not she enjoyed life at Apollo's sprawling Athens home.

Actaeon still didn't think it was right that Athena didn't watch over the city named after her, but she didn't carry the kind of favor with Zeus that the other gods did. She got shafted during *who gets what time.*

Actaeon fiddled with the handle of his espresso cup. The evening was drawing to a natural close, thank creation for that.

"Hand to Athena, his mother talked to him in a dream." The voice drifted from another table.

Actaeon shouldn't be eavesdropping. Their conversation about the friend of a friend of a friend, wouldn't be interesting on most days. Tonight? It blew his own evening out of the water.

Cassandra used her fork to section off another tiny square from the pastry in front of her. Though she'd complimented the food on several occasions, her tone was flat, as if she read from a script.

"No shit," a man said. "Gillian? She died four years ago."

Actaeon wanted to turn and seek out the group that was talking.

"You're making a mistake, you know." The shift in Cassandra's voice caught him off-guard, and he met her gaze. A new kind of clarity stared back.

He didn't like this any more than what came before, but it was different. "About what?"

"The woman—Lexi? She'll never be yours."

Actaeon clenched his jaw. That kind of direct comment was enough to push good graces aside. He didn't understand why he was drawn to her. What made fate decide they were meant for each other. Not that he cared what fate thought, but he wanted to explore more with Lexi.

It might be inexplicable and undefined, but what Actaeon had with Lexi was real, growing, changing, and unquestionable.

None of that meant he'd shut down this conversation. It was the most distinct thing Cassandra had said all night. "What do you mean?" He was wary.

She let out a clipped laugh. "A child like that? She literally threw a tantrum in your foyer when you stopped paying attention to her."

He clenched his fist under the table. "She wasn't feeling like herself. It was hardly a voluntary reaction."

"Whatever you have to tell yourself."

"This isn't a matter of denial. I witnessed it with my own eyes. She wasn't *throwing a tantrum*, and this evening is over." He shoved his chair back.

Cassandras chin quivered, and tears welled up in her eyes.

Which was bullshit. That she'd pull the same stunt she accused Lexi of… Anger surged inside Actaeon.

"Can I get you anything else, sir?" Their waitress paused next to him and rested a hand on his arm.

A glow grew around Cassandra, and the dishes on the table rattled. "Don't touch him." Her voice came out low and threatening.

The almost blinding white light around her was bad. If Actaeon could see it, it wasn't an aura. She was drawing light to herself. She didn't wield magic. Not the vibrant, combative kind.

"*Cass.*" Actaeon kept his posture casual, despite every muscle in his body tensing for a fight.

The waitress backed away quickly. "I'm sorry. I didn't mean to offend."

Cassandra extended her fingers and flicked her wrist.

Instinct and adrenaline propelled Actaeon between her and the waitress before he registered what was happening. A shard of light flew from Cassandra's hand, and struck Actaeon in the chest.

Pain spread from the burn, and he sucked in a sharp breath through his teeth. It felt like Apollo's magic. It wouldn't kill him, but it might leave a scar, and it fucking hurt.

"What are you doing?" He snapped out the question. Around them, people scrambled back from their tables, knocking chairs and dishes to the sidewalk. The rapid shift in mood was bad enough. The fact that Cassandra had never wielded power that way before, especially sunlight, was worse. But striking out at a random person was unforgivable, missing memory or not.

With a twitch of his fingers, his hunting dagger materialized.

So did Apollo, standing between Actaeon and Cassandra.

"What in Tartarus is this?" Apollo's question shook surrounding buildings.

Great. Now they were putting on a show for everyone who had their cameras out.

Cassandra's pleasant smile returned, and she looked up at Apollo. "No big deal. No harm, no foul."

"Is that so?" Apollo glanced at Actaeon.

Actaeon clenched his fist around the hilt of his blade. "It's not so." He stalked forward, prepared to finish this fight.

"So much for trusting you, nephew." Apollo grasped Cassandra's hand.

Before Actaeon could retort, Apollo and Cassandra were gone, and so were the crowd and café. He was on the front step of his house.

"No, seriously. What the fuck was that?" he asked the empty air.

Icarus stood at the counter in the main floor of his shop. His work area was downstairs, but he was trying to keep business hours, to keep his mind occupied. . He stared at the row of shelves on the adjacent wall, but didn't register them.

Over the millennia, he'd seen more people die that he cared to count. Lost countless friends and acquaintances. He grieved for all of them, though the sense of loss was more muted these days. Time and overexposure had made him numb.

In a way, that made him sad, but if he sank into each passing, it would drive him insane, the way it had with Atlas. The decay of mankind's heart during the second world war drove him to kill himself.

There was more to George's death, though. Sure, he missed his partner, but he'd never had a death wish.

Icarus couldn't stop replaying that last conversation in his head. What was he missing? Why couldn't he grasp it?

The front door swung open, and he looked up. The woman strolling toward him, tight smile on her face, would be the perfect distraction. He wanted answers for the questions about George, but he needed distance.

The brunette with the blue-and-pink aura swirling around her would be the perfect way to let other thoughts rattle in the back of his head for a little while. Was she a daughter of Eros? No. Eros only had the one son, and he wasn't the kind of god who hid his escapades. Aphrodite? The colors were right, but this woman wasn't.

He didn't care who a person was—god, human, servant, or hero—they all had something to offer. And this woman offered a mystery.

She carried herself like someone who didn't want to be seen, but whose nature and presence defied that desire. Dark hair fell halfway down her back, framing a pale face, and blue eyes studied him.

"May I help you?" he asked when she was a few feet away.

She met his gaze, and some of the coolness evaporated from her expression. "I'm looking for Icarus?"

He stepped around the counter and approached her. "Are you a fan?" He got those sometimes—people who'd heard the old stories. Icarus wasn't important enough to make history books, but he also wasn't the kind of threat that required he be stricken from the myths.

But most people who came looking for him inspired by tales of flying on wings made of wax and feathers, knew what he looked like.

"I appreciate some of your work," she said. "I like mazes."

Irritation tickled his senses. "Daedalus built the labyrinth." Not the new one, but very few people knew about Hades' prison.

"Not that maze."

Caution raced through his veins at the words. "Then you'll have to be more specific."

She fiddled with a cuff on her ear, tapping her finger against the metal. "Might as well get this out of the way. Zeus sent me."

Icarus could guess where this was going, but he wanted to see how much she'd say if he let her keep talking. She wasn't Zeus' daughter. As brightly as she glowed, traces of her parentage should be visible in her aura.

Perhaps she *was* Aphrodite's. But the pink and blue were more of a recreation than a natural result. The colors were right, but the pattern was structured—more like a fractal than an organic flow.

He was barely aware of stepping forward, until she took a step away. She wore a tattoo on her neck. It might be a god mark, but most heroes that knew who they were didn't brand themselves with their parents' names. Besides, hers said *Truth*, and it didn't belong to any of the gods.

"What does Zeus want from me?" he asked.

"A new prison for Hades." Her voice was firm, despite the heave of her chest.

The air between them was charged. Talk about the ultimate mystery. She was stunning. Compelling.

Understated but impossible to ignore. A walking dichotomy.

How had he never met her before? A woman with this kind of power? There should have been rumors about her existence. *Something.*

"He let someone break the last one," Icarus said.

She licked her lips. "And that person is very sorry and wishes they could take it back."

As he searched her eyes, images flashed in his mind. Snippets. Desires. Of kissing the shine from her mouth. Of pressing her to the wall and seeing if this electricity was real. Of fucking her until they were both spent.

Of flying?

"Who are you?" He didn't want to guess. He had to know.

With each step Icarus took toward her, Lexi took one back, until she collided with something. Toasters and coffee makers rattled on the metal frame, and she gripped the shelves to steady both the appliances and herself.

"Who are you?" Icarus' gaze bored into and through her.

She collected herself. She wouldn't let that intense gaze burrow any deeper into her soul. Her heart hammered against her ribs. It should be with fear, facing this unknown entity, but it was a stifling need that stole her breath and threw her mind off balance.

"Is this a metaphorical question?" she asked. "As in, what's my meaning in life? Who am I?"

"It's a literal question. I'm a literal kind of guy." Each time he looked her over, heat raced along her skin.

And the images that filled her head—maybe they were a side effect of being around heroes? Aphrodite help her, if she fantasized about screwing every one she met. This hadn't happened with Heracles, though. She'd just wanted to punch him.

If Icarus didn't recognize her, the illusion was working. The new face. The adopted glow. "Can't you see it in my aura or smell it on me, or something? Everyone else can," she said.

He dipped his head closer, and her pulse kicked up to a billion. Desire raced through her veins. "You're not going to lick me, are you?" She tried to keep her tone light. Cerberus and Actaeon could smell who she was. Maybe this guy had a different approach.

"Only if you beg."

That was tempting. She could almost feel his tongue gliding along her skin. She smirked to hide the reaction, and shook her head. "Cocky much?"

"You have to beg for that, too. Besides, I'm more of a hands-on kind of guy." He trailed his fingertip over the mark on her neck, never making contact. "Why *Truth?*"

His touch hovered close enough to her skin the electricity flowed between them. If she looked down, she swore she'd see the sparks. She bit the inside of her cheek, to prevent her gasp from escaping.

The front door of Icarus' shop clanked open, startling her. "Sorry that took so long," Cerberus said.

Icarus looked at him, then back at Lexi. "If he's Cerberus, that makes you…"

Fuck. "I should have asked you to stay outside," Lexi thought.

"Am I interrupting?" Cerberus' question echoed in her head.

Icarus glanced over his shoulder, at the mirror behind him. He met Lexi's gaze in the reflection and scowled. "Nope." He put several feet between them. "My answer is a hard *no.*"

"We haven't gotten into details yet." She'd almost forgotten that was why she was here.

He glared at her. "You broke my fucking labyrinth." The smooth seduction was gone, replaced with raw irritation.

The instinct to apologize, and make everything all better, nudged her senses. Fuck that. She didn't do anything wrong. "I said I was sorry. Besides, it wasn't technically me."

"You were the catalyst, so it doesn't matter if you're here for toaster parts. The answer is *no.*" Icarus turned on his toe and stalked away.

"You're right. I should have stayed outside," Cerberus thought.

Icarus would have found out anyway. Lexi was grateful it happened sooner, rather than later. The disguise was grating. The teasing, though… She wanted that back.

Icarus paused and whirled back around. He looked between Lexi and Cerberus, and then landed his gaze on her. "He shares your aura. Your actual one, not that bullshit lightshow. I thought it was a rumor, but you have a servant. How'd you do that?"

"Magic?" Lexi tried to laugh. She didn't know how far the answer would get her, but it was the best she had.

Cerberus crossed the room to stand next to her, a scowl marring his expression. "Loyalty and benevolence."

The fascination Icarus watched them with was almost tangible. Inspiration struck. Everyone wanted to know how she'd formed the bond with Cerberus, and though she didn't have answers, she did have something to offer this intriguing man. "I don't know how it happened, but I'll tell you everything else if you hear me out."

"Be careful with your phrasing." Cerberus' warning might as well have been a shout in her head.

"Deal," Icarus said and gestured toward the back of his shop. "You look like a coffee kind of woman. Or will this require something stronger?"

The about-face cranked Lexi's suspicion to *Maximum.* "Just like that? You're not going to negotiate?"

Icarus shrugged. "Nothing to negotiate. I'll hear you out, as in, you'll explain that Zeus wants me to spin my wheels on another prison that can't contain your father. Then, when I've listened, you'll tell me *everything* about the events leading up to your successfully making a pact with a servant."

"Define *everything*." Lexi didn't mind a good barter. Not like what Zeus forced her into, but this seemed fair.

"Careful." Cerberus said the word at the same time he thought it. The echo was jarring.

Icarus crossed his arms and tapped his foot. "*Everything* is everything. Yes or no?"

"Are you sure that's what you want?" Cerberus stepped in front of Lexi and stalked toward Icarus. A growl cut through his voice. "You want to hear about the death? The betrayal? The sex—"

"You're not deterring me." Icarus stood his ground.

Cerberus paused with only a few inches between them. "The years of online chatting that frequently broke down into giggles and winky faces? You want a play-by-play of the late-night geeking out—"

"No. Fuck no. Yawn?" Icarus sighed. "You don't have any idea how you made the bond."

Lexi shook her head. "Cerberus was dying, and I didn't want him to. A bunch of words were exchanged… I may have threatened a few gods. Not that any of them heard me except for Artemis."

"I'd have paid to see that. Are there actually any details to share?"

If Lexi said *no*, would he shut her down? It didn't matter. She'd made Zeus' request, and nothing more was required of her. Except she hadn't expected to be intrigued by this man.

Because that was what she needed—to be fantasizing about another hero. *Not*.

"It was stressful. It hurt like nothing I've ever experienced. I can offer those details." Cerberus' voice was strained. Whispers of that agony ran between him and Lexi, gnawing at her bones and aching in her soul. She hated that he'd gone through that.

It was also the first thing she'd felt from him since he walked in the shop. He was shutting her out.

"My answer is *no*, to the new prison for Hades question." Icarus almost sounded apologetic. "Kill the bastard. Don't try to lock him up again."

"Zeus said that wasn't possible." If she pushed this angle, could she glean enough information from Icarus to decipher Zeus' lie?

"He'd know better than I do, but I suspect there's a way."

That wasn't helpful. "So that's it? We're done?" The entire exchange was easy. Straightforward. Lexi should let it go.

Icarus shrugged. "You can't help me. I can't help you. So, uh… ciao, toots?"

"Great. Thanks." Cerberus hooked an arm around Lexi's waist and steered her out of the store.

The familiar contact shoved the odd conversation with Icarus to the back of her mind. Making things right with Cerberus was far more important. A pain grew in her chest at the idea of fighting with him. The moment they were outside, she turned to face him. "Now, can we talk?"

"Sure. Never do that to me again." The edge was back in his voice, slicing through her.

"Do… what?"

"Make me choose between protecting you and obeying you."

Oh. She should have guessed that the couple of hours that passed since they left the mob behind were more likely to aggravate Cerberus than calm him.

"What were you going to do? Start biting arms off? They couldn't hurt me," she said.

His growl was like sandpaper over her hurt. "None of us is *actually* immortal. You remember that time when I nearly died? You don't know how far your powers extend. What if the angry mob had ripped you apart?"

Underneath the anger and frustration, she felt his hurt. His concern. That sliver of fear that he could still lose her.

She understood that worry. Lexi didn't want to imagine life without Cerberus. "I didn't mean to piss you off."

"What did you think it would do? You can't make a habit of decisions like this. It will get you killed."

"That's my choice." She hid a wince. The words came out wrong. She didn't want to die, but she wouldn't be responsible for letting him kill others.

"And you take my decision away by ordering me to act against my will."

No. She wouldn't let him spin this back on her. "I'm sorry you're upset. I'm not sorry about what I did."

"That's fine. You don't have to be. I'll see you at home." He turned away.

Unbelievable. She was trying to talk this through, and he was pouting? "You're just going to storm off in a huff?"

"I'm going to take care of business. Believe it or not, I had a life before you, and it didn't cease to exist because you came along."

The retort knocked the air from her lungs and left her speechless. All she could do was watch him walk away.

CHAPTER FIVE

Actaeon trekked back to Apollo's house, and hammered on the door for several minutes. There was no answer.

He called Artemis, to see if she had any insight into the Cassandra event. There was no answer.

He was starting to see a pattern.

So he'd tried to take his mind off the evening by reading. He couldn't focus. When he heard the front door *snick* open, relief trickled through him. Lexi and Cerberus' company would be a welcome distraction.

The door slammed shut, and his relief evaporated.

Cerberus wasn't here. Actaeon only smelled Lexi. A moment later, she stormed past the living room, footfall heavy on her way to the stairs.

"Whoa." He called, keeping his tone light. "Are you all right? Where's the puppy?"

Lexi whirled. "*Holy fuck*. Could you not, with the stupid fucking nickname, every fucking chance you get?"

Actaeon held up his hands. "I'm sorry. It's habit. I'll try to stop."

"I can't believe you had to be asked. He's told you he doesn't like it."

Whatever Actaeon had walked into, he was ready to backpedal out. Thank Athena she wasn't throwing balls of sunshine, like Cassandra had. "Do you want to talk about what happened?"

"No. How was your not-date?" Snideness filled her question.

"She tried to blow up a waitress, and Apollo intervened."

Lexi gave a barking laugh and crossed her arms. "Bummer. So sorry to hear it."

Her frustration and hurt and disappointment washed over him. He might not share an emotional bond with her, the way Cerberus did, but she radiated a jumble of feelings. None of them was sympathy.

The bulk of her feelings might be directed at whatever happened with Cerberus, but Actaeon suspected he had a little part in how she felt. "I'm sorry I went." He poured sincerity into his words.

"Because your dead girlfriend tried to blow you up?" Her words were harsh, but some of the tension faded from her posture. She may not like what he had to say, and that was her right, but at least he'd know that he meant it.

"Because it hurt you. Because she doesn't deserve my attention. Because she's my past, and I want you to be part of my future."

Lexi frowned and let her arms fall to her sides. "You don't owe me anything. I can't expect you to structure your world around my feelings." But the catch in her voice said she didn't mind the consideration.

He was a fucking idiot. Cassandra had showed up, and instinct told him to help. It seemed like listening to that instinct got him in trouble as often as not. "What you think and feel is important to me. I shouldn't have let her influence that."

Lexi rubbed her face and exhaled noisily through her fingers. "I don't have a comeback. Yay, I guess?"

He hated seeing her this way. "What happened?"

"I don't want to talk about it."

"What would you like to do?"

"Like you care."

"You know I do. You wouldn't be here if I didn't." He wanted to cross the distance between them and wrap her up. Fight away whatever was eating her. He doubted it was the kind of thing he could fire an arrow through, though.

"Why?" Desperation leaked into her voice. "Why do you care? How do I know you won't turn around and run back to Cassandra the moment her day is worse?" It wasn't a hostile question. She searched his face.

He deserved that. "I won't. I promise. I care because I care."

Lexi hugged herself. "You barely know me. Every time you say you're done with me, you change your mind. Why?"

He hated to hear her phrase things that way. He untangled her arms, to grasp her fingers. Some of the lines faded from her forehead. "I'm not done with you. That's not what happened with Cassandra. I…" How was he going to phrase it differently than before?

"Feel responsible for her. I know. I heard." Lexi clenched her jaw.

That wouldn't do.

He guided her to the couch, sat down, and tried to pull her into his lap. She sat next to him instead.

That was fair. He didn't like it, but he got it. "You and me getting to know each other comes with time, and we have a lot of that. But you're not the only one fumbling your way through things."

"But…" She sighed.

He waited for more, until he realized she wasn't going to finish the thought. Actaeon draped an arm over her shoulder. His relief when she didn't pull away was more potent than he expected. "I don't know what I feel for you. It's not fate. Don't think I'm doing this because I buy into the notion that a red string means I should care. I want to know more about you, and figure out what this is. I like having you around."

"What if you get tired of me?"

What had he done to make her ask that? *Stick up for the woman who killed her mother*. Yeah, that had been stupid. "I don't see it, but I can't promise."

She stiffened, and he kissed the top of her head.

"Don't discount whatever this is because it's not set in stone," he said. "I'm up for giving it a chance if you are."

"I kind of wish I could call you a liar and mean it. That would make this easier."

"I won't apologize for telling you how I feel. Do you want to talk about what happened?"

Lexi draped her legs over his, as she leaned her back against the arm of the couch. She looked at him. "We went to the market, like you suggested, and it was a lot of fun."

"Until...?"

"Someone recognized me. Things turned ugly—*mobs of people backing me into a corner* ugly—and I ordered Cerberus not to hurt anyone. He got mad, a bunch of other stuff happened that made things worse, and he walked away pissed off and said he'd be home later."

"Ah." He understood without question Cerberus had been upset. And if the hellhound snapped at Lexi, it made sense she was angry in response.

"You're going to take his side." The hurt in her voice wasn't as potent as before, but it was back.

He rested his hands on her legs, pulling up her jeans enough to rub a thumb over her ankle. "I'd tear someone apart for you. Before you ask, I can't tell you why, except that I would. I begged my mother for asylum for you. I was willing to try to kill Hades—"

"That wasn't for me. That was to save people."

"It was to save *you*." Yes, the others mattered, but he couldn't deny what his primary motivation had been.

"So you *are* taking Cerberus' side."

Actaeon didn't see it that way. "I'm pretty sure I'm taking your side. You want me to be mad at the pup—at Cerberus, and I will be."

"No. Don't twist things that way." A hint of warning leaked into her voice.

"Fine. I understand where you're both coming from. This is a fight I can't take sides in, except that I hate to see you hurting."

Lexi dropped her head back and let out a long groan. "What was I supposed to do? Let him tear someone to shreds?"

"I don't have an answer for you. How'd you get out of it?"

"Zeus zapped us out of there before things got ugly. He wanted a favor for a favor."

Lexi felt raw inside. Actaeon believed everything he said, but she couldn't fathom how it was that easy. Jumping to Cassandra's defense, and then abruptly regretting it. Suddenly knowing what he'd done to piss Lexi off, when he'd glossed over it hours ago.

When she was growing up, Dad was her confidant to a point, but there were some things wasn't comfortable sharing with him. There was no one else until Cerberus, and so much of their conversations online had to be limited, to keep her hidden.

She was learning to open up to him now, but she still held back. There were some things she worried might disappoint him.

It was different with Actaeon. She felt like she could say whatever was on her mind, but didn't know if that was a good thing.

"What Zeus he ask for?" Actaeon's touch was comforting. It sent energy zooming through her, and chased away the shadows in the corners of her mind. When he was on her side, it was nice.

When he wasn't... Was she being childish about Cassandra? No. If she was *just* an ex-girlfriend, maybe. But the things Cassandra had done...

She couldn't tumble down that hole. She needed to talk, Actaeon was listening.

"He wanted me to talk to this Icarus guy. To ask him to make a new maze. Zeus said it had to be me because I needed to apologize for breaking the last one. But that didn't seem to make a difference." Her apology hadn't quite been sincere. She suspected that wouldn't have mattered.

Actaeon raised an eyebrow, and his grip tightened slightly on her ankle. "So Zeus waited until you were out with Cerberus, just the two of you, and he had a chance to get you to owe him. I can tell you why."

"Enlighten me." She wasn't in the mood for anymore guessing games.

"You met him, didn't you? Icarus? You talked to him for a few minutes?"

"Yes…" She wished it had been longer. Not that it mattered.

"It's been more than a week since you formed the servant's bond with Cerberus. By this point, everyone in the pantheon knows about it, and they all want to know how you did it."

It was too simple. "He did seem hung up on that."

"It's that simple." Actaeon echoed her thoughts. "And it's why Zeus sent you and Cerberus. Icarus told you *no* today, but he's going to keep coming back to you and the situation, until he has an answer."

She shouldn't like that idea. She should be focused on mending things with Cerberus and figuring out what the fuck was going on with

Actaeon. The last thing her heart needed was to be lusting after some random third guy, and hoping he'd ask for another chance to talk to her.

"Awesome." She kept her tone flat.

Actaeon gave her a dry smile. "If you'd like another opportunity to talk to Icarus, I can put you in front of him. Fifty-fifty chance you'll get a better response with me there than you did with the dog."

"Seriously?" She twisted her mouth at the hound reference.

"Habit." He almost sounded apologetic.

"Say I do want another shot at talking to him." There was no question. She wasn't going to show that card, though. "What falls on the other side of that fifty percent?"

Actaeon's wince was telling. "He refuses to ever see you again. But I'm going to a funeral tomorrow, and he'll be there. It's for a mutual friend."

That sounded inappropriate. "I'd rather not discuss politics—what would you call it?—while relatives are mourning their loved ones."

"It's the best place for civility. After more than three-thousand years, funerals are footnotes. Gatherings for the living."

She shivered in spite of herself. She hadn't attended many funerals in her life, but Dad's still haunted her dreams and devoured her psyche when she dwelled too long on his death. "You make it sound so cold."

"George—the man who passed away—is with his partner in the afterlife. They're reunited and happy together. Do you want me to mourn that?"

"No." Envy spiked inside at the reminder that death meant being reunited for most people. For everyone in her life it had just been an end. "I'd like to go with you…"

"But?"

"I don't own any dresses." Or much of anything. If it didn't fit in her backpack, she left it behind. It was an excuse, but it sounded good. She didn't want to be surrounded by mourners. Fake. Obligatory. Oblivious.

"I'm sure I have something you can borrow."

She didn't know how to respond to that. "They're not Cassandra's old clothes, are they? You didn't keep them from way back when, in case you did find her?"

"I didn't save Cassandra's things, and I wouldn't offer you her clothing. I've hung on to some of Artemis' things."

Lexi laughed, partly with relief that he easily rebuffed her concern, but cut it short when she realized he was serious. "You want me to wear your mother's dress?"

"She's not using it and she's got good taste."

"That's not weird to you?" Lexi wasn't picky about where her outfits came from, as long as they were clean, but this seemed odd.

Actaeon's raised eyebrows implied he believed otherwise. "Sisters share clothes. Mothers and daughters. Friends. If it's a big deal, we can go shopping. Or you could illusion yourself up something."

He made it sound so benign. This was one thing she was willing to admit wasn't worth overreacting to. "If no one minds, it wouldn't hurt to look."

"I promise, if you've never worn a Rhapso creation, you're in for a pleasant surprise. Nothing fits like nymph clothing." He extracted himself from under her legs, stood, and tugged her to her feet. "Come on."

Lexi let him lead her toward the rear of the house, to a room she hadn't been in yet.

"Are you free?" Cerberus' tentative question nudged her thoughts.

Relief tricked inside, but she wasn't willing to let it reign. *"Actaeon's letting me shop for dresses in his closet."* That was appropriately vague and casual. She hoped.

"I'm sorry," Cerberus said. *"I understand why you did what you did."*

The corner of her mouth tugged up. *"Me too. I mean, but all that stuff you said, back at you."* She paused, considering her words. *"I know why you wanted to protect me, but I'd make the same decision again."*

"I know. You're willing to put the world above yourself. It's one of the many things I love about you. It's also one of the many reasons I can't let you."

She clenched her jaw. That meant this could happen again.

"I'm not trying to make you angry," Cerberus said. *"I'm heading back there in a few hours, if you'll have me. We'll have this conversation face-to-face?"*

That would be better. This wasn't a solution, but it was a good start. *"Of course I'll have you. I'll see you in a little while. But you're not changing my mind."*

"No. I don't expect to. I love you."

"I love you too." She liked being able to say that, even when things were tense. Would she ever reach that point with Actaeon?

Was it worth worrying about right now?

The wall that had kept Cerberus' emotions blocked off from her vanished, and she could feel him again. The flow of affection surged in. She'd missed this so much, despite it only being gone for a few hours.

Actaeon had crossed the room. He flipped a switch, and light spilled out from a huge walk-in closet.

Why am I doing this?

The thought came from nowhere. She'd done what Zeus asked—passed the request for a new prison for Hades along to Icarus—and gotten her answer.

Why was she jumping on another chance to speak to Icarus again?

Lexi had two incredible people to fall in love with, twice as many as most ever got. And while one was up in the air, Cerberus was hers alone. She definitely wasn't seeking out Icarus to explore the strong pull she felt toward him.

The answer was simple—Hades needed to be kept in his place. If Icarus could do that, she needed to plead with him to reconsider.

That was the only reason.

CHAPTER SIX

Lexi sat in bed, trying to focus on a book. Actaeon had hundreds of them in his library. Some of them were even newer than a century old. He wasn't much of a genre reader, though. She'd plucked a leather-bound HP Lovecraft book from the shelf.

It turned out the Old Ones weren't so scary, when the real gods were more callously destructive.

She set the book aside, and scrubbed her face. Sleep wasn't happening.

It wasn't unusual for Cerberus to take off in the middle of the night. Sleep was optional for him, just like it was for Actaeon.

But this was the first fight Lexi had with him, and despite the mental apology, she wanted him here, to cement that things were all right.

She tried to keep the desperate whining out of their bond—at least he'd left that open—but she let the longing flow through.

He wasn't speaking to her mentally. He was sending back reassurance.

It helped, but it wasn't a long-term solution.

"I'm home," Cerberus' voice in her head was one of the most beautiful things she'd ever heard.

"Can I ask where you've been?"

There was no answer. She frowned. Did they need to make up first? She understood that he wouldn't tell her everything, especially as life went on, but the snub dug deep.

He stepped into the doorway. "You can ask, and I'll answer."

She hopped from the bed, crossed the room in a few short steps, and hugged him tight.

Cerberus squeezed back, and kissed her on the top of the head. "I'm sorry."

"It's okay. Or, it will be." She took a step back, and grasped his hands. "Where were you?"

"Touching in with old contacts. People I knew when I worked for Hades. Trying to get a good idea of who I could still trust."

She nodded. It seemed like a smart thing to do.

"It didn't have to be now, but I needed to think." Cerberus searched her face.

She didn't have to guess that he was looking for understanding. She couldn't offer that quite yet. "I see."

He tilted his head back to study the ceiling, before meeting her gaze again. "I can't let anything happen to you." Warmth and concern lined his words. "Not because I serve you, but because I love you and I'd be lost without you."

"I get that." And she did. She felt the same. "But those people…"

"You don't want to see anyone hurt who doesn't deserve it, and even then you hesitate. I understand." He brought her hand up to kiss the back of her knuckles. "I'll respect that until I don't have any other choice."

She couldn't argue that. Or rather, she could, but she was tired of fighting, and it seemed like a reasonable compromise. "Thank you."

"Come here." He bent to hook one arm under her legs, and steadied the other behind her back, and lifted her up.

She let out a tiny laugh, and wrapped her arms around his neck, letting him carry her to the bed.

He kissed her on the cheek, pulled back the comforter, and set her on the sheets. "Don't move," he said.

"As you command." She gave him a mock solute.

Cerberus shed all of his clothes except his boxers, the climbed into bed with her. He nudged until she rolled on her side, to press her back to his chest.

This was good. It was right. *"I'm lucky to have you,"* she thought.

"Luck isn't any more reliable than fate. We earned this."

It was a good point. Months and months of getting to know each other online. Finally meeting in person and realizing despite the shit storm they were in the middle of, they fit together. *"Whatever it is, I love it. I love you."*

He kissed the back of her neck. *"I love you too."*

Regardless of what she and Actaeon might have, it wasn't anything even close to this. She hated the thought the instant it popped into her head. Way to ruin a perfectly good moment.

"Where'd you go?" Cerberus asked aloud.

She hadn't meant to shove him out of her thoughts. She forced herself to drop the wall that had gone up instinctually, and let the ideas flow between them. These thoughts were difficult, but she didn't want to hide them from him. "Someplace I shouldn't have."

She might want more with Actaeon. There was a pull she couldn't ignore. Right now? They were barely more than friends with benefits. Was it a benefit if it had only happened once?"

"There's no reason to rush things," Cerberus said.

"But Actaeon…" She didn't know how to finish the thought.

Cerberus rested his chin on her shoulder. "You're not responsible for his actions. What he did with Cassandra? I can't explain that, and it's not either of our places to make excuses for him. You'll either reach a point where you understand who he is, and still accept him, or you won't. Neither outcome is wrong, and you don't have to figure out anything tonight. Or even next month. Or next year."

She wasn't used to looking at her future beyond tomorrow. It would take some time before she was okay with *the answer will happen, just not yet.*

Icarus felt awkward being in George and Ralph's house, now that the owners had moved on.

Esper had inherited it. The paperwork would take a few more days, as would most of the things that needed to be done, but there was no doubt she owned it now.

Still, he was adjusting. He paused in the kitchen, letting the memories wash over him. He was here to help her get things in order. Ensure funeral arrangements were made, insurance claims started, and everything else she wasn't prepared to face while she grieved.

Esper was in her mid-twenties, so she didn't need him, as her godfather, to be her legal guardian. That didn't mean she couldn't use the support.

So many things had happened in this room. In this house. George and Ralph starting their life together. Bringing Esper into their world.

So much love and hope and pain and loss radiated from the walls.

He hated seeing Esper mourn. Guilt gnawed at him. A mortal death hadn't hit him this hard in… he couldn't remember the last time.

Esper bursting into tears every few minutes made things worse. Not that he blamed her. He sat at the kitchen table. He needed to numb his mind, or he'd never make it through the next few days. But being here reminded him of George's call. The coffee they never managed to have…

Icarus had done everything he could, but it didn't feel like enough. He'd missed *something*.

"Icarus?"

Hearing Esper use his full name dragged him from his thoughts. She was sitting in a chair on the other side of the table, watching him. "I'm sorry, what?" he asked.

"You were someplace else. Was it nice?" Her smile didn't reach her red-rimmed eyes.

He shook his head. "It really wasn't."

"This is all my fault." Her voice dropped so low he barely heard her. She clasped her hands and turned her gaze toward them.

He reached across the table to cover her hands. "It's not. You're never responsible for someone else's actions."

"Intellectually, I understand that. But I can't ignore that nagging feeling that if I hadn't…" She swallowed a sob.

Icarus felt her words. They gnawed at his core and mirrored his own tumble into grief. But this girl who only had a few decades of life behind her, and may not have many more in front of her if she hadn't inherited her father's immortality, needed his support. He shoved his own doubts down. "If you hadn't what?" he prompted kindly.

Her frown deepened and her chin quivered. She closed her eyes, and took a deep breath. "I lied to him."

"I'm sur it wasn't a big deal. What did you tell him?" This was the kind of conversation that called for tea, or something else soothing. But Icarus didn't want to interrupt her, and risk stalling the dialogue.

"I told him I hadn't seen Daddy Ralph recently."

Icarus' gut clenched, but he kept his reaction from his face. "How recently?"

"Don't be mad, please. And don't tell me I'm crazy." Grief coated her words.

He squeezed her hands. "I'm not mad, and you're not crazy. Gods call themselves our benevolent overlords. Your godfathers are three-thousand-year-old immortals."

"But that's just the way the world is."

He supposed to her, that was true. "It hasn't always been."

She pulled her hands from his, and twisted her fingers around each other. "Have you ever seen a ghost?"

"I've talked to people who have died." He didn't want to discourage her, but he also couldn't lie. That wouldn't help.

"But you went to the underworld to do that."

Icarus nodded. "I did."

"Do they ever come here?" Esper asked.

The grandfather clock in the hall ticked out the seconds while he searched for an answer. "They've never come to me personally, but I've also never fought a griffin. That doesn't mean it doesn't happen to others. Esper, you can tell me anything. I'm not going to judge you."

She pulled her sleeves over her hands and fiddled with the cuffs. "Ralph came to me in a dream. He said he missed me. That he wanted Daddy George and me to join him."

"When did that happen?" Icarus made sure only sympathy shone on his face. The story sounded too much like George's.

"The first time was a few weeks ago. I guess around when that Hades thing went down."

That Hades thing. Talk about understatement. "Before or after?"

"After, I guess." Esper shrugged. "I thought they were nightmares. School has been stressful. I know Ralph's been gone a while, but I've been missing him more lately. George has been… not quite here for a while now." She sobbed. "I shouldn't have blamed him. I don't blame him. But I thought…

I thought I was dreaming about Ralph because I wanted the support of at least one father."

"It's not your fault." Icarus hated to see her suffer this way. "When did you realize these weren't just dreams?"

"Don't get mad." Her plea was timid.

"I won't. I promise."

"I couldn't sleep after I had the dreams too many times. Trenton was worried, so… he got me something to help."

She was concerned Icarus would be mad about her taking drugs to get some sleep. There were so many worse things in the world. "Did it help? Whatever it was?"

"It was tea. Something of his great grandfather's. It helped. The dreams went away."

Trenton was her best friend. They'd grown up together. Atlas was his great-grandfather. Trenton hadn't inherited any of those titan abilities, as far as Icarus could tell. He didn't even glow the way Esper did. But he knew more about his lineage than she did.

"I'm glad it worked. As long as you're smart and safe about it, that's what matters," Icarus said.

"I was. I am. And it did. But then, I saw Ralph a few times when I was awake."

That was definitely odd. "Did he walk up to you on campus?"

"He appeared in the corner of my room while I was studying. Shadowy and transparent."

"Like a ghost."

Esper nodded. "And then George called me and asked if I'd been seeing Ralph. I was scared. I didn't want him to think I was insane, so I said *no*. And then the night before…" She sobbed, and the dam holding back her tears broke.

The crying wracked her body, and she turned in on herself.

Icarus stood and moved next to her. He helped her uncurl, and pulled her to her feet. He held under until the crying stopped. "You don't have to tell me if it hurts too much."

She sniffled and hiccupped, then dragged the back of her hand across her face. "George left me a message that night. The night he die…" She faded into another gasp.

"It's okay. I'm here," Icarus said soothingly.

"I didn't hear my phone ring, because I put it on silent before I go to bed. He said Ralph needed him. That was I was strong and I'd be okay and he knew I'd make him proud. He promised he'd be watching me from the underworld. I'm so sorry." She was crying again.

He didn't care that she was soaking his shirt with snot and tears. He squeezed her. "It's not your fault. I mean that, and I'll tell you until you believe me. None of this is your fault."

It was Hades fault. Icarus had no doubt. He didn't know why, but he'd make the bastard pay, whatever it took.

CHAPTER SEVEN

"What the…?"

Lexi's unfinished question drew Icarus' attention.

He looked up from his table, to find her standing near the doorway of his workshop, wearing nothing but a T-shirt and panties. The desire that nudged him today rushed over him, raising goosebumps everywhere.

"Do you sleep in that?" she asked.

He looked down, to see he wore the same jeans and button-down he'd had on earlier. He must have fallen asleep working. "Good dream."

She pursed her lips but rapidly shifted to a smile. "I probably shouldn't be dreaming about you."

She held herself with the same confidence as earlier. There was no attempt to hide the fact that she was in her underwear.

Icarus took a step and found himself in front of her. The way her breath hitched sent heat spilling through his veins. *Really good dream.*

Lexi held his gaze, making no effort to put distance between them.

He hooked his thumb under the elastic of her panties and traced along her skin, never moving below her hip, despite the desire pulsing inside.

"I fell asleep at my workbench," he said in answer to her question. "I lose track of time, I pass out." Why was he explaining himself to his own dream?

She shifted her weight, pressing her hip against his palm. "That makes sense."

"Glad to hear it. What are you doing in my dream?" And why was he asking her that?

She looked between them. "Pretty sure it's *my* dream."

Sassy fantasy. He liked that. "How do you figure?"

"I'm the one in my underwear."

And he'd like very much for her to be in even less. "Not sure how that proves your point." He dragged his gaze over her again, studying the long, pale legs, round hips that led to a narrow waist, and full breasts. *Creation,* he had a good imagination. "Unless you're Morpheus."

"No." Lexi shook her head. "If this were Morpheus, I'd see through the illusion."

Fascination warred with arousal. "And you talk like you believe this is your dream. My subconscious is a fucked-up place."

"That's my line."

He liked the banter, but he wanted more. To live out the fantasy that had flashed through his head when they met. "Agree to disagree?"

"You're capable of that?" she teased.

He dipped his head until his mouth was a breath from hers. Invisible sparks rushed between them, dancing along his skin. "I'm capable of a lot of things. I have a feeling even more with you."

She licked her lips and leaned closer.

He closed his eyes to kiss her, and missed. When he looked, she'd stepped out of reach.

The smile she gave him was apologetic. "Maybe next time."

Lexi started awake. The dream lingered, filling her head and heating her to the core. It didn't matter that the contact with Icarus was brief and tame; desire pulsed between her legs.

It was Cerberus' voice that had interrupted the vivid dream, but he wasn't in their room with her. That wasn't unusual. He was either downstairs, or out enjoying the night in his hellhound form.

Lexi kicked off the blankets and went in search of him. She was vaguely aware she was wandering through the house in a T-shirt and panties—the same things she wore in the dream—but as long as Actaeon didn't have company, she didn't care.

Need thrummed under her skin. The sensation didn't fade now that she was awake. She wanted a release, and while she could take care of things herself, it would be much more fun with a partner.

She wandered downstairs, toward the light spilling from the living room. Actaeon sat in an easy chair, reading. *Aphrodite,* that was sexy.

He looked up when she paused in the doorway. "Weird dream?" he asked.

Can everyone see inside my head? She shook aside the question. Actaeon wasn't in her head, and Icarus hadn't been either. "You could say that. It was really…" *Intense? Sexy? Fuck,* she was horny.

"Arousing?"

That was putting things mildly. "Why would you say that?"

"I can smell it on you."

She'd forgotten he had an enhanced sense of smell. It made him a hunter. She frowned, not sure what to do with his observation.

"Don't do that." Actaeon's smile was both reassuring and playful. "It's a good thing."

"Really?" Her pulse hammered in her ears. They hadn't had sex since that first time in the bar restroom, but it wasn't off the table. Cerberus was okay with it. She grew wetter the longer Actaeon watched her.

"I have the perfect solution," he said.

There was only one she could think of, and she suspected they were on the same page. "Do tell."

He crooked his finger and motioned. "Come here."

"Is that an order?"

His smirk was hungry and added a new layer to the prickles of lust filling her. "It's a strongly worded request." His voice was low.

She crossed the room, enjoying the way he watched her every step. When she was within reach, he grasped her fingers and pulled her the last few inches.

Lexi straddled his lap, liking the rough texture of his slacks against the insides of her thighs.

She expected the contact to chase the clouds from her head, the way touching Actaeon tended to do. Instead, as their auras mingled and danced, she plunged deeper into the lust that penetrated her thoughts.

Actaeon dragged his fingers up her back, drawing her to him, and cupped the back of her neck. "I forgot how good it feels to have you this close."

"Me too." She draped her arms over his shoulders and fell into the crush of his mouth against hers.

The bond she shared with Cerberus was intimate, soothing, and nothing like this. Actaeon's caress—his fingers digging into her scalp, his tongue sparring with hers—breathed life into her.

When she pressed her chest to his, her shirt rubbed her skin, tantalizing every needy nerve ending. Their auras wound more tightly together the more their bodies tangled, until it was impossible to tell where her energy ended and his began. The way his ice sent heat spilling through her veins was disconcerting and alluring.

He yanked her shirt off and lowered his head to her breast, to flick a tongue over her nipple, before drawing it into his mouth. He nipped the swollen bud hard enough to sting, and she gasped.

"Good?" His lips vibrated against her skin.

She pressed into his tongue. "Definitely good."

When Actaeon dragged his fingers up her spine, she arched closer to him. With each suck and lick, she worked her hips, grinding against his hard length.

Lexi worked her way down the front of his shirt, undoing each button she encountered, then shoved it off his shoulders. Why had they only done this once? Every touch from him was a new high, thrumming inside.

He moved back to claim her lips, kissing her hard and holding her captive. His grip was demanding, and she loved being needed this way.

With each rock of her body, she pressed against the seam of his slacks. His erection nudged back through the thin cotton of her panties, digging into her clit. She felt like a teenager again, getting off on dry-humping.

She rode the edge of climax, but this wouldn't push her over.

"Stop." Actaeon gripped her hips. She gave him an exaggerated pout, and he kissed her bottom lip. "Not for long. I promise." He nudged her back a few inches on his legs and undid his trousers.

She reached between them before he could, to grip his shaft and work him free. The sharp breath he sucked in through his teeth was musical.

He lifted her without any notable strain, to move her forward again.

She shoved her panties aside, and he slid inside her. He stretched her out, but there was more to the feeling than that. She felt him as if every inch of them touched at once. It didn't make sense when she put it to words, but the sensation was incredible.

Actaeon caught her ear between his teeth. "Finger yourself." His breath was hot against her cheek.

Lexi stroked her clit. She groaned at the different points of contact. Orgasm sped up on her, speeding through her body and lighting up her senses.

He pounded inside her hard and fast. His grunts grew louder when she came. Did he feel her release? Energy wrapped around them, binding and freeing and drawing out her climax.

The edge didn't fall away from her pleasure. She knew when he was close, not just by the sound, but also by the pulse under her skin. When he came, spilling inside her, she felt the heat. The charge in the air. His climax and desire, woven with hers.

He kept up the frantic pace as ecstasy faded, and then slowed to a stop.

Lexi let herself collapse against his chest and rested her cheek on his shoulder. "Holy fucking mother of Eros."

"*Language.*" His teasing was breathless.

She laughed at the playful scolding. "Sorry."

"Mhmm." He pressed his lips to her neck. "Better?"

"Much." Like this, she could almost pretend she didn't remember the dream that brought her down here in the first place.

Icarus was jarred from his dream by his muse's rapid departure.

Muse. Was she?

The shared moment replayed in his mind, vivid and fresh, as if he'd lived it rather than fantasizing—Lexi's scent, her warmth, the challenge in her eyes.

She was inspirational.

He was sitting in his workshop, where he'd fallen asleep. The biggest difference was now his erection pressed against his zipper, begging for attention.

He rubbed his cock through his trousers, wishing it was dream-Lexi's hand grasping him instead.

"Pleasant dreams?" Morpheus' voice came from behind, startling him.

Icarus swallowed his surprise and spun on his stool. He should have known it was too good to be just his subconscious. "You'd know, I suppose. Why'd you send me the gift?"

"It wasn't me." Morpheus shook his head. "I couldn't see it. But you did do a lot of groaning."

Icarus wouldn't focus on that last part. "I didn't think it was possible for you to not see a dream."

"Neither did I."

That was as disconcerting as waking up to the god of sleep watching him. "Why are you here?"

"For information. I was going to get it the normal way—"

"Invading my dreams? That kind of normal?"

"—but someone beat me to it." Morpheus smirked.

Icarus didn't know how he'd kept Morpheus out of his head, but he was grateful to know the dream was his own. "What kind of information do you want?"

"I want to know how you trapped Hades."

Lexi's answer from earlier raced to the front of his thoughts, and he let it roll off his tongue. "Magic."

"Heh." Morpheus' chuckle was strained. "I'm looking for more specific details."

"Trade secret." It was something Icarus wouldn't share. Couldn't. Especially now. Which was the reason he told Lexi *no*. And it made him doubly grateful Morpheus hadn't been responsible for the dream.

He didn't dare think about the *how* of trapping Hades now. He was being paranoid, since he was awake, and Morpheus couldn't see inside his head, but he couldn't risk it. No one could know why Persephone had to be the key last time.

"I must know how to contain him." Morpheus' voice took on a hard edge.

"You *serve* Hades. Trouble in the underworld?"

Morpheus didn't look amused. "Hades is building an army of the dead. Your friend George was one of thousands."

Icarus shook his head. It made too much sense. The call from beyond the grave, the sudden shift in George's mood, what Esper saw—it was so ludicrous, it had to be a god's plan.

"He'll destroy us all," Morpheus said. "When there was balance, he was happy to let things ride. To let his brothers rule above, while he ruled below. When Zeus and Poseidon forced The Enlightenment, they destroyed the equilibrium."

"Fuck."

Morpheus tossed an SD card on the table, and it landed with a deceptively soft *plunk*. "He knows whom he's gathering. If you don't give me the information, give it to someone. Hades needs to be restrained," he said and vanished.

An army of the dead. It was so cliché. So contrived.

Icarus picked up the plastic clamshell holding the thumbnail-sized card, and turned it over and over between his fingers. A pit grew in his chest, telling him once he watched what was on this, he couldn't unwatch.

He needed to know.

He grabbed his phone from where it sat a few feet away, pulled the current card, and popped in the new one.

Maybe someday he'd figure out how to read these damn things just by holding them between his fingers. The thought was enough to amuse and distract him, as he browsed his home-grown operating system, to the files Morpheus provided.

For the next few hours, he tumbled into a pit of viral videos.

A CEO caught on security cameras talking to no one, right before he crashed through a window he shouldn't have been able to break and plummeted twenty stories to his death.

A girl in a locker room—she looked like she was in her late teens—telling the empty air she'd record their conversation, so the world would know someone had back for her. Then she set her recording device on the ground, stepped into the showers, and slit her wrists.

One video after another showed similar events—people talking to no one, before ending their lives. Usually in violent ways.

Revulsion bubbled in Icarus' chest, and he tossed the phone aside, not caring where it landed.

Morpheus was right. This extended far beyond what Esper and George saw, and it needed to stop. Icarus needed to find Lexi again.

Icarus should look forward to that, rather than dread the outcome if she was required to become the next key.

CHAPTER EIGHT

Actaeon needed an outlet for the adrenaline pulsing inside. He straightened the lapels of his suit jacket and felt like he was preparing for a fight, as he strolled up George's front walk with Lexi and Cerberus.

All three were dressed appropriately to the mourning. Lexi had passed on the dresses and gone with a pants suit instead. Like any nymph clothing, it contoured to fit perfectly when she tried it on, and she looked stunning.

"Any particular reason you're nervous?" Cerberus asked him. He wore a suit.

"I'm not nervous."

"Wound tighter than a spring."

Actaeon wouldn't push the argument. This was the wrong time to pick a fight. "Icarus and I had different ideologies when it came to dealing with The Enlightenment."

That, and a few hundred years ago, they went their separate ways as lovers for the last time.

Actaeon knew it had been the right decision, but it left a kind of tension between him and Icarus that time hadn't completely dulled.

"Imagine that." Lexi's sarcasm was marred by its own chord of stress. "Is this where the fifty-fifty comes in?"

Actaeon knocked on the solid walnut door. "Pretty much. It's not as though it's a grudge. Just a minor disagreement."

"I don't want to know what kind of variance there is between your definition of that and mine," Lexi said.

The door swung open, and Esper greeted them. Grief made her look older than her early twenties. Red rimmed her eyes and heavy shadows hung underneath. She managed a weak smile when she saw Actaeon. "Uncle Ace." She threw her arms around his neck with a sob.

Her grief hurt him. She'd avoided so much pain by being here, but some things couldn't be escaped. He returned the hug. "How are you holding up?"

"I've been better."

"I imagine." He let sympathy spill into his voice. "Esper, this is Lexi and Cerberus." To them, he said, "Esper is George's daughter."

Lexi gave her a kind smile. "I'm sorry for your loss. I know what it's like to lose a parent."

"Pleasure to meet you." Cerberus gave a brief nod. "I wish it were under better circumstances."

Esper stepped aside. "Thank you. Uncle Russ is in the sitting room, if you'd like to see him."

Actaeon kissed her on the cheek. "I would. I'm here if you need anything. Not just today, but at all."

"Thank you." Esper ushered them into the house.

Pockets of two and three people were scattered through the home, crowding the place. Actaeon was glad to see such a turnout to mourn George's passing. Funerals might be for the living, but it was gratifying to see George had an impact on so many.

"*Uncle Ace* and *Uncle Russ*?" Lex asked, at the same time Cerberus said, "Who is she?"

Maybe Actaeon should have explained Esper before they got here. Where she came from wasn't one of those things he thought about much these days.

He spotted Icarus at the far end of the sitting room, speaking with an older woman in a tight-cut black dress, who leaned in close each time she said something.

Icarus cast a bored gaze around the room. Rescuing him from the conversation offered Actaeon the perfect excuse to take his time coming up with better answers to Lexi and Cerberus' questions.

"I'll re-introduce you," Actaeon said, and cut a straight path to his old friend.

Icarus met his gaze, then looked past him his eyes growing wide. He said something to the woman, squeezed her arm, and walked away before she could reply, to stop in front of Actaeon. "You know the brat." There was only curiosity in his words.

Actaeon bristled at the nickname for Lexi. "Intimately, and don't call her that. Where do we stand?" He spoke quietly, not wanting to disrupt the mourners.

"Are you still martyring yourself by refusing to take a side?" Icarus's gaze kept drifting to Lexi.

Actaeon was grateful for the subdued atmosphere. "Are you still selling your brain to the highest bidder, for the sake of discovery?"

"No." The corners of Icarus' mouth tugged down. "Not since Hades."

"Same." Actaeon's tension was evaporating.

Icarus clapped him in a brief hug. Centuries ago it might have meant more than a friendly *hello*. Not now. "Then we're good. How do you know these two?"

"Let's get through the afternoon, and I'll buy you a drink and explain."

"It's going to take more than one, but you're on."

"This is surreal." Lexi's voice was low. "The two odd men out in the list of immortals, and you're bros."

Bros. Right.

Icarus's dry laugh mirrored Actaeon's thoughts.

"We'd like to get started," a man called from the front of the room.

People filed into the folding chairs that had been set up facing a temporary podium surrounded by flower arrangements.

There weren't enough seats, so the funeral goers spilled into the hall and the next room. Actaeon and Icarus led Lexi and Cerberus to the back.

"Don't think I missed that you ignored my question," Cerberus growled in Actaeon's ear. "Who—*what*—is she?"

Actaeon glanced at him. "Have some respect, pup—please. After we leave."

Lexi was quiet, taking a spot between Actaeon and Cerberus, and watching.

Icarus stood behind them. "Don't think I missed the ambush, either," he murmured, head near Actaeon's.

"Don't think anyone missed how much you appreciated the surprise," Lexi said as she glanced over her shoulder.

Actaeon shook his head, unsure of what to make of the exchange. This was going to be interesting.

Esper stepped to the podium, to deliver her eulogy. Prometheus would be proud, if he had the sense to appreciate the girl. She kept a tentative grip on calm, as she spoke about her stepfathers with respect and adoration.

When she lost her composure and started sobbing, Lexi squeezed Actaeon's hand hard enough he felt the pressure in his knuckles. He glanced at her, to see unshed tears in her eyes and that she held onto Cerberus as well.

He hadn't considered the setting might be tough on her, despite not knowing the deceased. He hadn't drawn the parallels between her life and Esper's.

A heavy weight pressed in on Lexi the moment they stepped into the house. It wasn't all the people— she accepted the crowded nature of the world—it was what they carried with them.

Grief and longing and regret clogged her pores and filled her lungs until she couldn't breathe.

She shoved the sensations aside while she talked to Icarus. Smiled through the introductions and the banter. Ignored the strange glow around the girl—Esper—that was unlike anything Lexi had ever seen. It wasn't bright, but it was… fractured. Like broken glass, glinting in the light.

But when Esper started speaking, the oppressive weight became whispers, and then shouts, in Lexi's head.

Sobs.

Screams.

Cries for another chance.

For forgiveness.

For vengeance.

And when the girl at the podium broke into tears, Lexi felt the grief through every inch of her body, crushing her until she nearly passed out from the overload.

"Are you all right?" Cerberus' concern mingled with the cacophony. His touch was another set of emotions to deal with.

She wavered on her feet, looking for something—anything—to ground her. Her fingers brushed Actaeon's, and the fist around her lungs loosened. She gripped his hand for all she was worth, letting it tether her.

He glanced at her and squeezed back.

Lexi clawed past the chaos, as it fell away, and resurfaced in her own thoughts. She wanted to wipe away the tears on her cheeks, but she didn't dare let go of the lifeline keeping her attached to reality.

"What was that?" Cerberus asked.

She tried not to let the question terrify her. Or rather, the lack of answers. *"I don't know. I'm fine now, though."*

She spent the next few hours convincing herself of exactly that and not letting go of Actaeon or Cerberus for more than a few seconds at a time. Breathing became easier as people filtered out of the house until only a few remained.

"You owe me a drink," Icarus said.

Actaeon nodded. "Should we say our farewells?" He kissed Lexi on the cheek, then whispered, "Be right back."

She fought back the panic when he let go of her, but the oppressive pressure was gone. Evaporated with the mourners. Or it was a panic attack, brought on by seeing a girl in her twenties deal with losing the man who raised her when her ethereal parent wasn't there.

Lexi drew in a shaky breath, and watched Actaeon and Icarus hug Esper and exchange a few words with her.

Cerberus pulled Lexi in, so her back was to his front, and wrapped his arms around her waist. "I won't apologize if I'm asking this too much." His breath was warm and comforting on her neck. "Are you all right?"

"I don't know."

"I'm here however you need me to be."

She was so grateful for that.

The four of them left the house, and Lexi felt more of the pressure fade in the outside air.

They walked a few blocks to a local bar. By the time they arrived, she felt more like herself.

The brightly-lit pub didn't resemble those Lexi frequented. The group didn't even look out of place in their funeral best.

And when Icarus ordered a round of beers, he didn't pay in barter. There was no hesitation as he tapped his phone against the machine to use digital currency. He led them to a booth in the back corner of the room, away from everyone else. Not that there were many people in here, at four in the afternoon on a Wednesday.

Lexi suspected that would change over the next couple of hours.

She slid into her seat, with Cerberus by her side and Actaeon across the table. Icarus took the spot next to him.

Lexi needed to feel normal, but everything was off by a degree. Tilted just enough she didn't fit. "*Uncle Ace* and *Uncle Russ*?" She forced the teasing into her voice.

"Don't." Actaeon shook his head, but he didn't look bothered. He took a long drag off his beer, before setting the bottle down with a sigh. "She's Prometheus' daughter."

"Well… fuck me. You're serious?" Disbelief rolled off Cerberus.

That must be significant. "As in, barely lucid, bleeds energy, tried to kill you in Las Vegas, used to be chained to a rock—"

"Yes. *As in.*" Icarus leaned in, forearms on the table. He fiddled with the label on his bottle but didn't drink. "The long-story-short version is that Prometheus was finally clawing his way back to sanity after The Enlightenment. The one good thing that came of it, was that after thousands of years in chains, he was free. He met someone. Fell in love. They had a baby."

Nausea surged in Lexi's gut, and her head spun. She knew where the story was going. At the very least, she could approximate.

Actaeon met her gaze and frowned. "Esper was only about six months old when her mother died, and Prometheus… It severed the tentative grasp he had on this world. Icarus knew George, who was looking to adopt, so we made sure she had a good home."

"Right." Lexi didn't know which hit her harder—the similarities between Esper's story and her own, or the differences. "And the nicknames?"

"George didn't want her to know who we were," Actaeon said.

"Your picture is in history books." She turned to Icarus. "And people write songs about you."

Icarus shrugged. "When she was learning to talk, she didn't know that. By the time she found out, it didn't matter."

That must have been nice. Not the losing-her-real-parents thing, but being placed in an upper-middle class home, with a loving father, by a pair of doting *uncles*. It sounded more pleasant than living isolated in a middle-of-nowhere town, and then spending several years running, never daring to tell anyone who she was, before being sucked into a bullshit series of twisted threads of fate.

Lexi swallowed her bitterness. Esper might not have an easy life ahead of her, either. And the girl having a different path wouldn't change Lexi's any.

"Wow." Cerberus shook his head. "I don't have any other words for it."

"She has an aura, but she's never shown hints of gifts," Icarus said. "And now you know the whole story."

Lexi finished her beer. The alcohol hit her empty stomach, and while it didn't give her a buzz, it did take the edge off her tension.

Cerberus waved the waitress over for another round, and Lexi sent her gratitude in his direction.

Icarus focused on her. "Enough about something that happened decades ago. I want to know about recent history. Who are you?"

"You asked me that before, and you know the answer." Verbal sparring was a familiar realm for Lexi. A pleasant distraction.

"That's not what I mean. You can't keep holding out on me. Did he"—he nodded at Actaeon—"tell you that I like finding answers?"

"He told me you're manipulated by knowledge," Lexi said.

Actaeon held up his hands. "Not my phrasing. Accurate, but I was more diplomatic about it."

Cerberus barked a laugh. "You?"

People were spilling in for the evening, and chatter filled the air.

"*Anyway*." Icarus never took his attention from Lexi. "First you taunt me with this whole hero-with-a-servant thing and tell me you don't know—"

"I don't."

"And then you show up with a second guy on your arm. Where do I submit a resume to be a part of your harem?"

Lexi didn't care for the phrasing, or the whisper of heat at seeing more of Icarus. "I don't have a *harem*."

"We're fated mates." Cerberus sounded smug, until Lexi winced mentally. *"I know you don't care for the phrase, but it's true,"* he sent her.

"It's okay. Fate or not, I still love you." She didn't want to pick a fight with him. Not ever again. Those few hours of arguing hurt too much.

And somehow they were on their third round of beers. Lexi downed this one as well. The buzz was kicking in, pushing aside her weird freak-out from earlier.

"Hmm…" Icarus snapped his fingers, and the jukebox a few feet away lit up. Music spilled out. A few people glanced toward them, and a couple moved to dance, but for the most part everyone ignored them.

"You are a fascination, aren't you?" Icarus said.

Lexi shook her head. "Nope. I'm just a girl."

Icarus snapped again, and the song changed.

Lexi didn't recognize it, but the music had a decent beat, and the opening line was, *Take this pink ribbon off my eyes...*

"It's called I'm Just a Girl, *and it's probably older than your stepdad,"* Cerberus told her.

Icarus stood and extended his hand. "If I can't apply to be in your boy band, dance with me."

"You're relentless and absurd." And it was helping her feel better. She nudged Cerberus.

"You can tell him no, *"* he said.

"Are you jealous?"

Cerberus rolled his eyes and scooted out of her way. "You know how I feel."

"I do." And she wouldn't have it any other way. She brushed her lips over his, then took Icarus' hand.

He spun her into him and settled his palm on her hip. It'd been a long time since she danced for fun. As he led, some jumbled combination of a structured step and club-style grinding, it occurred to her how much she'd missed it.

She laughed when he spun her again. As she faced him, he drew their hands up to head level, palms together.

Her brain stalled at what she saw. A thread, distinct and vibrant, ran from her little finger to his.

Why hadn't she noticed that before?

Because she'd gotten used to the faint cord that always connected her to Actaeon and Cerberus..

This was different, though. It wasn't blurred or faded.

She broke all contact and took several steps back.

"Did I do something wrong?" Icarus watched her, concern on his face.

She pressed her palm to her forehead. She didn't need to be tied to every other fucking person she met. There had to be a mistake. "I just got dizzy."

"Are you hear…" Actaeon trailed off when she shot him a look.

Icarus looked between them. "Is she what?"

Lexi sank onto the bench next to Cerberus. "No. It's not voices."

"You hear voices?" Great. Now Icarus was back to looking at her like a curiosity.

"No." She spat the word out more harshly than she intended. "I mean, I hear Cerberus. Servant's contract."

"And others," Actaeon said. Lexi glared at him, and he shrugged. "You're talking to someone who might have answers."

"Hmm…" Icarus sat opposite her.

Her irritation surged, possibly exaggerated by that red string that ran between them, which she couldn't ignore now that she knew it was there. How did no one else see it, and how dare fate continue to make decisions on her behalf? "I'm not a fucking experiment. Don't look at me like one."

"That's not what I'm doing." Icarus sounded contrite.

She needed to calm the fuck down. "I only heard them the once"—twice if she counted today, which she didn't, because today was a panic attack—"and it was probably Apollo's fault. Or Cassandra's."

"*Fuck*." Actaeon grimaced.

Icarus' attention was no longer on Lexi. "Cassandra? What haven't you told me?"

"It's been less than half a day. There's a lot I haven't told you," Actaeon said.

Lexi was grateful to no longer be the center of attention, but she didn't like that vibrant cord that stretched and shrank and passed through objects without pause, running between her and Icarus.

And she definitely wasn't looking forward to explaining it to Cerberus and Actaeon.

There was no way she was telling Icarus.

CHAPTER NINE

Icarus knew Cassandra had *seen* Actaeon come for her in the underworld. Since Actaeon did that decades ago and hadn't found her, Icarus figured her soul hadn't survived.

It was nice to know that wasn't the case, but the missing-memory thing was strange.

The other details of their story were far more fascinating. He could almost feel the adoration flowing between Lexi and Cerberus, and wasn't surprised the promise made as Cerberus died was sincere.

Icarus still wanted to know why Lexi had done something only a god should be capable of, but he was building a picture in his head.

Actaeon's obsession, if it could be called that, was fleeting. Icarus didn't have to ask or delve deeper. His old friend was a sucker for the tormented soul, whether or not they were a soulmate. Morpheus… Cassandra… At least Icarus had never dealt with that. He didn't suffer nearly enough to hold Actaeon's attention for long stretches of time.

Abrupt and irrational anger surged in Icarus, at the idea that Actaeon might do the same to Lexi—treat her as a gauntlet for suffering, and nothing more.

He shook the thought aside. "So what you did in my shop—what Hades said you could do… That extends beyond changing your appearance."

Lexi stared at him, eyebrows raised. "The entire story—that's what you took from it?"

"The rest is standard stuff. Convoluted traps set by the gods, that overlap and cancel each other out. But illusions…"

She nodded at Cerberus. "He pulls his possessions out of a pocket reality that exists on another plane. I just make imaginary things."

"—st heard from my boyfriend. He's back. I'm s—"

Icarus blocked out the background conversation. "Illusion isn't the same as imaginary."

"We tried to explain that to her," Actaeon said.

"—oncement in about ten min—" The bar was getting crowded, and the snippets of conversation were distracting.

Lexi held out her hand, and a screwdriver appeared in it.

Icarus's pulse sped up, propelled by intrigue. The tool itself wasn't special. Medium-sized flathead with a black and yellow handle. The Greek letters scratched on the side, which were only half visible, read *katektises ton kosmo kai parapano*. It meant *you've conquered the world and more*. He knew even without seeing the entire inscription, because he'd put it there. It couldn't be.

He reached for it, but his fingers passed through and brushed Lexi's palm, and the screwdriver vanished.

Invisible sparks traveled up his hand, and he met her gaze. Did she feel that? Was it an effect of her magic? "Why did you make that?"

Lexi dropped her chin into her palm, her hand muffling her words. "It's what popped into my head."

"It's getting late." Cerberus glanced at his watch. "Or crowded. We should get going."

Icarus had so many questions. The most insistent one was, *Why did Lexi recreate a screwdriver from* my *workshop?* "Come back to my place. I'll help with Hades."

"How much will it cost?" Actaeon asked.

Icarus glared at him. "You know me. I'm all about the information. But I'll warn you now, there's not a lot of opportunity for martyrdom in the workshop."

Actaeon opened his mouth.

"Turn on GNN," a woman at the bar shouted.

A few people groaned, but others chimed in their agreement.

The bartender switched the TVs over.

A familiar face splashed across all the screens.

"Fuck me," Actaeon murmured.

Icarus sank back into his seat. This was bad. Beyond bad. When George and Esper talked about seeing Ralph, it was more of a visage in the room kind of thing. More like a ghost. The man on the TV was very real. And looked very much alive.

Lexi looked between them. "Who's that?"

"Steve Jobs," Cerberus said.

"The fruit guy?"

Icarus shot her a glare. "Hush. Listen, and then we'll explain."

"I know a lot of you have questions." The voice that came from the speakers was distinct and belonged to a man who passed away nearly fifty years ago.

"Turn it up."

"Shut your face."

Icarus wanted to smack both of the people arguing. He flicked his fingers, and every speaker in the room turned all the way up, drowning out the chatter.

"—will come in time." Steve's voice grated on Icarus' eardrums, but it was audible now. "I'll take a few questions, but first I want everyone to know that yes, it's really me. Tests will verify that. My time here wasn't done, and Hades saw that. He's sent me ba—"

"Fuck." Lexi massaged her temples.

"—st gods don't answer prayers, but Hades does. He's done this for me, for my family, and for a world who needs to grow toward the twenty-second century. I'll take us in that direction."

The confidence in the words didn't surprise Icarus. Some people never changed, and Icarus had mentored Steve and his business partner, Steve, back in the day. "Arrogant bastard," he muttered.

"I need air." Lexi shoved her way through the crowd and out the door, before anyone could stop her.

Morpheus was right. Hades was building an army of the dead. Not zombies or vampires or anything so cliché. The god was far too sophisticated for that. Icarus grabbed Cerberus before he could bolt after Lexi. "Make sure she's all right—she'll appreciate it more coming from you—then we'll talk. Hades has to be stopped."

Lexi pressed her back against the brick next to the bar's picture window, tilted her face to the sky, and tried to fall into the empty space above her. She couldn't put words to why all of this bothered her so much, beyond, *Hades thinks it's smart.*

"Hey." Cerberus stopped in front of her and rested his hand on her cheek. Comfort and concern spilled through the bond, helping to calm her.

She managed a smile. "So he can bring people back from the dead."

"Apparently."

"You're surprised."

Cerberus pressed his lips to hers, then turned to help her hold up the wall. "I've never seen it done, but this is a different world."

That wasn't reassuring. "He's supposed to be weak. What does this become when he's back to full power? Or maybe a better question is, *What's the point?*"

"I don't know, to your first question. The point? Faith. Why worship anyone else, when he defies death?"

She could think of a lot of reasons, but the question was rhetorical. "What do we do?" There was no doubt she had to do something. She was the catalyst for setting the asshole free.

"The short version is, we get rid of Hades. Icarus said he'd help."

"My dancing was that good, huh?" She meant it to be a joke, but the words fell flat.

Cerberus kissed her again, then took her hand. "Let's hope he's not quite so superficial. If he's going to hit on my mate, he'd better be doing it for your sexy brain."

Mate. She knew Cerberus loved her, but the way he clung to the *fated* aspect of their relationship soured in her gut. It was a petty thing to let herself get hung up on. "I can't argue that. Shall we?" She fell into step beside him, and they headed to the repair shop.

She couldn't help but glance down at their intertwined fingers, and the ethereal red cord that flickered and blurred but bound them.

What she saw with Icarus must be different.

They reached his place, to find him and Actaeon waiting in the main shop. Icarus gestured toward the rear. "Come downstairs. I'll make coffee."

Half an hour ago, Lexi wanted to drink enough to get a buzz and have her thoughts blurred until she couldn't focus on anything specific. The news conference from undead tech-guy took care of that.

Coffee sounded good.

The group headed down a set of stairs and stopped in front of a basic, non-threatening wooden door. Icarus gripped the knob and pushed it open.

As they stepped into the room, Lexi's stomach dropped into her shoes. Not because the space stretched out farther than the eye could see—it was vastly bigger than the building above them—but because she'd been here before. In her dream.

"This isn't on earth." Cerberus' comment kept her grounded.

Icarus grinned. "Nope. It's the other side of the veil. Same concept as the labyrinth was. It makes the whole *if I imagine it, it comes to life* thing work a lot better."

"And the infinite space probably doesn't hurt either," Actaeon said.

How did her subconscious recreate this spot so perfectly? Was she picking up part of Cassandra's gift? As an oracle, would she start seeing the future, along with recognizing the truth of the present? Would it drive her insane?

No. She was overreacting.

She forced herself to ignore the eerie feeling of *déjà vu.* "You have a Tardis?"

Icarus chuckled and glanced at Cerberus. "I see why you love this woman."

"The geek references are just a hint of the *why,* but they don't hurt," Cerberus replied.

Icarus led them further into the room. "I think best down here. You came to me, so I assume you don't have solutions. Let's brainstorm."

He grabbed a remote control from a nearby desk.

The action drew Lexi's gaze to a screwdriver that sat a few feet away. The same design as in her dream from here, identical to the one she'd created in the bar.

No wonder Icarus had been stunned by her trick.

Icarus turned on the TV. "*As our story develops,*" he said in a booming, announcer-like voice.

The goofiness would have made her grin if her mind wasn't struggling to process so much.

"Tell me again why we can't just kill Hades?" Icarus asked.

If Zeus was telling the truth, wouldn't it be public knowledge?

"You saw the fight in Las Vegas?" Actaeon asked. "That was Heracles and me at full strength."

"That was you holding back, because of Prometheus, and Hades at full strength."

Actaeon narrowed his eyes. "Sure, I may have pulled my punches, but what I sent at Hades was all I had."

Lexi remembered how drained Actaeon was after that. She didn't doubt he'd given it his all. "Could we cut Hades off from his power, even temporarily? He did that to me. Cassandra did it to Cerberus."

"We might be able to, except…" Icarus looked at her, frowning.

"Except Hades can't be killed. Zeus told you that." Cerberus' tone was hard to read.

Or she didn't want to admit she heard a hint of despair in there. "Zeus was lying about something."

"Speak of the devil," Actaeon murmured and pointed at the TV.

Sure enough, Zeus was making his way across a marbled floor, toward a podium with rows of reporters and cameras pointing at it.

He stood in front of the room, not saying anything until the chatter died down. He had presence, so it only took a few seconds.

"Ladies and gentlemen." His voice boomed over the room. There were several mics in front of him, but he didn't need them. "I know there are a lot of questions after this afternoon's press conference from Steve Jobs."

He paused, and Lexi swore she felt it through the TV.

"I will not be doubted." Zeus' shout caused the broadcasting camera to shake, and people jumped in their chairs.

Lexi's heart leaped into her throat, and beside her, Cerberus tensed. The shift in ethereal pressure in Icarus' room said he wasn't the only one.

"Now, then." Zeus gave the cameras a flat smile. "It's fantastic that Hades is bringing back loved ones, but I can stop them from being gone in the first place. In fact, effective immediately, all Solstice sacrifices will cease.

"In addition, for those who are dying or recently deceased, they or their loved ones may petition us. We wish we could heal everyone, but there are instances where it's just a person's time. Hades is violating that simple directive—"

Icarus laughed. "Love how he spins this." Sarcasm dripped from his voice.

Lexi couldn't agree more.

Zeus continued. "—more you believe in us, the better we'll be able to help you. More faith, more prayer, and more tributes will ensure that more of you never have to lose loved ones."

Mute flashed on the screen, and Lexi looked up to see Actaeon holding the remote.

"Glad to see he's using the moment to his advantage." Actaeon's voice was bitter.

Icarus opened his mouth.

A loud *boom* filled the air and shook the ground, almost knocking Lexi off balance.

Icarus sprinted toward the door. "Something's wrong outside. That sounded like an explosion."

Lexi, Actaeon, and Cerberus ran after him.

They reached the main street, and Icarus stopped short. "*No.*" Shock and grief filled the single word.

Across the street, smoke spilled from a four-story building, and flames licked at the windows.

Every negative emotion ever created surged inside Lexi. She swallowed it. "We have to make sure people can get out."

Icarus nodded.

Lexi braced herself for an argument from Cerberus about her own safety. He hesitated for the briefest second, studying her. "You're right. We do."

They raced to the building and inside, trying to stay out of the way of anyone evacuating. Lexi coughed as thick, black smoke filled her lungs. This just happened, how was it already raging out of control?

Heat singed her skin. Terror filled her on behalf of anyone still stuck upstairs. They had to get these people out before someone was hurt or killed.

CHAPTER TEN

Actaeon had hoped for something to distract him from what was happening between Lexi and Icarus. A burning apartment building wasn't what he had in mind. Could he take the wish back?

The smoke billowing from the building grew thicker as they stepped through the front doors. "Four floors, four of us. Everyone take a floor," Actaeon barked. "How many units?"

"Sixteen total." Icarus shifted his weight from one foot to the other.

Actaeon understood the impatience. "Lexi, One. Icarus, Two. Cerberus, Three. I'll take the top. Sweep every apartment—closets, showers, anything with a door or that looks like a hiding space."

Lexi sprinted down the hall, and the rest of them up the stairs.

As Actaeon neared the top landing, the building rumbled and shook, and the floor swayed beneath his feet.

Concern and urgency swelled inside. It had only been a few minutes since the explosion. How had the damage spread so quickly? Heat assaulted him until sweat spilled from his pores. If it were regular flame, it probably wouldn't do permanent damage. But this felt otherworldly.

He reached the first door and kicked it open without hesitation. He couldn't linger too long in any place. It was critical he ensure each spot was clear, though.

"Hello?" he called. "I can help you get out of here."

There was no answer. That didn't stop him from searching. He checked under the bed, in the pantry, every place that looked big enough for a small person to hide in.

The children's toys littering the floor of one bedroom made him doubly grateful he didn't find anyone.

He raced into the hallway and to the next unit. Flames climbed the walls and crept in toward the middle of the floor.

A concussive force rocked the structure, and he wobbled on his feet as the second explosion threatened to bring the building crashing down. The sound of snapping beams followed, and the floor creaked under his feet.

Lexi. She would never forgive him if he went to check on her instead of finishing here. The next apartment door was open, and a quick but thorough check said the place was empty.

A wall of fire blocked him from Apartment Three. He sucked in as deep a breath as was possible, given the situation, and ran through it.

Pieces of his clothing burned away, and his skin sizzled.

He'd heal.

It was nearly impossible to see now. Actaeon ran crouched low to the floor.

He was almost ready to move on, when a movement out of the corner of his eye caught his attention. A man—a boy?—lying on the ground, struggling to crawl.

Actaeon knelt next to him. "Hey. Are you hurt?"

"Not badly." The boy's voice was rough. He was probably only sixteen or seventeen.

Actaeon helped him stand and hooked the boy's arm around his neck. "We have to go through fire. I'll keep you as safe as I can."

He half-ran with, half-carried the teenager to the end of the hallway, and paused at the top of the stairs. So far, they were clear. "Can you walk on your own?" Actaeon asked.

The boy nodded.

"Good. Run all the way down. Don't look back. Get outside."

Actaeon confirmed the boy was truly walking on his own, then raced to the last apartment.

The wall of fire tore away more of his clothing, and though his burns were healing quickly, it didn't keep him from feeling the mounting damage.

The final unit was unoccupied. Not even furniture or a shower curtain graced the inside. *Thank creation.*

Actaeon sprinted back to the stairs and down. He reached the top of the last landing and saw Lexi at the bottom, watching, worry heavy in her eyes. She let out a half-smile and shouted when she saw him.

He couldn't hear it over the screams and sirens, but he inferred something about hurrying.

He was a few steps down, when the building swayed again. The splintering of wood mingled with the auditory chaos. Time slowed to a crawl. Literally.

He struggled to maintain his footing, with the stairway threatening to give out beneath him. The ceiling above Lexi exploded in a shower of flame and plummeted toward her.

There was no way he'd make it to her in time. Even if he jumped, he couldn't knock her aside far enough.

"*Lexi.*" His voice wouldn't carry in this noise. A fear like he'd never known swelled inside.

She looked up, and her eyes grew wide.

Flaming debris showered around her, crumbling in sparks, and falling everywhere but where she stood.

When the cave-in settled, she stood in the middle of scorched debris, surrounded by a meter-or-so-wide circle of nothing but clear floor.

A creature landed in front of her, shaking the floor. The chimera had a lion's head, a goat's body, and a snake's tail, and was opening her mouth.

Actaeon charged in, tackling the beast. The impact snapped her jaw shut, stopping the flame that shot from her mouth.

They crashed through the apartment building doorway, splintering the frame and landing on the street. Screams filled the air, and a wide berth grew around them as the crowd backed up.

The onlookers didn't disburse, though. Irritation raked through Actaeon, mingling with adrenaline. Could he contain this and keep anyone from getting hurt?

And why the fuck was a chimera here?

Cerberus in hellhound form joined him. Actaeon had only fought with him once, against an illusion of Heracles, and the struggle was more like Heracles kicking their asses.

But Actaeon and Cerberus had found that rhythm once—the pace needed to help rather than get in each other's way—they could do it again.

The chimera was at least twice the size of hellhound-Cerberus. She swung her tail. Actaeon ducked, and she swiped his legs with her paw, throwing him off-balance and into Cerberus.

The chimera seized the opening to pounce at Lexi, who stood in the apartment doorway, watching.

Icarus screamed, "*Move.*"

Cerberus lunged, grabbing three of the chimera's legs in his jaws. The pair tumbled to the ground in a mess of limbs.

Actaeon gritted his teeth as he watched the beasts struggle. He couldn't use his bow. The risk of hitting Cerberus was too high. He'd need to go hand-to-hand, but with the snapping jaws and whipping tails, that looked even more dangerous.

He needed Cerberus out of the way.

The hellhound had agility, but the chimera had mass. Neither held the upper hand for long.

Actaeon didn't like this. He was a fighter. A hunter. It was what he did. When he came on obstacles like this, he took his shot, and whoever got in the way had to deal with it.

He wasn't used to caring if he caused collateral damage to a brawling partner. Most of them could handle it. Cerberus may not survive an arrow of moonlight to the knee.

"What do you need?" Lexi's question startled him. She had moved to stand next to him.

Nothing she could offer. He wasn't being rude—that was reality. "I need Cerberus to either move the fuck out of the way, or pin her down for about ten seconds." Long enough for Actaeon to draw his bow and aim. "Preferably with the chimera's chest exposed."

"Done," Lexi said. "He says don't miss. He probably can't do this more than once."

Their servant's bond let her ask. Fucking brilliant. Lexi moved out of the way.

Actaeon watched Cerberus tangle with the chimera, his fingers twitching to draw his bow.

The chimera landed on her back. Cerberus clamped a jaw around her throat, and pinned her. His body covered hers, but with the size difference, there was an opening.

If Cerberus moved while Actaeon was shooting though…

"Now," Lexi shouted.

Actaeon fired. He hit the chimera, but not in the heart. She bucked Cerberus off, and charged at Lexi.

Actaeon jumped between them, dagger in hand. He drove the blade up through the chimera's ribs.

Cerberus darted behind them, knocking Lexi aside. Actaeon didn't have to look to know Lexi was shielded. He drove the knife deeper.

The chimera erupted in a white-hot ball of flame that lasted a heartbeat before burning out and vanishing.

He should be heavily burned, but didn't have any more damage than before the chimera attacked. What the fuck?

Unspent adrenaline raced through Lexi's veins, telling her the fight wasn't over. To do *something*. She didn't know why she wasn't a charred husk after the chimera exploded, but it was one thing out of this whole event to be grateful for.

Cerberus was human again. He helped her stand, concern flowing from him.

"I'm all right. I promise," she sent him.

"Good. Everyone else is, too."

She smiled at the nudge of comfort.

Actaeon watched Lexi with concern. She felt lost and… useless. She hugged herself and let her gaze travel over the crowd. People had their phones out and were recording everything.

They were going to be internet stars. *Epic.*

Actaeon wrapped an arm around her waist. "We should make sure everyone is all right." He steered her toward Icarus.

He stood near an ambulance, talking to two women, one a couple decades older than the other, both sobbing. They were next to a man on a stretcher who wore a breathing mask.

Snippets of conversation drifted toward them.

"…surprised he's still alive…"

"…burns like that, he should be gone…"

The two paramedics moved out of earshot.

Actaeon and Lexi joined Icarus, who stepped back a little from the people he was with. "They're surprised he's still alive, especially for someone who wants to let go."

"You know them?" Lexi asked. How was everyone acting so calm, as if a giant, fire-breathing monster hadn't just attacked them?

Icarus raised his eyebrows. "I know pretty much everyone in the neighborhood. I've been here a long time."

"That sounds so strange. But amazing," Lexi said softly. Her attention kept drifting back to the three by the ambulance. What would that be like?

"I wouldn't have it any other way."

She was struck by the sincerity mixed with worry in his voice.

Icarus nodded at the man on the stretcher. "He summoned the chimera. His wife said he kept going on about seeing his daughter."

"The younger woman?" Actaeon asked.

"No. Her sister died several years ago. He was heartbroken. She was his baby girl." Pain filled Icarus' voice. "His wife says he's been seeing the girl for a few weeks. That he insisted his daughter wanted them to join her in the afterlife…" He trailed off with a frown.

Lexi had a feeling there was more to it than that. "What's wrong? Besides the obvious."

He shook his head. "Déjà vu. Anyway, he waited until most everyone was on their way back from the funeral, then summoned the chimera and asked her to destroy the building and everyone inside. He was going to take as many of them as he could with him, so they'd all be happier." Icarus' voice wavered. He scrubbed his face. "That's why it all went up so fast."

"You. It's you."

The shouting made Lexi's calming pulse kick up again, and she whirled.

"You're the reason this is happening." The injured man sat upright on the stretcher, struggling against the paramedic trying to get him to lie down. He pointed at Lexi as he shouted. "Hades wants your head. You will be destroyed."

The venom in the words drilled deep, and she struggled for a response to the screaming. What was she supposed to say to that?

The paramedics forced him prone and strapped him down, but his shouts continued after they shut the ambulance doors.

Phones were turned in her direction now, and a ripple of, *"Is it really her? It is,"* ran through the crowd.

Everyone pointed at her, and fear surged inside. Not for herself, but for what would happen to the onlookers if this got out of hand.

Cerberus was by her side, though she didn't register how he got there. "Come on. Let's call it a day." He took her hand.

"If you go back to my shop, it will let you in. I'll join you as soon as I've made sure people are safe." Icarus pointed them toward his building.

Lexi nodded and let Cerberus lead the way.

There was too much to process, and her mind whirred out of control. Hades was bringing people back to life? And now he was responsible for telling a man to kill a building-full of people?

Or was that last bit the delusion of an injured and grieving man? He recognized Lexi, so the blame fell to her?

She swore her body was ready to snap from the tension winding through it. This was almost worse than watching Actaeon and Heracles fight Prometheus and Hades. Then, the outcomes were limited and obvious—someone would win, and someone would lose.

She didn't know if this situation was related to any of the other strange happenings—to Hades, to her—or if it was all randomly unfortunate.

She and Cerberus stepped into Icarus' pocket reality of a workshop. Nausea filled her, carried on a fight-or-flight reflex with no outlet.

The instant the rest of the world was closed on the other side of the door, she gave in to the weakness pulsing inside. She leaned against a nearby wall and tried to breathe.

Cerberus paced a few feet away.

"Don't do that." She needed to step outside her head, and that meant speaking aloud. "Please? I need…" What? Comfort. An ear. To not feel so completely out of her fucking depth.

To learn how to cope with the world she was a part of.

He stood in front of her and rested a hand on her cheek. The touch helped calm her. "You only ever have to ask." Cerberus' reassurance ran through her like a salve.

"Thank you." How had she survived for so long without something like this? How did anyone?

"Talk to me. Even if the words don't make sense to you, it'll help, to get them out," he said.

"That man out there… What he said… What if he's right? What if this is my fault?"

"It's not. I promise. You don't even know these people."

That was exactly what she wanted to hear. So why didn't it comfort her? "But Hades—"

"What?" Cerberus searched her face.

The door opened, but she didn't pay attention. There was no threat in the air. It was Actaeon or Icarus, or both.

"Given that people are using his name, odds are good that Hades is behind a lot of this." She needed to sort out her concerns enough to vocalize them. "Especially if people are sacrificing themselves in his name."

"Which we haven't seen, but either way, that's him. Not you."

Not reassuring. "But it's like Actaeon says—so much of this stuff is self-fulfilling prophecy. I went after Mom with you and him, because everyone was working so hard to either make some bit of fate happen or prevent it.

"If you hadn't been there, if he hadn't been there, if we hadn't found Persephone… Cassandra wouldn't have decided Actaeon wasn't coming for her, she wouldn't have let Hades use her as a vessel—"

"And if Aphrodite hadn't wiped your memory, you wouldn't have gotten in Actaeon's cab." Icarus interrupted. "If Cassandra hadn't worn the siren earring to suppress her visions, she wouldn't have been assaulted by them once they came back, and she might have kept a grip on her sanity. If Persephone hadn't run… If Hades, Zeus, and Poseidon weren't massive dicks… Do you see how this is a destructive path to go down?

"It doesn't matter if you're the butterfly or the ripple of air its wings cause. You can't take responsibility for the world's woes because you made what you felt was the best decision at the time."

Lexi stared at him, words gone. The edge in his retort dug under her skin. And the matter-of-fact nature of his words anything but soothing.

It helped her feel better anyway.

He gave her a dry smile. "That being said, this Hades thing is right on the cusp of growing out of control. He needs to be eliminated."

"So you'll build him a new prison?" She let relief fill her.

"No." Icarus's response shattered her hope. "I'll help you find a way to kill him, but I won't build another prison."

Her frustration surged forward full force. "What if death isn't an option? Zeus said it wasn't."

"Zeus is a lying sack of shit. Everyone can be destroyed. We'll find a way. No prison. Period. End of story. No room for discussion."

She clenched her fist until her knuckles ached. How did this reasonable man flip to being the exact opposite?

CHAPTER ELEVEN

Icarus didn't want to explain this. There was the risk of someone else plucking the knowledge and using it in less-than-pleasant ways.

But after spending a few hours with Lexi, he had a much bigger concern—she was going to insist he do it anyway, despite the threat to her.

He didn't want to put anyone through what Persephone went through. He'd hated doing it once, but it was supposed to be a sure thing. Persephone was never supposed to be in danger.

Now that the labyrinth had been destroyed and he saw flaws in its construction that he didn't know how to fix, he couldn't ask that of someone again. Especially Lexi. He didn't know why, but he was drawn to her. It was a little maddening.

"Why are you being so stubborn about this?" Lexi was watching him.

He couldn't vocalize his answer. "Why are you? I'm offering death. A way to be done with this entire thing."

"Hades can't be killed," Cerberus said.

"Because no one has done it yet? If that were proof, then any god still alive would be unkillable." Icarus moved away from the group and deeper into his workroom. He didn't like the three sets of eyes watching him. "I'm saying let's put our heads together and figure out how to make it happen. We have the man who was his most loyal servant for millennia, one of the most powerful heroes out there, an actual magical genius, and his own flesh and blood. Between us, we should be able to find an answer."

Actaeon stepped in front of him. The man had menacing down on a good day, and all he had to do was stand there. Today, with half his suit burned away and irritation marring his face, he was borderline terrifying. "What aren't you saying?" he asked. "And why?"

"If you knew what, you'd know why." Icarus didn't have a problem telling him. They disagreed on a lot of things, but Actaeon could keep a secret. This wasn't the time or place to discuss it, though.

"You're going to explain eventually, anyway." Lexi's voice was clear and calm, and when he looked up, she held his gaze. "So we can keep running in circles, or I can say, *please*, and you can tell us what the issue is."

He chuckled at how simple she made it sound. As if the situation were a matter of black and white. Then again, he was making it that, forcing them to choose between death or capture for Hades. "Fine. Here's the deal. The reason the labyrinth worked was Persephone."

"Who was the key." When Lexi said the words, Cerberus flinched.

"And it wasn't because I sat in here and thought, *how can I make this entire setup more convoluted?* It takes a lot of energy to bind a god, and Hades *is* as strong as anyone. I couldn't figure out a way to guarantee the box would hold him, unless I had someone with his power running through them, to help me make the seal."

Icarus paused and watched as the collective *Oh*, spread through the room. "The harpies don't serve him. Persephone is gone. Cerberus is no longer his."

"And that leaves me." Lexi let out a long sigh. "There's no issue, then. Let's do it."

"*No.* Definitely not." Cerberus spat out his disagreement before Icarus could.

That was an easy sell. Icarus still had to convince Lexi, who was glaring at Cerberus, though.

"Not your decision," she said.

Actaeon shook his head and stepped forward. "They're right. You can't do this."

Icarus was grateful for the backup. "Even if you put your foot down and insist, it doesn't happen unless I make it happen."

Lexi looked between all three of them. and let out a bitter chuckle. "*Hi.* I'm sorry. Did every single one of you miss the part of the last hour or so, where some guy tried to blow up an entire apartment building because Hades told him to? Have you forgotten that when Hades was here, at full strength, he wiped out thousands, to prove he could? I'm one person. A person who's tired of sitting on my fucking ass and being helpless, while a god I helped free kills off the population.

"If the solution is to bind him through me, if that saves more than one other person, it's worth it." The conviction and sincerity in her voice was as alluring as the rest of her.

Icarus didn't agree with her logic, though. "Persephone wasn't the only seal, she was the"—he fumbled for the right word—"glue holding the spell together. The trials were there to distract, in case a well-meaning hero came along. But they were never meant to trap anyone, just to point you in the wrong direction." He fixed a pointed glare at all of them.

"It did," Actaeon said. "Until Aphrodite deposited us at Death's door, to get us out. Perhaps your biggest issue was a breakdown in communication."

Icarus let his stare turn withering. "Thank you for the vote of confidence." Sarcasm dripped from his voice. "*Perhaps* I'm not stupid enough to think any god was honest with me about what they put in place or their reasons for it. None of that changes my core point. Killing Persephone should have weakened the prison, not destroyed it."

"And…?" Cerberus let the word hang in the air.

This part was harder than letting Lexi know she was a solution. "And I was wrong. I don't know where I fucked up. I can't tell you why it didn't work."

"That's lovely." Cerberus sounded snide. "Lot of help any of this is."

Icarus didn't need anyone reminding him he'd screwed this up. "Fuck you. I'll get it."

Lexi stepped in the middle of all of them, arms crossed. "In the meantime, if I may—how about we don't take any options of the table? Zeus was hiding something when he said Hades can't be killed. Let's figure it out. If all else fails, put the cell in place and let me seal it, to buy us a little more time."

"Sure. Sounds like a plan." Icarus was willing to say anything, even lie, if it meant he could put off binding her to a new prison.

Lexi pursed her lips and narrowed her eyes. It was as if she saw right through him. "Next time, mean it." Her tone was cold.

He had a feeling he'd crossed the wrong line, and searched for a way to sidestep rapidly. "Go back to what you said about figuring things out. Zeus isn't exactly going to put up with intense questioning."

"No, but between the three of you, how many gods, servants, heroes, and scholars do you know? Someone has to have information about why Zeus would say what he did. And even if it's pieces here and there, we can build a bigger picture, right?"

And she was back to being sexy.

Actaeon seemed to consider her words. "What if we don't get enough pieces?"

"We don't get any if we don't look," Cerberus said.

Icarus clapped. "Great. It's settled, then."

Lexi was beyond frustrated. She didn't think there was a word for what raged inside. It was a sour cocktail of powerlessness, irritation, and fury. Would she be like these three in a century? Would it take two, before mortal life wasn't valuable?

That wasn't quite fair of her, but the way they were acting…

She swallowed the feeling. "Who do we talk to? What can I do?"

Cerberus winced, and her heart sank further. "We're going to need a lot of help with research. Here or back at the house," he said.

"You can hang out here." Icarus nodded at a doorway on a far wall. "That's a kind of electronic version of a siren gate. It sits at the apex of a ley line, and it'll take us anywhere else that has one. That makes this a good place to check in. I have a lot of access to information. We need eyes on that."

"And you're going to do best lying low. People aren't reacting so well to you, and we don't know which gods will be the same." There was Actaeon, with the blunt reality of the situation.

Lexi wanted to pout. Stomp her feet, cross her arms, and throw a tantrum. A little whisper in the back of her head insisted she'd get her way if she did. And with more than just Cerberus.

She didn't want them to yield because she demanded it. She was simply frustrated that they were right, and she didn't have more to offer. That had to change. "All right. Reading, I can do. Where's everyone else going?"

"Athena," Actaeon said. "We want knowledge—"

"We start with the goddess of knowledge." Cerberus finished the thought. "I'm going to go down my list of contacts."

Lexi hoped they weren't the same contacts that led him to her, because that took nearly forty years. She made sure the thought was tucked deep, away from him.

"And if there's anyone I can take you to meet that won't endanger the conversation, I will. We will." Actaeon probably meant the words to be reassuring.

Instead, they were a reminder that she was an obstacle. Someone to be worked around, rather than with. She didn't want the thought to make her bitter. Given they wouldn't even let her do the one thing she was qualified for—locking Hades away from this world—it was difficult to hold onto good will.

CHAPTER TWELVE

Actaeon wasn't letting Lexi become a key to a prison for Hades. It didn't matter what he had to do, in order to stop her. He wouldn't allow it.

If it was really as simple as hunting down an alternate answer, he'd make that happen. He'd apologize to people he'd wronged in the past. Beg for information. Be amicable to the gods. Whatever it took.

He had to admit Icarus' gate was a neat trick. A control panel offered a list of all available destinations. He had a stop to make before Athena. Fortunately, it let him use the same gate.

He'd have to do a little traveling, but that would be the case anyway. It wasn't like a bus line or even an airline, with stops in every major city in the world. There were frequently entire countries between two available points.

But it was faster than flying, and far less expensive than bartering with a god for the travel.

In Italy, he rented a car to get to the coast, then hopped a ferry back to Greece.

Given how things went with Cassandra last time, this could be a bad idea. But if Hades could bring back the dead, as with Steve Jobs, there was as good a chance as not that she fell into that category.

It took several hours to make the trip, and the time alone was disconcerting. Just a month ago, this was *status quo* for him. How did he already miss having others around?

One person, specifically.

That wasn't quite true. He was even learning to enjoy Cerberus' company. And it was good to see Icarus again.

The train of thought didn't sit well with Actaeon, though he couldn't say why.

The exterior of Apollo's home, from the courtyard to the foliage, to the building itself, was a mirror image of Artemis', but cast in warm-colored stone instead of cool.

In the mid-morning light it was stunning. As if it were built to bring the sun to life.

This was a bad idea. It would piss Lexi off. Actaeon didn't want to confront Cassandra again. But he needed answers, and Cassandra had had Hades in her head. She had to remember something.

Actaeon knocked, and his uncle answered.

"I could do this the way you did, and slam the door in your face." Apollo's greeting was dry.

Actaeon gave him a grim smile. "I appreciate your being the bigger man." He had to grit his teeth, to keep the sarcasm from building too sharply. "May I speak with Cassandra?"

"No."

Actaeon should have expected this. He was too distracted, and that was bad. "Would you like to ask what *she* thinks?"

"Hmm… No. That came out wrong. She's already said she'd rather not see you. I have a good idea of what she thinks."

This was ludicrous. Should Actaeon make this a demand, or say *please*? "Will you tell her I stopped by?"

"I will do that. But don't hold your breath waiting for a call."

Actaeon didn't like this, but he tempered his irritation. He didn't know how Cassandra would react if he forced his way into this house, and he needed her to talk to him.

Athena was his next stop. She owned one of the smaller islands, so it meant another ferry ride. Fortunately, she was a favorite local deity, so it was easy to find a boat heading in the right direction.

The trick would be getting her attention. It was her island, people made pilgrimages, and she even left portions of her home open for worship, but it was rare for her to make an appearance.

Between buying a ticket, waiting for the next ship, and the ride, it was early afternoon before he reached Donoussa.

He disembarked with the other passengers. Most of them followed the signs to the gift shop. From there, they could tour the island, pay homage to Athena, then come back here and buy woven trinkets and wooden statues.

Athena had a stronger base of worship than most of the gods. Subtle, but powerful. The sand and plants here almost hummed with faith. Every one of these tourists who bought something stamped with her name, who took it home and displayed it, was offering her a prayer.

He broke away from the group and followed a small path that wound away from the buildings.

There were other people back here—some tourists, but most employees. Signs marked the area, requesting that guests please be respectful and not disturb off-duty workers.

Athena had blessed each marker to carry the same suggestion as the words. Most visitors would read one, then felt compelled to head in the other direction.

Actaeon wasn't here for an employee. He'd reached a row of cabins for those workers who chose to live onsite.

There was a cabin at the end that most people thought stayed vacant. That was his destination. He entered Athena's house without knocking, and paused in the entryway.

The energy that flowed through the room was comforting. Athena was one of the few members of the pantheon who had always sided with the heroes over the gods. And her door was always open to them.

Unsure how long it would take to get her attention, Actaeon crossed the oak floor to a pair of cushions that sat at the far end of the room. He knelt on one of the pillows and prepared to wait.

She would know he was here. This was as much a temple as any house of worship for a god—imbued with Athena's energy and linked directly to her. Which also made the setting as private as possible.

"It's been too long." Her lilting voice startled him. She took a nearby cushion. "I'm glad you're here." She folded long legs beneath her, and her dark hair fell in a curtain around her smooth, tan face, draping down her back and almost touching the floor when she sat.

He hadn't expected her to arrive so quickly. "I'm sorry I don't visit more often."

Athena squeezed his hand in greeting before resting her own in her lap. "Me too. Social visit?"

"To begin with. I have an ulterior motive, but I also have time. How have you been?" He didn't need to rush things. It was nice to catch up with an old friend.

She gestured around her. "Business has never been better. Zeus may be an asshole, but this Enlightenment thing is doing wonders for my bottom line." A breeze fluttered through a window, ruffling her lightweight blouse and winding around them before vanishing again.

Actaeon swore he heard whispers, dozens of them, carried on the wind. "I can only imagine the things you hear and learn."

"It's amazing. It truly is. These people come from all over the world, with their cultures and their technology and their perspectives, and they imbue my little island with all they know and believe."

He wouldn't have the patience for it, but he understood why she loved it.

"I'm glad you're back in the game," she said.

"Does everyone know?"

"I haven't asked them. But you're hard to miss when you're not hiding."

"So I've heard." It shouldn't be an unfamiliar feeling, but registering on so many gods' radars made him feel exposed.

For centuries, he hadn't bothered to cover his aura. Then again, man had forgotten who the gods and heroes really were. Actaeon walked among mortals unseen. And because he'd lost his own faith, so to speak, shortly after The Enlightenment, it felt like he'd been masking his true self much longer.

"What can I do for you?" Athena asked.

"Can Hades be killed?"

Her laugh was shaky. "Cut straight to the point, don't you?"

"Almost always. I don't know a better way to ask."

She unfolded herself and stood. "Zeus doesn't believe that he can be. Or, that's what he says he believes."

"That's not good enough." Actaeon rose as well, so he could look her in the eye. "If Zeus and Poseidon had left well enough alone, Hades probably would have stayed in the underworld." Hades never cared about the trials of the living, until The Enlightenment. "That didn't happen, and he's going to make *everyone* suffer for it." It was information everyone knew, but he had to drive the point home, to ensure the threat was fresh in her mind.

Athena sighed. "I wish I had more to offer. There are some things even I've never managed to learn. Believe it or not, the gods don't want the means of their destruction being public knowledge."

That made too much sense. "Icarus says the only way to bind Hades is with his own energy. I don't suppose there's any confirmation on that?"

"It's probably true. It sounds reasonable. When it comes to Icarus, though, I never dare guess. He has so many things bouncing in his head, I can't comprehend half of it. Invention is a different language than knowledge."

"Where else am I supposed to look?" Actaeon couldn't keep the frustration from his voice. He hated to admit that Cassandra and Athena were pretty much his only two decent ideas about where to turn. He could start going down his contact list, the way Cerberus suggested, but that felt like a lot of wheel spinning, and it lacked subtlety.

There was no telling when he'd stumble on someone who held loyalties he didn't know about.

"There's always the library." She was talking about the books she'd rescued and hidden before Alexandria burned. Stashes of ancient tomes very few knew existed.

"I couldn't ask you—"

"To look on your behalf? You could, and you should. But my answer is *no*. If you want the information, go find it yourself. You know what you're seeking."

He hadn't expected that. "You'd let me wander through the library?" He was almost terrified and definitely humbled at the notion.

"I trust you. I'll send you in, and if you call my name when you're done, I'll bring you back here. But only you."

"It could take me eons to sort through so many books."

"You're exaggerating, but it will take a while. Did you have someone in mind to help you?"

"Her name is Lexi." She wanted to help, and she'd adore the place. Besides, there was no one he trusted more. He wasn't sure why it was so absolute, but it was.

"Persephone's daughter? The girl who bonded with Cerberus?" Of course Athena recognized the name.

"Yes."

Athena knitted her brows together and pursed her lips. She was silent for a few seconds. "All right. But only if I can meet her."

"I'm not sure if she's up for that."

"You, of all people, are familiar with how we work. I'm offering you something big. You can do me this little favor in exchange." Her voice was kind, but an underlying edge of *you don't have a choice* ran through the words.

He wouldn't use Lexi as a bargaining chip in any deal. "I'll talk to her. I'll tell her that's the condition. It's not my trade to make."

"That's fair. I'll see you in a few days, once you've had a chance to work things out?"

Actaeon agreed. They chatted a little longer, and he wished her *farewell*.

As he rode the ferry, he ticked off a rough timeline in his head. He needed another couple of days to talk to Lexi, then get back here. After that, who knew how much time, to sift through the library?

If Hades was using this string of events to regain his power more quickly, he could be back in a matter of weeks.

Suddenly time felt as fleeting and temporary to Actaeon as he assumed it did to most mortals.

A prickle ran up his spine and danced over his skin, and a distinctly non-human scent teased his sinuses. *Cerberus?*

Actaeon whirled, looking for the source. He searched faces, but none stood out. Something strange caught his attention out of the corner of his eye. It almost looked like an overlapped image of two dogs, as though the creature had two heads.

He focused on the dog, but it was a regular Russian wolfhound. Taller than the boy it stood next to, but nothing out of the ordinary.

Actaeon sniffed the air again, but the not-quite-Cerberus scent was gone. Perhaps it was a remnant, clinging to his clothes, or a vivid memory.

He looked at the dog again. Not even a Doberman, like Cerberus' three-headed form.

Actaeon rubbed his eyes. He needed to take a break if he was jumping at shadows. He would, when this Hades situation was dealt with. He'd take Lexi someplace remote, and spend a few weeks— months—getting to know her.

A short while later, the ferry pulled into the dock. He disembarked with the other passengers.

Another scent greeted him, this one unmistakable. It was a smell that had haunted his dreams until recently. He looked up, to see Cassandra waiting for him near the parking lot.

This ought to be interesting.

He approached with caution, searching for Apollo. Too bad he couldn't sniff out rapid mood shifts to crazy-fireball-throwing mode. With the crowds here, he didn't know if he could prevent someone from getting hurt.

CHAPTER THIRTEEN

Icarus pointed Lexi toward a spare laptop and logged her in. It was impossible to miss her etched in scowl.

"I get it. Research detail isn't the most super-neato-keen thing you could be doing." He tried to keep his voice kind. "It's what we're all doing, though."

She looked at him, and her expression softened. "They get to go on location. I sound like I'm pouting, but I'm trying not to. I've spent my life in the shadows, so I understand, but this feels like a whole new kind of prison."

"It's a temporary thing." He felt bad for her. It would be nice if there was time to come up with a solution.

She slouched in her seat with a heavy sigh. "Right. Because in the grand scheme of immortality, the next couple of decades will seem like nothing. For now? It's still a large portion of my life."

"Decades?" He didn't understand where she'd gotten that number from. "We'll be doing this for a couple of weeks—maybe a month or two—and you won't be locked up that entire time."

"Not like this. There's always another reason to hide, though. Who I am, where I live, or what my lineage is." She dropped her head into her hands. "I'm sorry. This is starting to sound whiny. But things like this?" She nodded at the laptop. "Getting online without having to jump through hoops, in the hopes no one discovers me? A foreign concept."

He pulled his stool closer to hers and settled in. She wasn't near enough to touch. He swore he felt the electricity flowing between them, though. "Not anymore."

"I'm logged in as you."

"You don't have to be. You're not a secret anymore. It's true that getting in the gods faces is dangerous right now, but there's no reason to keep pretending you don't exist."

"You make it sound easy." She looked skeptical.

"It is if you let it be."

Lexi shook her head and turned back to the screen. "Not sold."

"You know in Actaeon's company, you're not hidden anyway." He was pointing out the obvious, but her replies made him wonder if she'd realized it.

Her smile was tight. "I do know. But I'm safe with him."

Icarus didn't doubt that. Unless Actaeon was in one of his more fickle *save the helpless* moods. Icarus could point out that Actaeon didn't exactly boot Cassandra to the curb, but he suspected Lexi knew that. She was already living in the open. If she admitted it, she'd give herself more freedom.

"Give it time" he said. "I don't have a better pitch than that. Either you believe it, or you don't."

"I can't argue with that." She paused. "Or, I suppose I could, but I don't see a reason to."

The conversation faded away, replaced with the clacking of keys and the scratch of pencil on paper, as they both dove into their research.

Icarus wasn't writing anything specific down, but getting thought fragments out of his head helped him organize them. Sometimes words and images led to more. Other times, like now, he sketched random lines and let his mind work on its own in the background.

Lexi whimpered, and he looked up to see her frowning at the screen. She was engrossed, so he didn't bother her.

After a couple of minutes, there was another sound, this one more like a sobbing gasp.

He glanced in her direction again.

"It's nothing. Just the news." She met his gaze for the briefest moment before looking away.

The third time she made a strangled sound of horror, he dropped his pencil. "What is it?" Icarus didn't snap at her, but he wasn't going to let her shrug it off as nothing, either.

"Videos, blog posts, messages, about dozens of different groups—not individuals but multiple people—who are killing themselves in Hades' name. Hundreds have died in the last twenty-four hours alone. We have to do something."

The news burrowed deep under his skin. So many lives lost. For another god's ego. He had a hard enough time with the solstice sacrifices that came with The Enlightenment, but this was random and chaotic death. "What are we going to do?"

The way Lexi narrowed her gaze and pursed her lips almost screamed *heartless bastard*.

"I care," Icarus said. "You've seen that. But what do you want to do?"

"I don't know. Find the next group before it's too late?" Frustration filled Lexi's voice.

He liked the sentiment behind the idea, but not its lack of practicality. "We find one. How many dozens do we miss? If these are just the people going viral, how many more aren't?"

"I don't know." Her hands sat on the table, and she clenched her fists so hard, her knuckles were pale.

"You *are* doing something." He poured sympathy into his words. "You're doing exactly what needs to be done. Not every problem can be chewed through with three jaws full of teeth or shot at with arrows. If we get to Hades, this stops. If we take time out to hunt and peck one-off instances, he can get to hundreds more while we save a tenth that many."

Her jaw was tight, and she stared at him as though she wanted to say something.

"What?" he prompted.

"I feel so useless. I'm sitting here, staring at a computer, while so many lives… That fight with the chimera? I was a liability."

"Is that what this is about?" Icarus was on a first name basis with being dead weight in a physical fight. It had been a long time since it was an issue for him. His strengths lay elsewhere, but he remembered the resentment. A hero who couldn't do anything besides *think*. Who wanted that?

"It's one example," Lexi said.

"I think I can help." His solution wasn't the same as what he'd discovered in himself, but it was similar.

"How? Please don't feed me more lines about what we're doing being important. I understand that, but it's not comforting."

Icarus stood, grasped her fingers, and pulled her to her feet. At the contact, a shock raced through him. "Show me that trick again. The one you did with the screwdriver." He tried not to think about the fact that she'd summoned a tool she'd never seen, from mid-air.

"Asking me to perform party tricks isn't much better." Her stubborn attitude might be enticing, if it wasn't counterproductive.

"Fantastic." Sarcasm slipped into his reply. "That's not why I'm asking. I want to see what you're capable of. You wanted to accomplish something?"

"How does this—"

"I don't know. But we're going to figure it out."

She held out her hand like last time, and a dagger appeared. He recognized the shape and color—it looked like the one Actaeon summoned. It sat on display as if it didn't have any weight. It shouldn't be balanced on her hand at that angle.

Icarus reached for it, and it vanished. "I can't touch it."

"Because it's an illusion." Lexi's retort had a hint of *well duh* to it.

"This was explained to you? Just because it's an illusion doesn't mean it's not real."

Lexi crossed her arms and stepped back from him. "I've heard it. It doesn't make any sense, though. I know what I summon isn't there."

Icarus wasn't sure why this was important for him to figure out, but he tended to follow the inspiration, and his insisted he learn what Lexi could really do. A different thread pushed him to focus on her specifically. How kissable her mouth was, even when she was upset. The swell of her breasts when her arms pushed them together. Her sharp wit.

He closed the distance between them again and tugged her arms apart. He grasped her hands and let the desire flow through him, to dance with everything else inside. "Who did you face in the labyrinth? When you first arrived?"

"Me? No one. I showed up in a vast void of nothingness, with no one around me."

That was interesting. Her description sounded like the space he used to build everything in, before any of it took shape. Her experience was an unexpected side-effect. He wanted to explore that but tucked the tangent aside for later. Now, he needed to get to a different piece of information, to put her on the same page as him.

"How did you move past that point?" he asked.

"I meditated? Basically I focused until I could feel Actaeon and Cerberus, and that was enough to make them… show up, I guess? I don't have a better word for it. We think we were all in the same place the whole time, but I couldn't see them because they were part of the illusion."

"Fascinating."

She frowned. "I don't like being your science experiment."

"You're not. I promise. Or perhaps a little, but I'm trying not to do that to you." They were getting sidetracked. *He* was getting sidetracked. He wanted to kiss her. Claim her. Feel her legs wrapped around his waist and her body pressed to his. "What did you see when you found them? Who were they facing?"

"I still never really saw that part. To me, they were fighting air. But according to them, it was Heracles."

Ouch. "And he was winning," Icarus said, filling in the next part of her story. He should have guessed Heracles would be the first challenge. The entrance was designed to feed off an individual's darkest traumas, and he had a hard time imagining a bigger one than Zeus' champion. Except maybe Hades. The result might be different if Actaeon and Cerberus were to step into a similar situation today.

And he was getting stuck on another tangent. "He was kicking their asses because he was tangible. *They* believed Heracles was there."

"Until I convinced them he wasn't."

Fucking stubborn. He was wrong—that wasn't irritating. It was sexy as fuck.

"Next you need to learn the other side of the coin. How to convince people what isn't there is."

"I can't." This time she pulled from his grip and returned to her seat.

He missed feeling her, and that bothered him. "Have you tried?"

She opened her mouth, and then snapped it shut again. Silence stretched between them, while he waited for a response.

Lexi got what Icarus was pushing for, and she didn't want to reject it out of hand. She'd pulled off a lot of things with her gift for illusions, including making other people vanish. But what he was asking felt beyond her grasp. She barely understood the concept of *it's not real, but it is*. How was she supposed to bring it to life?

Icarus moved behind her and settled his hands on her hips. The contact was too intimate, and at the same time too alluring. "Who got you the siren earring?" He nudged her to her feet.

"Cerberus."

"You can't ignore this gift. You've learned to use it as a parlor trick, which is a good start. I think you can wield it as a weapon." Icarus kept his head near hers, his warm breath falling across her cheek with each word.

When he did that, she wanted to offer him whatever he asked for. "I can't cut someone with my imagination."

"You know what you're wielding isn't real. No one else does, unless you tell them. You have to believe they won't know the difference."

She wanted to lean back into him and pull his arms tighter around her. But there was more to the desire that thrummed inside. Lexi wanted to believe this idea of his was possible. And to see what else they came up with together. And to discover if he understood other references besides her Tardis one. "I don't know how to do what you're asking."

"Have you ever wanted to fly?"

"That's your myth, not mine." She was familiar enough with his name to know the story of the man who flew too close to the sun and got burned. The problem was, that didn't stop her from wanting to join him if he tried it again—literally or otherwise.

"It's not a myth. And I'm happy to admit I was arrogant—possibly a little careless—but that doesn't stop me from wanting it still. You're not at all tempted by the idea of wings?"

"Incredibly." She didn't mean to say that out loud. "But you're talking about a flight of fancy— no pun intended—where I need to learn something that helps me make a difference."

He pressed his forehead to the back of her skull. The light pressure radiated from a single point until it hummed over her entire body. "Sometimes you have to treat yourself." Icarus' voice was almost hypnotic. "You can't save the world if you lose *you* in the process. I know. I've seen it happen."

She didn't want to dwell on the idea of losing herself, or on the hint of sadness that crept into his tone. "I should start with wings?"

"Only if that's what you want. You should start with *something*."

"All right. Wings it is."

Before she finished speaking, his touch fell away. She fought the urge to reach behind her and grab for him.

She didn't have time to consider the impulse, as he moved into view. The intensity in his gaze stole her breath and amplified her thoughts.

"Summon them, or whatever you call it," Icarus said. "Don't focus on the tangible part yet. Give yourself wings."

"I won't be able to see them. Not clearly. My illusions are always translucent to me." The idea filled her with doubt.

"I'll tell you how stunning you look in them. And you will."

His certainty bolstered her. She pictured wings. As large as her body. White and feathered. Attached to and unfolding from her shoulder blades.

"*Wow.*" His awe washed over her, making her cheeks heat.

She made sure to keep the image in her mind. "You're just saying that."

"Do I strike you as that type of person?"

"No." It was something he had in common with Actaeon. "So… now what?"

"See if they work. Flex them. Imagine how you think it should feel."

She followed the prompts. If she flexed her shoulders, arched her back in the right way, would the wings move?

"Use them to lift you off the ground."

Ridiculous. She was doing this his way, though. She could almost feel her feet leaving the ground. She looked down. Nope. Wasn't happening.

She closed her eyes and tried to envelop herself in the picture she was painting. Flexing wings she'd created. Letting the air wrap around her. Floating.

It wasn't working. She'd feel it if it was. She wasn't going to get the hang of this. Not today.

A touch ran along the spine of one wing. Or she was imagining it. It was light and sensual and right.

"Open your eyes." Icarus' voice slid into the vision.

She did as prompted. His arm was extended, and he stroked her feathers.

She looked down. *Holy fuck*, she was about two feet above the floor. She gasped and dropped, to land hard and fall to her knees. Laughter bubbled up in her chest. "I did it."

"I told you."

"I'm glad one of us believes in me."

"It better be both of us now." Icarus offered her a hand.

She accepted, and he pulled her to her feet, bringing her to a stop with only a few inches between them.

"What else do you think I can do?" Her question came out breathier than she intended.

"Name it. Green Lantern that shit."

She caught her bottom lip, smirking at the comic book reference. "Giant mallets?"

"If that's your thing." Icarus' hands were on her hips again, guiding her back. "I was thinking more real-world practical, like the dagger, but what the fuck? Go for broke." His mouth hovered millimeters from hers.

The glee from what she'd accomplished mingled with the energy crackling between them. She draped her arms around his neck, desperate to close the remaining distance to his lips and terrified of doing so.

He lifted her to sit on a stool, and slid between her legs. Her body fit around his, snug and right. Instead of short-circuiting her thoughts, he set her mind on fire. So much spilled through her head at once. The past. The now. Possibilities. Ideas.

Need.

He crushed their mouths together. She moaned into him—or maybe that was Icarus, moaning. She didn't know where he stopped and she started.

This was real and vivid, and she wanted to fall into it forever. Icarus nipped her bottom lip, then licked the sting.

"I don't know how, but you've crawled into my thoughts and won't leave. And I wouldn't have it any other way." His voice was a dry rasp.

She wrapped her legs around his waist, trying to feel as much of him at once as she could. "It's a good place to be."

Her nipples strained against her shirt, and dampness grew between her legs. There were too many clothes in the way. She wanted to explore every inch of him. Kiss along his chest. Drag her nails up his bare back. Feel the hard length that was digging into her stomach, buried inside her.

There was nothing in her past that compared to this. Not even…

A sliver of doubt joined everything else. *What about Cerberus? Actaeon?*

Lexi summoned the last of her willpower, slid her arms down, and pressed her palms to his chest, pushing him away. She wanted to touch her swollen lips or let him do it. Instead, she hopped from the stool and put several feet between them.

It wasn't easy, but pretending she didn't see the hurt in his eyes was harder.

"Okay." Icarus licked his lips. "Will you tell me why?"

"You know why. I'm in a relationship."

"Right. The whole *I let fate tell me who to love* thing."

She winced at his sharp tone, and tried not to look at the red string glaring at her, connecting her to him. "That's not true. But I do love Cerberus, and his opinion plays a huge part in my actions." Why didn't she mention Actaeon? Because she still didn't know how she felt about him. The conversations were good… sometimes. The sex was great. That didn't equal love.

"What aren't you telling me?" Icarus searched her face.

How did he know? She ached to say something, but her heart wouldn't let her. "Nothing that will make a difference."

"The pull between us is real."

No. It couldn't be. She had a good thing. "Lust is a powerful motivator."

"You had the dream too."

"I don't know what you're talking about." She wouldn't be able to roll out the denials much longer. She was already hating how much lying this required.

Icarus held her gaze. "Me. You in your underwear. That was real. I don't know who was in whose thoughts, but we were both in the same place."

Lexi swallowed a whimper. "If you're dreaming about me in my underwear, you don't need a real-life version."

"It may not be a life-or-death requirement, but I sure as fuck want you, and I could see it becoming more."

"It's not going to happen." The denial ached more than she thought possible. "Conversation over." The words shredded her on their way out, leaving a pit inside.

How was that one of the hardest things she'd ever said?

CHAPTER FOURTEEN

"I need to know what's going on in my head," Cassandra said, as Actaeon approached. "You've been the closest thing to open with me since I got here."

This was a mistake. Lexi would be furious if she found out. Actaeon didn't know another way to get his answers, though. "I'll answer your questions if you'll answer mine."

"That seems fair."

He didn't trust her around crowds. Not after what happened last time. "Someplace else."

She twisted her mouth. "A spot with fewer people for me to blow up in a misplaced fit of jealousy? All right."

This wasn't the same woman he talked to a few days ago. She was more lucid. More interactive.

He gestured with his head, away from anyone else. "Walk along the beach with me?"

"If the situation were different, I'd swoon at a request like that." She jammed her hands in her pockets. "Sure. That sounds nice."

They strolled in silence, as the crowds thinned. Actaeon would get his answers, and then walk away. It was as simple as that.

Cassandra was close enough her arm brushed his occasionally. After several minutes, she gave a throat-clearing cough. "It's not normal to be locked away by gods. I remember that much. Apollo is kind, and he apologizes a lot, but he hasn't let me leave the house since… well… You know. He keeps saying he owes me. That he's responsible for me. What does that mean?"

"What did he tell you it meant? I'm not a mind reader." Actaeon had a hard time believing Apollo was apologetic about anything.

"He won't tell me. Apparently I'm better off if I don't remember."

Actaeon hated this. It was one of the biggest reasons he'd distanced himself from the gods. Arrogant assholes were always making decisions for their constituents, based on the gods' best interests. But they framed it as *this is for your own good.*

A few feet away, waves lapped at the sand, coasting in gently before rolling away again. The water was no longer Poseidon's domain. Would someone else step in to claim the sea? Or would it be one of the biggest places on earth that was free from a god's influence? It was hard to believe Zeus would allow that.

How many other gods would die before this was over? And would their deaths be a good or a bad thing?

"I'll answer any specific questions you have. But you have to keep in mind that, once you learn—re-learn?—a thing, you can't unlearn it," he said.

She glanced at him, her lips pursed in a bitter smile. "Apparently that's not completely true."

He recognized that look. The amused sarcasm. He used to adore that expression. Lexi's was better—more confident, less manipulative, and sexier. "Touché. I want you to tell me you understand it anyway."

"I understand. Once it's out there, it can't be taken back." She was definitely more with it today. "Besides, my knowing doesn't change what happened or what will happen."

His mind stumbled on the words. She used to say something almost identical about her visions of the future.

"Who am I?" she asked.

A frisbee flew overhead, and a beach-goer charged in front of them to snag it. He gave Actaeon and Cassandra a sheepish nod, then jogged back to his friends.

Where to start, with a question like hers? "First of all, you're a lot older than you look."

"So I'm what? Forty? Fifty?"

"Three-thousand and some."

"Oh. Okay." She sounded as though he'd told her, *It's twenty-three and breezy outside.*

Maybe her response wasn't that odd. She'd been immersed in the immortal side of things since she returned, and even without her memory, she'd come pre-programmed with knowledge of a post-Enlightenment world.

It still seemed like an understated reaction for someone who didn't recall their past. "You were born an Oracle," he said.

"I can see the future?" The question should be one of disbelief, but her tone was flat.

This wasn't right. Uneasiness clawed through Actaeon. "You *could*. I don't know if you can anymore or not. Myth says Apollo gave you the gift, in order to seduce you. That's not true. You were born with it. But when you turned Apollo down, he cursed you so no one would believe the future you saw."

"Oh. That sucks." She might as well be complaining that her toast was overcooked.

Sucks was an understatement. "It almost drove you mad." The first time, but not the last. "Over the centuries, Apollo's obsession shifted, and he eased up on the curse, until what you saw spoke for itself."

"How much later was it before you and I fell in love?"

"I—" That was a peculiar tangent for the questions to take. Had he told her they used to be in love? It must have come up in his house. "It's been about forty years."

"Apollo took centuries to get over me and even now has regrets, and you moved on in a couple of decades." Emotion crept into her voice.

It was awfully warm out here, for the sun being so low in the sky. Actaeon wanted to say Apollo tended to be obsessive. It was why Actaeon didn't get along with him. He kept his posture casual, but adrenaline raced through his veins. He needed to be ready for anything. "I'm a different person than my uncle."

"Buy me an iced coffee." She nudged his shoulder with hers, pointing him toward a kiosk near the edge of the beach. "I meant what I said about Lexi. She's a melodramatic child, and she'll devour you from the inside out, leaving you an empty husk."

He bristled at the words. "That's not *quite* what you said, and I disagree."

"That's your right. Regardless, thank you for telling me the truth about Apollo."

He didn't have to ask why she was so certain he'd told the truth. "How long have you had your memory back? Was it ever gone?" What was her game?

"You wound me. Why would I lie about something like that?"

When they were a couple, a conversation like this would have led to sex. How fucked up was that? "Everyone has their reasons."

"I was telling the truth when I wandered onto your little stretch of beach. I didn't remember a thing. At dinner, something happened in my head. It was as though my mind fractured. After Apollo fetched me, I was a wreck. Couldn't think. Nothing made sense. Have you ever gone mad and then come back from it?"

"Almost." They reached the coffee hut. "Usual?" he asked.

"Depends on what you think the usual is."

Actaeon looked at the girl working the register. "Large iced dirty chai, with an extra shot. And a bottle of Souroti."

"Sounds like you remember too." Cassandra leaned her weight against him.

Her touch was like rough scales cutting his senses, and he put several inches between them.

Cassandra straightened without flinching.

The cashier handed him his water, and he and Cassandra stepped aside to wait for her drink.

"I still feel it," she said. "The fractures in my mind. The splintered thoughts. They look like a broken window. But it's like I have a repaired one, too. The cracks are in my head, but they're not a part of me anymore."

Actaeon didn't like where this was going. "That sounds good."

"Everything came back to me that night. *Everything.* The visions. Dying in Las Vegas. Finding Persephone in the underworld. Realizing you were never going to come for me. That you were there for Lexi."

"Dirty chai," the barista called, then handed Cassandra her drink.

"Thanks." She grabbed her cup and took a long sip, meandering back toward the water.

Actaeon didn't have a response. He wouldn't apologize for that choice. He was starting to regret this one, though he was compelled to find out where all Cassandra's tangents were going.

She glanced at him. "Like I said, I feel the madness underneath it all. It's not gone. The drive that convinced me it was okay to let Hades use me as a vessel. That compelled me to kill Persephone. And the blackness. There was nothing after that." Her step faltered, and she pressed her palm to her forehead. She let out a shaky sigh, then resumed walking. "Hades pulled me from the nothing. He saved me."

The shift in her voice sent ice sliding down Actaeon's spine. Despite the haunting words, her matter-of-fact, clinical tone had returned. "That's a lot to process at once. I'm sorry you had to go through it."

"It's all right." They'd reached the edge of the water. She stood close enough that the surf lapped over her toes and sandals. "Hades explained it to me."

This was so much not better. "Explained what?"

"He promised to send me back to you. He's made the promise to hundreds and kept it. But none of the others were oracles, cursed by a god. I came with unexpected side-effects. He was trying to figure out how to fix me, and now he has. My mind is whole again, for the first time in centuries."

"That sounds incredible." Or unbelievable. Actaeon didn't know if he should push for answers or walk away. Nothing about this situation was right.

"It is." She turned to face him, and her expression softened. "Actaeon, I'm not trying to come off as cold. Or as the psycho ex. Or whatever else is going through your head. Losing you hurts. I'm trying not to feel it, but it's there."

"I understand." He wished he didn't. Not about her specifically, but when it came to dealing with loss, it wasn't easy to toss it aside and forget it. That didn't make him feel any for her.

"I figured you would. Another thing we've always had in common. When did you fall out of love with me?"

"I can't pin it to a specific moment. I looked for you after you died. I would have, even if you hadn't told me about the vision. I couldn't find you, and I mourned for years. Decades even. Until I realized I was doing it out of habit, and not because I felt it anymore."

"I see." Her hands fell limply to her sides.

He was surprised she didn't drop her drink. "I'm sorry. You wanted the truth. That's it."

"And then you replaced me." Her gaze was turned toward her feet and the foaming surf.

"That's not the right way to describe it."

"It's okay." She sank to the ground and pulled her knees to her chest.

He crouched next to her, at a loss for words. He wasn't going to apologize for the way he felt, and they'd covered most everything else. Except entire reason he was here—that touchy subject of Hades. If Actaeon broached the topic, which Cassandra would he get? This sad woman? The cold one? The vapid one from the other day?

She glanced sideways. "You told me the truth, and I promised you answers in return. What do you want to know?"

"You're on speaking terms with Hades?" Actaeon was hesitant to ask.

She nodded. "And I can travel back and forth between here and the underworld. He's given me an all-access pass. I can take you to see him at any time."

"I don't intend to come face to face with Hades again until I'm ready to destroy him."

"I know. But I'm going to show you why he's the winning side."

His laugh slipped out before he could stop it. "Not likely."

"You say that now." She set her drink between her feet, locking it in the sand. "You also swore after I died that you wouldn't take sides ever again. Four decades is *nothing* in our world, yet you fight for Artemis now."

"She shares my values."

Cassandra picked up a rock and rolled it over in her hand. The waning sunlight glinted off the smooth surface. "Artemis is a means to an end for you. Hades can be too. Besides, I want you back. I'm not going to force it on you, and I'm done badmouthing Lexi. It's fair to warn you I remember why you and I fell in love, and you'll remember too, once you've spent some time with me."

She'd shown him so many faces since she showed up, he had no idea who Cassandra was anymore. "If I tell you right now that none of that is going to happen, do you give up and walk away, or do you keep answering my questions?"

"I appreciate the honesty. It's good that you're up-front about your intent to use me. And I'm not going to stop trying."

That sounded like a bad thing. He wanted information, but the pit in his gut said this wouldn't end well.

CHAPTER FIFTEEN

Lexi followed Icarus upstairs, to a floor above his shop. He'd been quiet since she pushed him away. Polite but removed.

Up here was like a different world from the rest of the place. Unlike his workshop, it felt like it was still on this plane. Polished hardwood stretched down a long hallway in one direction, and stopped abruptly at stonework in the other. A small kitchen lay on that side, filled with granite counter tops and stainless steel. The look and feel was a combination of cramped and high-end.

It worked.

"You can sleep in here." Icarus' comment drew her attention. He was already at the other end of the hall, in front of an open door.

She joined him. The bedroom had the same feeling to it. Dark furniture that held a bright shine, minimal decoration, and no color. She had a feeling he didn't spend a lot of time up here. Nothing radiated his energy or inspiration.

"Thanks." Lexi gave him a tiny smile. If she hadn't fallen asleep in front of the computer, she might be able to argue that she wasn't tired.

"I'll grab you something to wear, so you don't have to sleep in the nymph clothes."

She watched Icarus vanish into a different room. She'd offered to go home. He explained there wasn't an open gate near *home* and she wasn't imposing by staying here until her *friends* got back.

Lexi didn't care for the words he put weight on. The gesture was kind, though. She wanted to be angry at him for shutting her out over a kiss, but that wasn't what he was doing.

He knew she wasn't telling him everything, and he hated the lies as much as she did.

Icarus returned and handed her some clothes. "Here. Come back downstairs after your nap."

"When does it get easier?" She frowned as the question crossed her lips, not sure what she meant.

"Which part? Watching people die, naturally or otherwise? Witnessing the selfish games those who live for centuries play? Or not having to get regular sleep?"

Lexi met his gaze, and turned away at the hurt that stared back. "All of the above."

"Try to get some more rest. I'll see you in a few hours."

She closed the door after he left, and sank onto the bed. What was she doing? It was a vague question, but she couldn't grasp any thought long enough to make it more specific.

She stripped down to her panties, set the borrowed suit aside, and picked out a T-shirt from what Icarus provided. As she unfolded it, a faint but familiar scent greeted her. Ozone and bodywash, masked by fabric softener.

Lexi couldn't wear this. It smelled like Icarus. How did Actaeon and Cerberus put up with that kind of sensory input all the time? It would drive her nuts.

A yawn threatened to split her jaw. Sleep called. At least the sheets only smelled like fabric softener.

She slid under the covers and closed her eyes. The sleep that caught her off guard downstairs hovered out of reach now.

Instead, an odd sensation tickled the edge of her mind. A voice.

"—she didn't—"

Then another

"—want her back in—"

Then several more.

"—time he didn't—"

"—know she didn't have a—"

"—good night at all—"

None of it made sense, but the chorus grew, more voices chiming in with each breath she took, until her skull ached.

She refused to lose her shit. Especially here. She tried to focus. If she dove into the noise instead of pushing it aside, she could hear complete sentences. Pleading for help. Offering comfort. Threatening.

A gentle touch brushed across her cheek, startling her. "Hey. Where are you right now?" Cerberus asked.

Lexi forced her eyes open and focused on him. "Where did you come from?"

"I had a pause in searching, and I came back to make sure you were all right." His touch, the concern in his eyes, his presence—it all helped ground her. "Are you?"

The chatter in her head didn't vanish, but with him here, it was easier to ignore. "The voices are back." She didn't have the same sense of distress as the previous two times. It was what it was.

"Come here." He tugged her fingers.

She sat up, and the blanket fell away. When the cool air brushed her bare skin, she remembered she was mostly naked.

The way Cerberus trailed his gaze up her torso, eyebrows raised, erased any awkwardness that tried to surface.

"You lost your clothes." Heat mingled with his teasing.

"I wasn't comfortable, sleeping in what was loaned to me."

He climbed into bed next to her. *"You need rest."*

Lexi lay with her back pressed to his chest. *"I'm not sure that's happening. But we're not expected anywhere for a few hours, right? We can stay here?"* It was a selfish request, given all that was going on in the world.

"I vote yes. *I can even offer a distraction if you'd like."*

Snippets accompanied the suggestion, of Cerberus making her moan in pleasure. Exploring each other's bodies... *"I like your idea of a distraction."*

Lust and desire spilled between them, his amplifying hers and vice versa. She yanked his shirt over his head, to trail her fingers along his chest. Heat and need flowed through their bond. She traced along his scars, following the fractured path of faint white lines down to his stomach, then dragging her fingers up his spine to pull him close.

He pressed his weight into her, pinning her to the mattress. He lay kisses along her neck, her collarbone, and her breasts. When he caught a nipple between his teeth and tugged, she moaned and ground into him.

The sting of his bite lingered on her skin and hummed in her thoughts.

"You like that?" he asked. His satisfaction mingled with her delight.

"I'm not a fragile doll. You can be a little rough."

His uncertainty flowed through their bond, but they had time for him to figure it out.

Cerberus wedged her legs apart with his knee. The rough fabric of his trousers was tantalizing against the inside of her thighs. She held his head captive as he licked and sucked her nipples.

She pressed into his mouth, riding the feedback loop of arousal, until she was squirming and on the edge of climax.

"I'm burned out on rough," he thought. *"But I can do fun."*

"Fun how…" Her question trailed off when he kissed down her stomach. Her core was slick with desire, but he skipped over it, and continued to lick light trails along her legs.

She twisted to get closer to his mouth. He pressed a hand into her hip, applying enough pressure to keep her from moving too much.

"Not fair," there was no weight in her protest.

His chuckle vibrated against her skin. *"I disagree."*

He finally moved back up, drawing his tongue along her outer labia before licking deeper. She arched her back into his mouth. He drove his tongue inside her, and she clenched around it.

"Better?" he asked.

Getting there. So, so close to climax. He was enjoying this as much as she was—seeing her squirm with anticipation. He finally moved to her clit, nipping lightly. The bite rocked inside, and she tasted herself through his tongue.

Her moans turned him on as much as his touch did her. He sucked on her swollen sex, coaxing as she ground into his face. She knotted her fingers in his hair, clenching her fists when she came. The euphoria of orgasm engulfed her, but it wasn't enough.

"I need more."

She didn't know which of them thought it. Both, probably.

Lexi tugged Cerberus back up as he undid his jeans. She hooked her feet at his waist, and helped push the rest of his clothes to the ground. Skin met skin, and her heart sighed with contentment.

The rest of her body needed to be closer still.

He rolled onto his back, pulling her on top with zero exertion. He lifted her like he would a pillow.

Maybe she should be a little terrified he could break her, but there was only ever safety and desire with Cerberus.

She straddled his legs and hovered over him, teasing. His need and amused frustration carried through her veins.

He wrapped a fist around his shaft and thrust up, driving inside her. The penetration filled her body and mind, and she tumbled the rest of the way into their connection. As he rocked against her, she lost herself in him. In them.

With his hands on her hips, he set a steady pace, building to a fast, frantic pounding. The intensity pushed her close to orgasm again, but not over the edge.

When he came, spilling inside her, their energy mingled and blurred until they were one. His climax pushed her into another of her own.

She rode the pleasure until the edge faded away. It didn't vanish, though.

"Favorite thing ever? Fucking you," Cerberus said.

She rolled to the side, to lay her head on his shoulder. *"Making love."*

"Call it what you want. It's still my favorite."

"Even better than the second season of Firefly?"

He laughed. "Even better than."

They lay there, hearts beating in unison, letting the air conditioner provide the background noise.

"How'd it go? Your contact-list hopping?" Lexi finally asked.

"Are you sure you want to know? This isn't exactly relaxing conversation." Despite the words, amusement and self-satisfaction flowed from him. He was pleased by what he'd discovered, and knew she would be too.

She let out an exaggerated sigh. "I have to find out, sooner or later."

He chuckled and pulled her closer. "I found something, but I think you're the best person to pursue it."

"You're not just saying that?" She could feel his sincerity, but her inability to help so far made her need the reassurance.

"I'm not. According to Eros, Aphrodite may have the information we need. She's something of a scholar when it comes to death and Hades."

Lexi hadn't expected that. She thought he'd say something about needing to be disguised or hidden, to get into some place. "Why? If no one knows much about him, what makes her different?"

"Her favorite son, Adonis, died thousands of years ago. She was heartbroken and sought out everything she could to use as a bargaining chip. Things were different back then. The information about the gods was newer—less muddled by time and interpretation. They felt more invincible in those days, too, so they held less back. Aphrodite is persuasive, so if anyone uncovered anything, it was her."

Lexi felt bad for the goddess, even though it happened long ago. "If she did learn anything, she never used it, since Hades is still here."

"You'd have to ask her for details."

Of course. "I don't know how to get a hold of her. Do you have a phone number?"

"Actaeon or Icarus can probably get you one. Eros didn't offer, and I didn't ask. It's probably easiest to go to one of her temples and pray."

"That makes sense." It also churned her gut. The last time she was in one of Aphrodite's temples, the goddess wove her influence around Lexi and Cerberus in a not-so-subtle nudge, to get them to sleep together. It wasn't that Lexi had been unwilling, but she didn't appreciate having the choice taken away.

Cerberus kissed the back of her head. "I understand. You'll be going in alone, if that helps."

"As long as she hasn't decided I need to screw someone new." The comment almost died in her throat, and she was surprised she kept her tone even.

"You know that night didn't change how I feel about you. I loved you before."

Lexi smiled at the reassurance. "I do. I'll never get tired of hearing it, though."

"Are you sure you don't want to sleep?"

"I won't be able to."

Cerberus sat up. She rolled onto her back, to watch him. Cords of muscle ran down his neck to his arms, and tattoos snaked up a chiseled chest. She did enjoy looking at him.

"Come on. We'll shower. You need some clothes that are actually yours, and then we'll find the closest temple."

Lexi didn't like the small, dark pit inside that ached at the thought of seeking out Aphrodite. The goddess had been good to her when Lexi was little, and sent followers to help her a couple of times since. But Aphrodite had just as many black marks in her *Fuck with Things* column, and Lexi wasn't looking forward to seeing which square this encounter would land her on.

CHAPTER SIXTEEN

Lexi and Cerberus approached the plain shop front Icarus had pointed them to. It was buried in the middle of several others on the street, but sure enough, the lettering on the window said *The House of Our Lady Aphrodite. All Are Welcome.*

It turned out the place was only a few blocks from Icarus' shop. Which struck Lexi as eerily convenient, but if she kept drawing assumptions about everything and never found real answers, she was going to drive herself insane.

For instance, Icarus had been perfectly polite and kind when she and Cerberus came back downstairs. He kept his distance. He wasn't flirting.

She wasn't going to think about that until later. She needed to speak with Aphrodite first.

Cerberus wrapped an arm around her waist and pressed his body to hers. He tangled his fingers in her hair and kissed her hard. The passion that spilled through him filled her veins and helped soothe her.

"Is this for show, for Our Lady?" she asked.

"No. It's because I like kissing you." Cerberus drew his mouth along her jaw and down to where her shoulder met her neck. He bit her hard enough to sting, drawing a gasp, then licked along the fresh mark. "That's for her. And you. See you back at the shop?"

Lexi smiled and squeezed his hand. "Yup."

As he walked away, she stepped through the front door. On the outside, it was nothing like the temple from her childhood town. But the moment she cleared the foyer, it was all the same. An open floor, circled by stone benches, with cushions decorating the ground. The wall was painted frescoes of Aphrodite and her priestesses acting out pretty much every sexual position Lexi was familiar with.

She tilted her head to the side, to decipher one of the images.

And some she couldn't comprehend participating in unless she could turn her bones to rubber.

Was she supposed to call out? Cerberus said to pray, but that felt superfluous. Aphrodite was aware the moment anyone stepped into one of her temples, and a hero's faith didn't bolster a god's power, so it wasn't as though Lexi's prayer mattered.

She sat on one of the padded seats, tucked one foot under the other knee, and kicked her free leg back and forth. If she looked behind the dais at the front of the room, would there be books tucked away, like when she was a child? Unlikely, but she enjoyed the memory.

Seconds turned into minutes. How long was she supposed to wait?

Shadows crept across the floor as the sun moved through the sky. Maybe she should ask Actaeon if he had Aphrodite's phone number.

Aphrodite appeared in front of her. "I'm sorry I kept you waiting, child."

Ambivalence surged inside. This goddess was capable of so much good, and so much deception in order to achieve her goals.

"It's all right. I figured you were busy." Lexi was too weary to fake sincerity.

Aphrodite waved her fingers, and a bench relocated, allowing her to sit across from Lexi, their knees only a few inches apart. "You don't sound like you're in the mood for chatter. What can I do for you? Ask anything, and if it's in my power, you can have it."

Why are you so willing to help me? Why did you erase my memory before I met Actaeon? Why did you coerce me into having sex with Cerberus? Don't you trust this fate *you put so much faith in?* All questions Lexi wanted answers to. If she started down that tangent of accusation, she was worried she'd piss off Aphrodite, and right now she needed one answer above all others.

"I'm told you're something of an expert when it comes to Hades."

A frown ghosted across Aphrodite's face, before her pleasant smile flitted back in. "I have more information that most. It depends on what you want to know."

"Zeus says Hades can't be killed, because he's a god of death. But everything, everyone, every particle, can be destroyed somehow."

Aphrodite shook her head. "Not in Hades' case. I'm sorry. And this recent string of deaths is helping him recover faster. I haven't seen it, but I can guarantee that's the case. The dead—hero, mortal, even those gods who died rather than getting destroyed—make him stronger. It was why he was always content to rule in the underworld. Why he never faded the way the others did. Death is that one thing in life that's certain."

"I see." Lexi's gut churned at the idea. It was true, then. He needed to be locked away, and she was the only key they knew of. The real trick would be convincing the men to move forward with the plan regardless. "I guess… thank you for your time."

"That's it?" Aphrodite searched her face.

Lexi shrugged. The avalanche of other questions rushed back. Where to start?

"How are things going with Icarus?" Aphrodite asked.

A shiver of ice ran down Lexi's spine. "Who?"

"Oh, child. You're a few blocks from his house. Traces of him are still on your lips."

Nope. Not possible. She'd been with Cerberus. She'd showered. Brushed her teeth… "How long have you known?" That was the last question Lexi wanted to ask.

"Since the first day I met you. About all three of them."

It was a good thing Lexi didn't bring Icarus with her. *Fuck.* "You didn't think it might be a good idea to tell me, instead of twisting the situation and lying to me and manipulating me?"

"Absolutely not. The way you're reacting now? Do you think it would have been better if I'd said something? If you pushed them away out of spite, you might never know love—that elusive, incredible thing most people search for their entire lives yet never find. You would have surrendered it willingly."

"What about fate?" Lexi spat the last word.

"Being fated for someone doesn't mean you end up with them. I can't see the future the way Cassandra did, but I can see the threads of fate that intertwine through love. The potential. The various outcomes. And if you didn't meet these men in the order you did… It's complicated."

Complicated. One of the biggest bullshit brushoffs ever. "Are you saying I wouldn't have fallen for Cerberus? Because I've loved him for a long time. Since before I met any of them in person."

"I'm not saying otherwise. Cerberus is your heart, child. And the heart will wound you again and again, as long as you fight it. With Icarus, though, you would have become so wrapped up in each other, the rest of the world might as well have ceased to exist."

"First of all, I'm not fighting anything with Cerberus." The words tasted sour, and Lexi didn't want to examine why. "And you're talking about what sounds like a dangerous obsession. I'm not that kind of person."

"You value your intelligence above all else. Your stepfather helped foster that in you, and Icarus is your mind. You trust your thoughts. You give your head the final say. And Icarus is the same."

No. Lexi didn't see it. Wouldn't see it. *That's your head speaking, just like she said.* "You said fated love wasn't a sure thing. You could be wrong."

"I'm not."

Anger surged inside Lexi. Part of it was at herself, for considering what Aphrodite had to say. For wanting it to be true. For denying it was. She directed all her rage outward. "Fuck you and your arrogance. You're wrong. Icarus is a silly crush. He's new. He's different. That's it. I'm the same to him. Something he's never seen before. It's not *fated love*. We'll get bored with each other. I have Cerberus and Actaeon."

"I won't argue with you about this." Aphrodite stood. "You asked why I didn't tell you. You've proved my concern was legitimate."

"Great. Fantastic. This has been super helpful." Lexi let the sarcasm pour from her words. *You're being a brat.* She was refusing to let someone else dictate the direction of her life. That wasn't irrational. It was smart. "Thanks for nothing," she said and strode from the temple.

Frustration and anger churned inside, as she stepped into the afternoon. The sun warmed her face, but it didn't do anything for her jumbled thoughts—the battle that raged between the bit of her insisting she only had herself to be angry with, and the part that wanted all of the gods to rot in Tartarus, for fucking around with her life the way they did.

A high-pitched whine brought a halt to it all, and Lexi stumbled. *What the fuck?* She pressed a palm to her forehead, and the noise grew louder.

It was sharp enough to fill her head and ache inside her skull. She stumbled again. Her knees slammed into the concrete, and a new pain jarred her.

The whine grew louder. Like someone had recorded a scream, looped it, and jammed the speaker into her ear, to play at full volume.

Her hands flew to her ears. She needed to lessen the noise. She brushed the siren earring with her palm, and the screeching intensified.

It was so loud, she struggled to access any of her other senses. Objects danced in front of her eyes, but she couldn't make sense of the shapes. The sharp tang of copper coated her mouth.

She fumbled with the earcuff, but her fingers didn't work. They refused to grasp anything long enough to be effective.

"Stop." She swore she spoke the plea, but the sound never reached her.

Was that music, buried in the noise? It wasn't a pleasant song. More of a chanted threat.

It had to be a siren. But why?

Answers could come later. Now, Lexi needed this to stop. Each time she touched the earring, the noise worsened. She gripped it and yanked. Pain jolted through her, but even that was muffled by the agony the music caused.

Her ear would heal. She hoped. She forced herself to hold on as tight as she could, and ripped the cuff away.

A new kind of agony spilled inside, radiating from the wound. Her hand was wet and sticky, and she tried to focus on it. Blood. That made sense. She was bleeding.

The music didn't stop. Was it louder now, or did the fresh wound just make it seem that way?

"I didn't anticipate seeing you again." The voice blended with the screeching, sounding like a threat and a song at the same time.

Lexi clenched her jaw and forced herself to focus on the words. To follow them back to an aura. It wasn't an easy thing to do, with the multi-tiered assault.

Her mind caught a strand of something ugly.

"You're also weaker than I assumed. I'm probably overdoing it," the voice said.

The noise faded to a dull roar, and Lexi's world solidified. She wasn't kneeling on the sidewalk anymore, despite what her knees said. Sand and surf crept up her calves. She looked up, to find Lorelei standing in front of her. A translucent cloud of an illusion—a stunning woman with porcelain skin— overlapped the siren's true self, not hiding the twisted features.

"What are you doing to me?" Lexi winced at the rasp in her voice. It even hurt to talk.

Lorelei crouched, putting herself at eye-level with Lexi. "Breaking you."

CHAPTER SEVENTEEN

Icarus felt the shift in the air when his mechanical portal opened. Cerberus was here since he left Lexi at the temple. It had been a couple of hours, so Icarus hoped she was getting a lot of good information. When she returned, she'd come through the front door.

That meant the new arrival was Actaeon.

Icarus glanced over his shoulder out of habit. When he saw Cassandra step through with Actaeon, surprise and concern replaced complacency.

He didn't appreciate the assumption that it was okay to bring her back here. One more bit of bullshit to deal with. Lexi was fucking with his head, thought he was convincing himself not to let her move in and take up mental space.

Besides, he didn't have the details behind why Cassandra was no longer dead, and she hadn't been stable when she was alive. Her being with Actaeon... Who knew how the fuck that was going to play out?

"Everyone knows everyone?" Actaeon gestured around the room.

Cassandra smiled. "I believe so. Nice to see you both again."

Cerberus growled.

Icarus didn't blame him. "Are we inviting everyone? Should I make plans to expand the place?"

"She has information." Actaeon had angled his frame, so he was half in front of her.

"Splendid." Icarus wasn't in the mood for this. "A lot of people have information. That doesn't mean I want them waltzing into my place uninvited."

Cassandra looked around the room. "Where's Lexi?"

A chill raced up Icarus' spine.

"She's visiting an old friend." Cerberus' voice was as much growl as words at this point.

Cassandra shook her head. She almost looked regretful. "No she's not. She's done with Aphrodite."

"How do you—"

"*Oh fuck.*" Icarus cut Actaeon off, as some of the pieces fell together. If introductions weren't needed, she had her memory back. Which meant— "Do you have access to your oracle gift?"

"I do. But that's not how I know. Did Cerberus ever tell you the sirens made a pact with Hades?"

"Sirens are neutral." Actaeon sounded like didn't believe his own statement.

Cassandra's frown deepened. "So are the two of you. Correct?" She looked between Actaeon and

Icarus. "No one's neutral in this war." A hint of sadness ran through her voice.

Cerberus shifted in a blink, a three-headed dog replacing his human form, and lunged. He knocked Actaeon aside and pinned Cassandra to the wall, one set of jaws latched onto her shoulder. "Where's Lexi?" His question rumbled through the room.

"I don't know."

Actaeon summoned his dagger.

Cerberus rested a second set of teeth near Cassandra's throat. "You're fleshy. We can make you suffer."

"And Hades can bring me back again and again." Cassandra spat the words. "My answer doesn't change. An oracle can't see through siren magic." She looked at Cerberus. "Hades promised her to Lorelei, in exchange for you. Nothing comes free. You know that."

Icarus didn't know if he was more furious or ill over the situation, and he couldn't deny the worry that raced through him for a woman he barely knew, but who haunted his thoughts.

Cerberus' form flickered, before solidifying again. "I paid my fee."

"That's not what I'm talking about." Cassandra looked at Icarus. "Make them tell you everything. Find her."

Fuck it. If she was going to string them along with what might not even be real, they needed to stop listening. Icarus pointed to a door a few yards away.

"Put her in there." It was a room on a different plane of existence, and it would hold most heroes. He hoped she hadn't picked up any skills he didn't know about, that would allow her to break the door down.

Actaeon grabbed her arm and led her to the room, slamming the door and flipping the lock once she was inside. He turned back to Icarus and Cerberus. "How are we supposed to find Lexi?"

"Your bond works like any other servant's bond, doesn't it?" Icarus asked Cerberus.

"It does. But she has to open her mind for me to get in, and I can't sense her." Cerberus shook all three of his heads and was human again.

"*Damn it.*" Actaeon threw his dagger, and it embedded itself in a far table.

"Watch it." Icarus wouldn't have his place destroyed by a foul temper. "Stop freaking out, and walk through this with me. Cerberus, keep your mind as open as you can."

"And explain what Cassandra meant when she said this was in exchange for you," Actaeon said.

The way Cerberus was glaring, he might as well still be in dog form. He had the deathly challenging stare down. "She's your psycho girlfriend. You tell us."

Icarus wasn't going to referee this match. Actaeon would win, and Lexi would be upset, and Icarus wasn't in the mood to clean up puppy parts. "It only matters if it tells us where Lexi is. I doubt that's the case." He needed to think. What did they know? "Sirens have to follow the same rules as the rest of us. Their power works on an audible frequency, but they're not gods. They need a gate, like any daimon, to take someone with them to a new place.

"And that"—Icarus nodded at his gate—"is the only one in this town."

Cerberus let out a long sigh. "Which means, unless Aphrodite moved Lexi, she's still here."

"Do we go door to door, asking if anyone has seen a siren?" Actaeon looked like he was considering the ridiculous idea.

Icarus didn't blame him. If Cerberus couldn't feel Lexi, they weren't left with a lot of options. Asking Cassandra more questions and hoping she told the truth? Which one was the bigger waste of time?

Few things made Icarus feel more powerless than a lack of answers.

Actaeon let rage spill through his veins, as he stepped into the room Cassandra was locked in and closed the door behind him. The hinges and seams vanished, and they were in a four-walled white box, with a matching floor and ceiling.

"You didn't think to mention this about Lexi sooner?" He spoke through clenched teeth. "As in, any time in the last several hours, when I could have done something about it?"

She watched him with wide eyes, the stench of fear radiating from her. "I didn't expect it to happen yet. I thought, if I came back here, I could tell her directly. She sees the truth of the now, right? I didn't think you'd believe me, but she'd see I was telling the truth. She's not supposed to already be gone."

"Stop." He clenched his fist until his knuckles ached. "All these masks and moods you're wearing… How in Tartarus am I supposed to believe anything you say?"

She shrank back against the wall, gaze never leaving his face. "I'm not… I can't… What is this place?"

"I don't know. Something Icarus dreamed up. Don't change the subject."

"I can't hear him in here." Her voice was tiny.

"Who?" But Actaeon already knew the answer. "Hades. What did he do to you?"

"I told you. He brought me back. He rebuilt me, to be his vessel. To get to you."

Actaeon couldn't do this. "Where's Lexi?"

"I don't know. With Lorelei. That's the best I have. I really am sorry."

"I'm sure." He hammered the side of his fist on the wall. The door appeared as it opened, and Icarus let him out.

"Time for the door-to-door approach?" Cerberus asked.

Actaeon moved into the room, and jiggled the temporary-prison door handle to make sure Cassandra was locked in. "Yes."

Icarus stepped in their path, looking at Actaeon. "Don't you have another way to contact Lexi?"

Actaeon stared at him, trying to make sense of the question. "She's a bit off the grid, so I can't exactly call her cellphone."

"Not like that. I mean…" Icarus glanced at Cerberus, then turned to Actaeon again. "They share a link. Do you have something similar?"

"I'm not a servant." Actaeon hated trying to figure out what was going on in Icarus' head.

Icarus clenched his jaw and turned away, to pace. He raked his fingers through his hair, moving his lips though no sound came out. "Dreams… Thoughts… Emotion…" he murmured. "As in, talking to her in her dreams or something? Is that a thing she can do?"

"Like Morpheus? Not last I checked."

Weird dream?

You could say that.

The snippets of conversation with Lexi from a few nights ago raced back. Actaeon didn't want to ask, but he had to know. "Can *you* talk to Lexi in her dreams?"

"What?" Cerberus' tone changed.

Icarus paused mid-pace. "I think I can. But we'd both have to be dreaming, for me to do that."

White-hot envy surged inside Actaeon. How did Icarus and Lexi share something so impossible and intimate. He'd been in her dreams? Actaeon shelved the implications. More important things were at stake. "Great. Stay here, take a nap, and we'll go search."

Actaeon would burn the world down for vengeance if something happened to Lexi.

Lexi's head throbbed, begging her to stop. Stop thinking. Stop struggling. Stop everything. Each time she tried to focus, Lorelei's song grew louder, threatening to split her skull.

"Cerberus and Actaeon had so much guilt." Lorelei's words harmonized with the foul music. "They tortured themselves far better than I ever could. But you… You deny so much. It can be in front of your face, and you refuse to accept it. You're not a martyr. Your mind is a sandbox for mayhem."

Lexi didn't know what that meant, but it reinforced her determination not to beg. This was excruciating, but she could deal with it.

The song changed, and the pain vanished, like a switch had been flipped.

"Hey." Cerberus's voice was kind. He was in front of her, his hand on her cheek, his gaze searching her face. "How are you?"

"This sucks," she thought.

He frowned and didn't respond.

Why couldn't she feel him? The physical contact was nice, but the emotional connection was missing. "Did I do something wrong?"

"I don't know. Did you?"

The lack of anything was similar to when he walled her off. "No." *I didn't tell you about Icarus.* But of course she didn't. There was nothing to tell.

He glided his hand along her skin, to trace the edge of her ear. That should hurt, shouldn't it?

No. Why would it?

Her earring. She'd ripped it off. Cerberus should be a double-image—hellhound overlapped with man. But there was no three-headed dog.

It should make sense, but reason was out of her grasp. She fumbled for answers, and they slipped through her fingers.

The world around her adjusted, becoming solid. She recognized this place. It was Lorelei's hut in Hawaii. But it was an illusion. It had to be.

The throw rugs under Lexi's knees felt real enough, as the weave pressed against her jeans. The song floating through the air was familiar. Comfort and love. She remembered that.

"Cerberus." Lorelei appeared at the opposite end of the room.

Cerberus was no longer by Lexi's side. He stood in the doorway to the hut. "What?" He sounded gruff. Irritated to be here.

Why couldn't Lexi feel him?

"Come in. Sit. May I get you something to drink?" Lorelei asked.

Cerberus crossed his arms and leaned against the doorframe. "I'm fine. What can I do for you?"

"You owe me a favor."

"Hello?" Lexi sent him the mental greeting.

He didn't even twitch, let alone look at her.

"What do you want?" He ground the words out.

Lexi might as well be invisible. How did he not see her in the middle of the floor? She stood, putting herself in his line of sight. "Cerberus?"

He looked right through her.

Great. She was trapped in a bad TV episode. The one where she was a dream. Or a ghost. Or existing on a different plane. And couldn't interact with anyone.

Lorelei said something about breaking her. That had to be what this was—a twisted series of events, meant to tear Lexi down.

She wouldn't let that happen. She'd wait and watch and look for an opening. If this was an illusion, even though it was one she couldn't see through, she'd find a way out.

"It's not so much what I want, but what Hades wants." Lorelei studied her nails as she spoke.

"I don't answer to Hades."

"No, but… Favor. And before I ask, I want you to remember you made this promise to me before you formed the bond with Lexi. My request overrides her desires."

Lexi's gut churned at the thought. This was a trick. A literal mindfuck. She wouldn't be sucked in.

"That's swell," Cerberus said sarcastically. "What are you asking me on Hades' behalf? I won't hurt Lexi."

Lorelei buffed her nails on her sleeve, then went back to studying them. "I'm not willing to push and see if I can request that or not. Besides, that's not what Hades is asking. He wants Icarus dead."

"No." The protest slipped from Lexi's throat, and she clamped her mouth shut. It didn't matter. No one looked in her direction.

Mindfuck. It's not real. She's trying to break you.

Cerberus hesitated. "She won't like that."

"You won't tell Lexi. There are details to this favor. You had to anticipate that. Say nothing to her. Don't act until I tell you." Lorelei produced an envelope from nowhere and held it out. "The rest is written down."

Cerberus crossed the floor, within inches of Lexi. She wanted to reach out and touch him, but she didn't know which would be worse—making contact or passing through him.

He snatched the letter from Lorelei. "So I just sit and wait?"

Lorelei handed him a dagger as well. "And use this."

"Then the favor is finished? We're square?" Cerberus had adopted a cool, emotionless tone.

Lorelei nodded.

The scene faded, leaving Lexi in a void similar to what she'd experienced when she first entered the labyrinth. Nothingness in every direction, including up and down.

"Nice show," she shouted. "What happens next? Do you show me the day my mother died, on a loop? No. Because you weren't there. Do you make me think the people I love are dying, over and over?" She didn't care that there was no response. The siren was listening. "Do you stick me in a combination of kind and cruel loops, until I'm useless and sobbing for you to stop? Because it's not happening." Lexi pushed to her feet. "You already told me what you're up to, and you won't fucking break me."

"I won't do any of those things." The music was loud and harsh again, and Lorelei sang her response. "All I have to do is show you the truth. You're big on that, aren't you?"

"Fuck you." If this was like the maze, Lexi could meditate her way out of it. If she focused hard enough, she could do what she had then, and follow her aura to where it mingled with Actaeon's and Cerberus'.

"Cerberus." The hut was back, and Lorelei stood at the opposite end of the room.

Cerberus stood in the doorway to the hut. "What?"

Lexi squeezed her eyes shut and tried to ignore the conversation that was identical to the one she just witnessed. This wasn't real. There was no truth in it. It was an illusion.

Just because it's an illusion doesn't mean it's not real.

CHAPTER EIGHTEEN

Lexi stopped counting the loops after two hundred. If the scene took about five minutes to play out each time, she'd been in here for…

Her brain refused to do the math.

No one stole her mind, damn it. Almost seventeen hours.

"Bill Murray did this better," Lexi called.

"Cerberus." Lorelei stood at the far end of the room.

Lexi could get up and walk around in here, without ever running into Lorelei or Cerberus. The furniture was solid, but she passed through the people.

She'd pulled faces at them. Spent several rounds shouting profanities at illusion-Lorelei. Studied Cerberus from every angle imaginable. Sung over them.

Her singing tended to make the music louder, and that hurt her head, so she'd given that tactic up quickly.

"You know what the awesome thing about torture is?" Lexi asked. "You do the same thing enough times, and your victim's mind becomes numb. They start blocking it out."

"This isn't torture. This is reality." That was singing Lorelei, not imaginary-vision one.

She's telling the truth.

Nope. Lexi didn't buy it.

You feel it. It's part of you. She's showing you something that already happened.

Bullshit.

Why don't you believe it?

Because Cerberus wouldn't. He couldn't.

Couldn't what? You've seen him kill. And you know how seriously the gods and their ilk take their barters.

Great. She was talking to herself, to avoid an illusion meant to drive her insane. Wonderful.

"Cerberus."

The loop started again.

Lexi groaned and stomped her feet. "Stahp."

The behavior wouldn't do her any good, but it was something different.

She tried meditating several times and hadn't felt anything. But there had to be a way.

The scene had played so many times, she had it memorized. She used the background noise as a rhythm to set her breathing to, and focused inward on her own power. There was nothing else there.

Then there was a separate glow. Not one she'd noticed in the past, but distinct and bright. She followed it, and it wound deeper inside her head.

"Thank you," singing-Lorelei said.

What?

"*Alexandra.*" Dad's sharp voice startled her, and her eyes flew open.

The setting had changed. She was in the home she grew up in—the pink house buried in a tiny little Utah town in the mountains.

She sat on her bed, the ancient Star Wars comforter wrinkling under her weight, and her stepfather was in the doorway of her room.

"What the hell were you thinking?" His loud words bounced off the wall.

She shrank back. It was rare for Dad to be this angry. What *was* she doing? "I wanted to know what the new boy could do." The voice that came out was small and young. She knew this memory and what came next. "He glows lime green. It's so pretty, Dad. I just wanted—"

"We've talked about this, Lexi. You can't do this." The anger was already fading from his voice.

But she was upset that she'd made him mad to begin with. Her bottom lip quivered. "I know, but he's nice, and I wanted a friend, and I didn't let anyone else hear me ask."

She wasn't supposed to tell anyone she could see auras. According to Dad, it was because people still resented the gods, and it was dangerous to admit she was affiliated with them.

"There it all is." Lorelei's song danced along the tension of the dream.

Looking back, Lexi understood Dad's point. When she was six, this had been worse than being grounded. "He can make the water dance," she said. "He promised not to tell if I didn't."

Dad settled on the bed next to her. "But he did tell. And you just did, as well."

"But…" She didn't understand his rules. "Do you want me to keep secrets from you?"

"I want you to not put yourself in situations where there are secrets to keep."

The scene faded, but it left a new ache behind. An emptiness, that one of her strongest memories of Dad was when she disappointed him.

She'd learned her lesson. For a few years, anyway.

And here she was, lying in the bed of a battered old pickup, next to the hottest guy in school. Everyone wanted to know Connor, and so many girls were jealous he'd gone straight for Lexi.

Lexi fell hard and fast for his stunning dark eyes she could drown in, his body that looked sculpted from stone, and the gorgeous aura of gold and silver weaving around him.

She was no longer a casual observer in these memories. She was reliving them, as her old self. She knew what was coming next, but no matter how hard she willed herself to leave, teenage-Lexi was content here, under the stars.

Conner propped himself up on one elbow and trailed a finger down the middle of Lexi's chest. The woven blanket they'd tossed over themselves was too heavy in the summer heat, and she was tempted to kick it off.

The twinge of pain between her legs was a pleasant reminder of what they'd done. He took her virginity, but she had a feeling she was nowhere near his first, though he was her age.

She didn't care, because she had him now. This stunning specimen.

"Is it your dad or your mom?" he asked.

They'd stayed away from the topic of their parentage so far, but she trusted him.

You shouldn't, she screamed in her own head.

"My dad," she said. "You?"

He laughed. "Dads."

Both parents were gods? Surprise and awe spread through her. "You're a god?"

That smirk of his was enough to make her squirm in anticipation again. "I guess so. Who's your dad?"

"It doesn't matter. He's dead." She might be okay sharing a little information, but she'd seen enough of Hades in the history books to know it wasn't a good idea to admit her bloodline.

"None of the gods are dead."

Lexi shrugged. "Don't know what to tell you. That's how it is."

"How have you survived for so long in this place?"

"What do you mean?" She liked it here. It was lonely, but she suspected anyplace would be, and there were fewer people here, so it wasn't as obvious.

"It's so *boring* here. These people survive on loyalty and hard work and that kind of no-one-really-buys-it bullshit. You belong someplace like New York or Berlin. The pantheon would love you."

Lexi giggled. "That's not what your grandma says. She says if I ever met one of the originals, I'd roll my eyes so hard, they'd pop out of my head."

Oh fuck. Realization spread through her as she re-lived the memory. That was the other reason she'd trusted him—he was *Dottie*'s grandson, visiting grandma for the summer.

Aphrodite. Her first boyfriend was a child of Eros. No wonder she'd been smitten.

It was surreal, having access to so long ago and feeling it as if it happened now, while her current thoughts overlapped. Was this anything like what Cassandra went through? Seeing multiple threads of time simultaneously?

"I'm serious." He skated a hand up, to tease her nipple, and brushed his lips over hers. Each touch danced through her veins like the brandy in the liquor cabinet that Dad didn't know she'd tried.

"When summer gets here, I'm done in this place. You could come with me," Conner said.

"Dad would never. He loves it here."

He stared at her, brows knitting together. "I didn't say him. Just you. Leave it behind. Come see the world."

"I couldn't. I can't. He's my dad."

"No. He's your stepfather. In fifty years, he'll probably be dead, and he'll most likely forget you twenty years before that."

The words hit hard, and Lexi's euphoria vanished in a gasp. "No, he won't."

"Zee…" He dragged a thumb along her bottom lip. "I'm not trying to be mean. You know these things. Love, devotion, commitment—they're all lies and illusions."

The pain that rocked inside teenage-Lexi mingled with the denial and reality of now. "Not with Dad," she said.

"With everyone. It's why I like you. You see that. You know we don't love each other."

It was true. She'd never thought that for an instant, though looking back, it felt like a callous thing for a fourteen-year-old to recognize. He wove a spell around anyone who caught his attention, and she never understood why they didn't see through it.

It was because his affection was an illusion.

"I don't know," she said. "I have to think about it."

He kissed her again. "You've got two weeks. The instant school is out, I'm done here."

He took her home a short while later. She crept into the house, careful not to wake Dad, and lay in bed for hours, staring at the ceiling and thinking about the conversation.

This wasn't right. That wasn't how the night went. She'd gone home and slept.

Hadn't she?

Murmuring from the front of the house drifted into her room, and she strained her ears, to hear. One voice was Dad's, and the other was female. She couldn't quite make out what they were saying. She crept down the hall, careful not to make a sound.

"I don't *know* how. But he came home and told me he was bringing the child of Death with him when he went back to Berlin." *Dottie.*

Lexi didn't remember any of this. It wasn't part of her past. This had to be part of Lorelei's attempt to break her.

But it's real. There was the fucking logical voice, trying to change her mind again.

"Come on out, child," Dottie called.

Teenage-Lexi didn't know how she'd been caught, but she stepped into sight.

"Why did you tell him?" Dad asked.

"I didn't… He saw what I was. I didn't give him any names. I just told him my dad was a god. I never said who. And I didn't say I was going with him, either."

Dad frowned and looked back at Aphrodite. "We can't stay here anymore," he said.

She shook her head. "No. He's a good kid, but he'll talk. And I can't keep you safe anywhere else."

"It's all right. We'll figure something out." Dad looked at Lexi. "You have half an hour, and you can fill two suitcases. Make it count."

"But—"

"*Now*, Alexandra."

She scurried away at the anger in his voice, and shoved as many books, memory sticks, and figurines as she could into her luggage. She tossed a few changes of clothes in as well.

"Lexi." Dad's voice boomed through the house. "We're leaving."

She sniffled away the regret and guilt building inside, and hauled her things into the living room. Aphrodite was still there, waiting by the door. She crossed to Lexi and rested a hand on her cheek.

"I'm sorry this is where we part ways," Aphrodite said, "but it was going to happen. Sleep in the car. Your stepfather will take you someplace safe. When you wake up, this will all feel like a bad dream. Connor brought you home at the end of the night, and you slept until your dad woke you up and said it was time to go."

Lexi gasped as the living memory vanished, leaving her in the void again.

"Oh, you're all sorts of interesting," Lorelei sang. "Not a martyr. Just a self-centered child, who would rather use the world around her and lie to them, to feel better about herself, than face the truth. Who knew that mark on your neck was ironic?"

Ambulance sirens blared, filling Lexi's thoughts and making her gut churn. She was in the living room of Dad's townhouse, staring at the splatters on the wall, unable to move.

No. *Please, don't make me relive this.*

Dad lay on the ground, his gut slashed open, and things that were supposed to be inside spilling out.

"No. Please." The words choked from her throat. "He can't be."

A paramedic knelt next to the body and pulled a sheet over him. "I'm sorry. We can't fix things like this."

"No-no-no-no-no." Lexi begged through her tears. This wasn't right. He couldn't be dead.

Someone rested a hand on her arm. "Miss? Did you call 9-1-1?"

She vaguely remembered doing that. She'd come home to find Dad eviscerated. But he couldn't be gone. They had to save him. "Please, do something?" She looked at the detective.

"There's not much to be done, in cases of ritual sacrifice." The officer sounded sympathetic.

Ritual…? "It wasn't. It couldn't have been."

The officer nodded. "Gargoyle claw was the weapon."

She'd told Dad they couldn't live in a city where Poseidon ruled. He insisted they were safest right under the gods' noses.

"I'm sorry. Is there anyone you can call?" the officer asked.

Lexi shook her head, barely able to see through her tears, as her stepfather's body was wheeled out on a stretcher. There was no one.

"Let's see what else you have that you're hiding from yourself." Lorelei's song drilled into Lexi's thoughts.

"I swear to every god who ever was or will be, I will gut you for this," Lexi growled at the empty air, her throat raw and her heart broken.

"Promises, promises. Which one should we play again, to discover what else we knock loose?"

Ambulance sirens blared, and Lexi stood in the living room of the last place she'd lived with Dad, choking on tears of sorrow and hatred.

CHAPTER NINETEEN

Lexi felt raw, inside and out. She didn't know how long she'd been forced to relive her past. And that stupid fucking image of Cerberus…

She wanted to curl up and take a nap. How many days had she been in here? A week yet? It felt like a million lifetimes.

Fourteen-year-old Lexi listened to Aphrodite talking to Dad in the other room. She'd heard it so many times, she was starting to imagine she could make out some of the words.

"—*sephon… she's not… tell any… goddess—*" That was Aphrodite.

If Lexi could fill in those words, she could probably make up entire sentences about what they'd been discussing.

The teenage version of her crept into a hallway.

Lexi screamed in her own skull to not do this. She was tired. They'd already been in bed. They could go back to sleep.

The scenery shifted, and she was back in Lorelei's hut. Lexi had put some pieces together. This place seemed to operate in a similar manner to the labyrinth's entrance. It plucked some of her sharpest memories from her head and brought them to life.

But it didn't seem as though Lorelei could read Lexi's mind. The place gave her past a shape, and Lorelei saw the manifestation. Something to be grateful for.

Lorelei and Cerberus spoke. About Hades. About killing Icarus.

Lexi grabbed a few cushions, spread them on the floor, and lay down. There was nothing for her to interact with in this scene. She could rest for a little while.

"As far as heroes and pasts go, yours is relatively tame." Icarus' voice startled her.

She jolted straight up and turned around, to find him sitting on a cushion behind her. "You're not part of this."

"No? Grateful for small favors I suppose, since these are based on traumatic moments. I didn't think you'd ever see me."

She reached out, expecting her fingers to pass through him.

He held up a hand, and she pressed her palm to his.

Lexi sobbed in relief. "How are you here? Did you find me?" His comment from earlier sorted itself out. "How long have you been here?"

"Meditation. Not yet. And through the Star Wars themed bedroom, and that whole awkward truck conversation. You and Conner? Really?"

The teasing threatened to make her smile. "Yes. Really."

"He's just a kid."

Lexi pursed her lips, but it felt good to be talking to someone other than herself. "He's the same age as me."

"Of course." Icarus kissed her fingers. "I'm still here, watching, the way you are. Except I think I'm in your head. When the scene shifts, even if you can't see me, I haven't left."

Ambulance sirens filled her skull, and grief set in. The change in scenery and mood gripped her chest and squeezed tight. Icarus was gone. Grief and panic surged back, as she watched the paramedic cover Dad with a sheet.

A sob bubbled up in her chest, and she tried to claw past the memory of grief. It was so difficult, though.

"Creation, Zee. I'm so sorry."

Icarus' voice in her head felt like when she talked to Cerberus, and that nickname… *"Only Conner ever called me that."*

"Why only him?" Icarus asked. *"It's cute."*

"I don't know. He came up with it, and I haven't really led the kind of life that lends itself to sweet nicknames." Was she really discussing this while she was trapped in a nightmare? *"Cute?"*

"Sexy? Appropriate? Whatever distracts you and lets me flirt at the same time."

She mentally rolled her eyes. *"You're relentless."*

"True. Where are you? I'll send the bruisers."

Bruisers. She liked it. *"I don't know. I was only a few doors down from the temple when Lorelei found me. After that, it's all a bit of a screeching blur."*

"I can start with that. We'll go door to door in that area, and then spread out from there."

What? A new type of hurt joined the scrambled mess that was her heart. *"You haven't already done that? I've been in here for weeks."*

"You only dropped off Cerberus' radar about fifteen minutes ago."

At least they hadn't forgotten about her. *"How did you know I was in trouble, then?"*

"Cassandra told us."

"Cassandra?" Lexi's world shifted again, and this time the scenery was new. Or rather, it was Icarus' shop, but at night.

"Fuck. I'm contaminating the place. I need to leave. We're looking. I promise."

Suddenly Lexi's head felt achingly empty. Should she have warned him about Cerberus?

No. That vision wasn't real.

"What's this? New trauma?" Lorelei asked.

Perhaps. But nothing was happening. *Contaminating.* Because it wasn't Lexi's memory. Panic surged inside. She didn't want Lorelei to discover Icarus had been here.

Lexi grasped the most awkward memory she had of the workshop. It wasn't even on the same scale as the grief of seeing Dad, dead in in a pool of blood.

It felt natural, to slide into her mind from just a few weeks—hours?—ago. The conversation about illusions being tangible. The wings. She wished she could have a third-person angle on this, like the conversation in the hut, so she could see the wings she'd created.

The moment ended in an intense kiss that she swore was as strong in the memory, and then the uncomfortable breaking apart. The stilted argument. The lack of conversation.

"This is traumatic to you?" Lorelei's song was gone, and she was speaking. "And you didn't break after a few loops? That's fine. We have centuries."

If this had only been a little while in the real world, it might take centuries for the men to find her.

Lexi wasn't looking forward to waiting. Especially when the ambulance sirens blared in her head again.

She tried to focus on the image of Icarus' shop, rather than the grief. If she thought about it, would it come back again? How did she make it do that the first time?

"Cerberus."

She was in the hut. Good. Mental break. She slid into the memory of the wings. The moments leading up to it. The dagger.

If she manipulated things in his shop and made them real, and this was a similar idea…

No. It couldn't be that easy.

The part of her mind that had been arguing with her since she got here pointed out that, if it *were* that easy, she wouldn't still be here.

She closed her eyes and pictured a dagger in her hand. She imagined it looking like the one Lorelei handed Cerberus.

The cool night air of her childhood home brushed her cheek.

No. She wasn't ready to slide into a new scene.

The hard lines of the truck bed dug into her naked back, and the woven blanket scratched her bare chest.

She wanted to stay outside of the scene, the way she did in the hut.

The twinge of pain between her thighs was a pleasant reminder she'd just lost her virginity.

Would that have happened with a mortal?

Odd thought to have.

But she didn't hear her younger-self's mind. She risked opening her eyes. Satisfaction spread inside. She wasn't lying in the truck next to Conner. She was watching herself in that spot.

It was a bit strange, sitting on the edge of the truck, looking at teenage-her giggling in post-coital bliss.

Lexi hopped to the ground, leaving the laughter in the background. Something dug into her palm, and she looked down.

She still held the blade.

"Nope," Lorelei sang the word, and the environment shattered in a shower of glitter.

Lexi smirked. The dagger was gone too, but she could bring it back.

"Pleased with yourself?" The siren's song caressed her ear. "You thought this was the worst I could do? I've been in the heads of the men you love. My dear, this was only an appetizer."

Lexi wanted to be smug and laugh the whole thing off. It was hard to do when Lorelei's song was capable of evoking terror, and the threat it carried promised worse.

"You let her escape?" Hades roar reached inside Lexi and squeezed her lungs until she couldn't breathe.

"I didn't *let* her do anything." Cerberus' voice came from her lips.

No. She could see the paws on the ground. Feel... extra limbs? She was Cerberus.

"*Lies.*" Hades' fury raged inside her, the same way Cerberus' emotions did when she was linked to him, but so much more painful and terrifying. "Your guilt spills from you in waves. How dare you deceive me? Find Persephone and the child *now*."

Cerberus nodded. It was almost dizzying, feeling three heads bob at the same time. "I will."

"And until then, you can live all the potential terrors they'll face if you don't," Hades said.

These memories weren't physical. They were rapid-fire splashes of threat that Hades spilled through Cerberus' mind. Persephone gutted in front of cameras, to prove Zeus' point. Baby Lexi sacrificed, for Ares' pleasure.

And so many more scenes of rape, death, and a million scenarios in between, that Lexi had to turn away from.

But Cerberus hadn't been able to. He put himself through that, to let Persephone go. To make sure Lexi wasn't born in the underworld.

Lexi tried to make it stop, the way she had before, but the threats shifted so quickly, she couldn't ignore their vivid gruesome nature.

Icarus opened his eyes, to find two pairs staring back at him. He hopped from the table he'd been meditating cross-legged on. "I know how to find Lexi and get her out."

"You were out for less than five minutes." Actaeon bounced on the balls of his feet.

Icarus had been in Lexi's head for hours, from his perspective. He didn't think she'd been exaggerating, but living it was different than hearing about it. It was critical they do this quickly.

"I believe she's still in town, and she's in something similar to the entrance of the labyrinth. There will be a doorway, and it will exist in a specific place..." Icarus searched for an appropriate analogy. "Like a Platform 9 3/4 kind of thing."

"Thank you. Someone gets it," Cerberus said.

Actaeon rolled his eyes.

Icarus wasn't going to ask.

"If it's local, you know where it is." Actaeon was already heading toward the door.

Icarus winced. "I don't."

He was met with twin glares of disbelief. "Why not?" Cerberus demanded to know.

"I wasn't going to set up the labyrinth here and bring that kind of trouble into this town." At the time, he justified to himself putting it in someone else's hometown. Now he didn't know why he'd thought that was okay. "But between the three of us, it will stand out to someone when we find it. We'll start with the buildings around Aphrodite's temple." If this prison was the same as his work, he should know it immediately, but since it was imbued with siren magic, he wasn't sure.

"Then what?" Cerberus was a static version of wound up, with his arms crossed and his fingers digging into his forearms hard enough he was going to leave dents.

"I believe Lexi's bound to the prison the same way Hades was in the labyrinth, except today, Hades is the key instead of Persephone. We need to—"

"Kill Hades." Actaeon headed back toward the room where Cassandra was.

"*No.*" Icarus would get through this faster if they'd listen. "We don't have time to figure that out. We need to—"

"Then how are we supposed to get her out?" Actaeon asked.

Cerberus straightened. "Transfer the key to someone who shares her energy. Me."

At least one of them was thinking. "Exactly."

"And then we kill the pup?" Actaeon sounded doubtful.

Cerberus nodded. "Fine. Let's do it."

"What? No. Fucking martyrs, both of you. Shut up and let me explain. We make Cerberus the key, and then he unlocks the door." Icarus paused, waiting for the next retort.

"What happens if we don't get to Lexi in time?" Actaeon asked the one thing Icarus didn't want to think about.

"You both know what Lorelei prefers as payment." Breaking people got her off. It was all a fucked-up game to her.

"Shit." Cerberus paled.

Icarus nodded. "How much does she know about the two of you that can be used against Lexi?"

Actaeon had stopped moving, and the glow around him was brighter than the lights in the room. "Fuck."

Icarus couldn't have phrased it better himself. Fear on Lexi's behalf squeezed the air from his lungs. If they took even an hour to locate her, she might not survive.

CHAPTER TWENTY

Lexi screamed at the pain that seared over her, but the voice that came out was Actaeon's. She didn't know when they were, but the reflection on the far wall showed him draped in lightweight robes, almost like a toga.

This was the least psychologically taxing memory Lexi had been shoved into, but Actaeon had a high threshold for pain, and being stuck in his head while he was tortured sucked. She would have passed out ages ago if this was happening to her.

Memory-Lorelei wore something similar to Actaeon's robes, wrapped tight and highlighting her figure. Her sweet, stunning reflection was a lie, and she preferred it that way. She liked to watch.

She dragged a knife down Actaeon's arm. Blood, dark and thick, welled up from the deep slice, covering layers of the same that had already dried on his skin. The cut closed up quickly, but it didn't heal. It left a glaring red gash next to neat rows of others.

Darkness licked the edges of Actaeon's vision.

Please let him pass out soon.

Memory-Lorelei leaned in, to caress Actaeon's ear with her lips. "You've stolen two of my favorite toys," Lorelei sang. "But this way you can see why I enjoyed them so much."

The words jarred Lexi from the agony. That wasn't what the siren said last time they were in this scene. Lorelei changed the memory, to talk to Lexi.

Lexi could do the same. Amid the constantly shifting landscape of mental and physical torture, she'd lost track of her discovery. Now that she had it, she had to focus on using it.

Her world didn't fade to black as Actaeon lost consciousness. Not like last time. She was stuck in his unconscious head for several seconds, before the scene shifted.

It gave her time to catch her breath and remember she might have a way out of this place.

She was Cerberus again, at some point during the Renaissance. He was a sculptor's muse, and the man he posed for was being hauled away for heresy, for his abominable renditions of a three-headed dog.

The guilt stole breath she didn't have and sent her drowning in anguish. She had to stay removed, despite feeling and hearing everything that passed through his head.

It took tremendous effort to summon the reminder. She didn't have the strength to do more.

"*Lexi.*" The voice was Cerberus'.

Of course it was. She was him. He was her. This was so confusing.

"It's actually *me,"* Cerberus said.

She would have laughed in relief, if it didn't take so much effort. *"You got in."*

"Yes. We know where you are, and we're going to unlock the door. But Icarus doesn't think that will be enough to free you. You still have to find your way to us."

"I can't do that." Every time she had enough of a grip on her own mind to act, Lorelei snatched it away.

"You can." His reassurance flowed through her. Talking to Cerberus this way was different than the conversation with Icarus. With Icarus, it was almost like he was in her head. Correction—as though they shared a mind. With Cerberus, it was more like face-to-face speaking, heavily doused with his emotion.

The instant he was gone, she'd be stuck with the vision's memories again. And how much longer until the door was unlocked? How would she know it was time to look? *"I'll try."*

"We'll find you. If you have to, sit tight until we get to you."

The concern and love and warmth evaporated, leaving her with the suffocating guilt of past-Cerberus.

His words wormed their way under her skin, though. Despite saying he believed she could do it, he didn't.

Her frustration barreled in, smothering external feedback. No way was she plopping down on her mental ass, to wait for the Three Musketeers.

The scenery changed to a place she hadn't seen before. Lexi recognized the sensation of being Cerberus. The guilt and the stretch of video displays on the sides of skyscrapers meant this probably took place in her lifetime. The disorientation of three heads indicated he was in his hellhound form.

His emotions and thoughts pressed in on her, but speaking to the real Cerberus had shown her how much a memory paled in comparison. She was able to hold onto herself long enough to focus.

Stepping outside of him would be a mistake. Lorelei caught on too quickly last time Lexi did that. If she concentrated, she could grasp the memory of making an illusion real. In her mind, she rebuilt the feeling of the dagger. Its weight in her hand. The sharpness of the blade and the engravings on the handle that pressed into her palm.

She didn't summon it yet. She needed the right moment.

It was difficult to strike a balance between blocking out the noise of being stuck in this vision, and hovering on the edge of summoning a tangible illusion. Fortunately, that meant her mind didn't have room for the distractions of torture.

The world around her faded, and she forced out an image. Her surroundings became a vast space of nothingness, similar to what she'd seen when she stepped into the labyrinth.

"You're alert again." Lorelei's song brushed her skin. "That won't do."

Lexi shoved everything she had into a concentrated point. When the dagger appeared in her hand, she felt it. She swung in the direction of the voice, slicing. When she hit resistance, she pushed harder and twisted the blade with as much force as she could muster.

Lorelei's scream sliced through Lexi, making her body feel like it was being forced through a cheese grater.

Lexi clenched her jaw and swung, and struck again.

Agony wrapped in a vivid song tore her to shreds. She fell forward when her target vanished. The noise stopped, and silence blanketed her.

Lexi rubbed her ears, to make sure they still worked, and cringed at the warm stickiness that slipped over her skin. She held her hands in front of her face.

Blood was coagulating on her fingers. The sight and faint scent of copper summoned a wave of nausea. She fell to her knees and retched.

Was this really her? It had to be. She sobbed in relief. It could be another step in Lorelei's torture, but the drying gore on her skin implied she'd done serious damage with her illusion.

Fuck. Did she kill Lorelei? She should be horrified at the thought. Killing was new for her.

Her or you.

That didn't make her feel better. She needed to get out of here. Where was the exit?

If this was like the labyrinth, was finding a path the same as well? She didn't require a meditative state to feel Cerberus, the way she had then. The instant she opened her mind, his familiar presence slipped in and wrapped around her.

Actaeon's aura brushed her senses, and a third strand wove through it all, sharpening her mind and helping her keep panic at bay. She grasped all three and yanked herself toward them.

Fractures spread through the nothingness, growing and splintering until it showered down around her. She cringed away from the debris, but as the shards struck her, they vanished.

Blackness engulfed her. She blinked several times and rubbed her eyes, but nothing appeared. A jabbing pain radiated from her ear. She reached for it and brushed the fresh wound from ripping out her earcuff.

She was back in her physical body.

A pale sliver of gray at her feet speared the darkness. The crack under a door. She wrinkled her nose at the dust in the air. Voices and the scuffing of shoes on the floor reached her.

She groped blindly in the dark, feeling along a rough wall until she gripped a knob. The door to the closet she was in swung open. Sunlight greeted her, and she shut her eyes tight, to block it out.

"Lexi." Cerberus' voice made her heart soar. He wrapped his arms around her.

She fell into the tight hug, pressing her cheek to his chest and daring to look again, now that her eyes had adjusted to the afternoon light.

Actaeon kissed the top of her head. "I'm glad you're all right. You are, aren't you?"

"My ear hurts like a bitch, and I've learned things about your pasts I thought would take me centuries to uncover, but yeah. I'm good." Her gaze fell on Icarus, who stood several feet back, hands jammed in his pockets. She wanted him closer. Part of this not-quite-group hug.

He gave her a tight smile. "Welcome back."

"Thanks. How far did I go?" She took a moment to absorb her surroundings. The floor was unfinished and stretched for several meters in each direction. Steel supports ran to the ceiling, loose cables and trash littered the floor, and graffiti decorated the sheetrock walls.

Icarus kept his distance. "Building next door to the temple. There was a call center up here until a couple of years ago. No one else has leased the place since."

"Why was I in a closet?"

"That's where the doorway is. It used to be a server room. I'm guessing they either had fantastic connectivity or the shittiest feeds ever, depending on who worked for them."

This was all so normal. Four people standing in the middle of an abandoned building, discussing local jobs as though she hadn't just been repeatedly dragged through a psychological shredder.

The reminder clenched in her gut, along with visions of Lorelei's blood coating her hand. She gasped and stepped back, struggling to find her breath. "There was so much blood." She held her hands in front of her, but they were fine. "Where… Did I…" She couldn't grasp her thoughts to form a full sentence. An onslaught of memories crashed around her—not all hers, but all ones she'd lived— and threatened to suck her back into torment.

And on top of it all, she couldn't shake the vision of stabbing Lorelei. How much of that was real? She sank to her knees with a sob, wanting to the visions to stop.

"…she didn't know…"

"…for her and her family…"

"…to go through the same…"

"…day, and she's told me…"

"…I just don't want…"

And now the fucking voices were back. She knotted her fingers in her hair and pulled until her scalp screamed in protest.

"Hey." Actaeon's voice cut through the chaos. He knelt in front of her and lifted her chin. His touch chased away the chatter and shooed her imprisonment to the far corners of her mind. "Stay with us, okay? It's a short walk back to the shop, and then you can rest. I'll carry you if you'd like."

She laughed weakly. "Carrying isn't necessary. I can walk."

"If you're sure." He helped her stand.

They took the stairs to the main floor and stepped out onto the sidewalk.

Actaeon's touch kept the terror at bay but she knew it was there. Her thoughts kept drifting back to it. Like prodding a wound, despite the ache each time. Having Cerberus on her other side helped, but it was more like a bandage than a cure.

Lexi needed a better place to focus. "Icarus said Cassandra told you I was in trouble. I assume there's a story there?"

Icarus walked a few feet ahead. At the question, he spun to face her, never breaking stride. "She's locked in a room, back in my shop."

Lexi didn't know what bothered her more—how closely that description matched the situation she left behind, or that Cassandra was alone at Icarus' place. No, she knew exactly what bothered her the most—Actaeon had to be the reason Cassandra was around. After he'd promised. *Sworn.*

Lexi pulled her hand away and shoved it in her pocket. "I hear you wrong. I must have." She glared at Actaeon. "You didn't bring her back into our lives. After everything…" Lexi choked on the memories. It was too much, combined with what she'd just been through.

Actaeon gave a strained laugh. "She sought me out. She has her memory back. And short version—she says she's sane now, but I don't buy it."

If Lexi wanted an external focus, this fit the bill perfectly. She could channel all her rage and frustration into an interrogation. " Let me talk to her. I'll tell you she's a liar, and you can kick her out."

Cerberus's grip on her hand tightened, and concern spilled through their bond. He didn't want to tell her *no*, but he wanted her to rest first. It was all there in a whisper of emotion.

Actaeon was silent.

Icarus turned away, to walk forward again.

Lexi didn't appreciate being shut out. She opened her mouth.

"Okay." Icarus' voice carried over his shoulder.

Lexi waited for Actaeon's protest, but all she got was the heavy press of growing tension. She'd focus on his betrayal later, and base her response on just how much he'd given up to bring Cassandra back into this mess.

When they reached Icarus', Lexi asked, "Where is she?"

"Do you want to rest first?" Cerberus nudged her toward the stairs going up. "You haven't slept in a while, and you just came out of a traumatic experience."

"It was a long-ass dream, and I'm not looking forward to going back." Lexi headed to the basement instead. "Down here?"

"Yes." Icarus stayed by her side. When they reached the room, he gestured to a plain-looking door on a far wall. "She's in there."

Lexi didn't break her stride. Slowing down meant doubting herself. Falling into her thoughts. On the other side of hesitation lay insanity.

Cerberus and Actaeon followed. Lexi wanted to tell them she'd taken on a siren; she could handle a well-animated zombie. She hadn't, though. Lorelei had trapped her in a different plane of existence. A world where fears and illusions were given shape and visibility.

Lexi faltered. Was that why she'd been able to summon wings the other day? Because Icarus' shop helped make imagination real?

She wasn't thinking about that.

She stopped in front of the door and waited for Icarus to open it.

Cassandra wore a hesitant smile, until her gaze landed on Lexi. "You don't look like you were fed to a siren."

"I got better." Lexi spoke through clenched teeth. Not really. But she would.

Cassandra pressed against the far wall and pulled her knees to her chest. "Please don't make me leave. I like it in here. I can't hear Hades in here. It's quiet in my head."

That wasn't even in the same hemisphere as what Lexi expected—bravado, smugness, confusion perhaps. But raw terror radiated from Cassandra. It was difficult to be angry with a request like, *Keep Hades out of my head*. Fortunately, Lexi had rage to spare.

Cassandra had agreed to the original pact. She might not like the consequences now, but she'd signed on for them.

And it had meant the death of Lexi's mother. Her thoughts seethed white-hot. "Actaeon says you remember everything."

"I do." Casandra occasionally darted her gaze behind Lexi, but mostly directed it at her.

Lexi swallowed the bile rising in her throat. "You remember killing Persephone?"

"Yes."

"Would you do it differently, knowing what you do now?"

Cassandra stared at her, unblinking. "No."

Lexi clenched her fist. Now might be a great time for that giant mallet. "Why did you come back?"

"Because Hades said you'd be destroyed. That I could have Actaeon. That everything would work out. But Hades was in my head. I don't want him there." Cassandra sobbed.

Acid churned in Lexi's gut. A range of weapons flickered in her hand, sliding from knife to sword to mallet and back again. She wasn't doing that on purpose. She refused to lose control for this woman. Could Lexi kill her?

The memory of Lorelei's blood drenched her thoughts and made her stomach churn. Maybe she could, but if Cassandra was Hades vessel, it wouldn't matter. "As long as she's in this building, I won't be." She looked at Icarus. "Your choice."

"She can give us—" Actaeon snapped his jaw shut when Lexi glared at him.

The fact that he had a protest, regardless of what it was, ached as much as the wound on her ear. Did he understand the impact of anything he said? Or was he just letting *help the sad person* dictate the direction of his life?

"It doesn't matter." Hades' voice filled the small room.

Lexi whirled back to Cassandra, who stood in the middle, terror replaced with confidence.

Fuck.

"She told me what happens." Hades spoke through Cassandra's mouth. "I know every step you're about to make, and I'll destroy you. Let me put this in terms you'll understand. This isn't an episode of Supernatural. You don't get to paint a demon trap on the ground and lure me into it. I know you're coming, and I know how you die. The question I leave you with is a two-parter. Do you think I'll do it on earth or in the underworld? And how badly will you fuck yourselves second-guessing your next steps? Too bad I forbade her from telling you what she told me."

Cassandra gasped and stumbled back. "Please lock the door and never let me out. Please."

CHAPTER TWENTY-ONE

Actaeon wanted to let Lexi rest. The haunted look on her face spoke volumes about what she'd been through. He wished there was time for that. "Hear me out. There's a reason I brought Cassandra here."

"I'm glad it wasn't because you like having her back in your life. That's not what it is, right?" Lexi didn't turn around.

The question hurt. "That's not why. She's working with Hades to destroy you, and the other gods. She's—"

Lexi let out a barking laugh. "That's sooo much better. Wow. Are you serious?"

"She can get us into the underworld and tell us where Hades is," Actaeon said.

Lexi shook her head and faced him. "Because that doesn't scream *trap*. She might as well have painted it on the side of the building."

Actaeon needed to do a better job of explaining his logic. He wasn't doing this to hurt her. He needed to diminish the pain. "You spoke with Aphrodite?"

Lexi paled. "Yes. But she only confirmed what Zeus said. Nothing new."

Why did she waver on those last words?

"Cassandra says the same—Hades can't be killed. Though I assume most of what she says is meant to deceive, whether it's true or not."

Cerberus wrapped an arm around Lexi's waist and pulled her closer. "Can we back up to the part where Cassandra remembers everything?"

"She says Hades healed her mind. She serves him, they both want Lexi dead, Hades in charge of humanity, and she's going to win my heart back." Actaeon hesitated on the last words.

Lexi snorted. "Sounds pretty straightforward to me. You're doing a shitty job of making your case."

"I don't know. We could ask her to be the key when we bind Hades. If she's his servant..." The venom in Icarus' voice bled with Lexi's irritation and left a vile film behind.

Cerberus scowled. "That sounds great. Until Cassandra kills herself to set Hades free." When everyone looked at him, he said, "What? After everything she's done, you think she's above that?"

Actaeon expected pushback. He knew it was dangerous to bring Cassandra into things, but he'd rather keep an eye on the threat than shove it aside and pretend it didn't exist. "We need to get in front of Hades, and she can put us there. And yes, I realize that says *trap*."

"Hades knows we're coming, either way." Thank creation for Icarus and his logical thought process. "We can pretend he doesn't, but even if Cassandra wasn't telling the truth about having seen it in a vision, the moment we step into the underworld, he'll know it. We have to plan with that expectation regardless."

"Which brings us back to the prison for Hades," Lexi said. "Having been trapped in one for a couple of hours, I vote we lock him in a similar cell for eternity."

"No." Cerberus' objection landed hard.

She looked at him, brows raised. "We don't have a choice."

This wasn't the way this conversation was supposed to go. "We'll find an alternative. We're not painting a target on your back by binding you to Hades." Actaeon grasped for a better argument. "I brought her back here so we don't have to sacrifice you."

Lexi glared at him, ice spilling from her. "Glad you've justified it. I already have a target on my back. She's not the solution."

"Lexi's right. We don't have another option than to make her the key, and we're running out of time." Icarus looked like the words sliced him apart to say.

Cerberus' growl wasn't surprising. "Are you going to at least figure out why it didn't work for Persephone?"

"I already have. It won't be a problem this time." Icarus raked his fingers through his hair and pulled up a stool.

Actaeon needed more information. "How does the key work with the prison?" When they found Lexi, he'd watched Icarus do something with a bracelet before snapping it on Cerberus' wrist.

"Magic," Icarus said.

"No. Details." Lexi crossed her arms. "I'm willing to put my life on the line to save countless others. It will be nice to do something, for a change. But I'm not going into this with an answer like *magic*. Give us details. For instance, why did you hide Hades in the middle of a labyrinth?"

"I didn't." Icarus' smile was laced with the kind of smugness that said he knew more than everyone else in the room. Actaeon hated that expression.

Lexi formed an *O* with her mouth. "The labyrinth was a distraction, wasn't it?" It was good to see her distracted as well. The shift in her expression was a welcome change from the haunted, murder-Cassandra look. "A way to draw in whoever was loyal to Hades, and get them lost in the challenges. Put them anywhere Hades wasn't." She almost sounded excited. That was disconcerting, given the topic, but it was better than the alternative.

"Exactly." Icarus' smile grew.

That explained why Aphrodite's city-in-the-middle worked the way it did. But there was a flaw in the design. "That's fine until one of your trials deposits the person right in front of your key." For instance, the exit from the town that took Lexi into the underworld.

"But it didn't. Persephone sought Lexi out. The key brought the means of her demise to her front door. That wasn't the doing of a trial," Icarus said. "But we'll need something new. A different place to store the prison. The way it works…" He pursed his lips. "All of us are polarized. The power flowing through us has a positive and negative side."

"So the prison is like a magnet." Lexi was picking this up with hesitation. "You take Hades' power, invert it through the key, and use it to repel him. If he's in a closed chamber, that prevents him from escaping."

Actaeon swore Icarus' eyes lit up with Lexi's explanation. Actaeon was both impressed and envious she and Icarus spoke the same language. What had transpired between them while Actaeon and Cerberus were gone?

Not breaking promises about never seeing Cassandra again.

"Hades still had access to me while he was in there," Cerberus didn't look as impressed. "To all of his servants. Lexi didn't when Lorelei took her. What's the difference?"

Icarus glanced at his hands and drummed his fingertips on his thumb. "All figured out. It won't be a problem."

Why was he lying?

"Mom wasn't Hades' creation, so the bond wasn't strong enough to lock Hades away completely." And why did Lexi cover for him, instead of calling him on it? "She was laden with his power, it was more painted onto her than a part of her. I'm as much my father as anything." She cringed and trailed off on the last few words. "If none of you has another solution, using me as a key is the only way. But I still want Cassandra gone. Anywhere that's not here. Get her the fuck away from me."

"How else are we going to get to Hades?" Actaeon didn't like that Lexi derailed the conversation into a decision to use her as a key, and stuck to her *no* when it came to the original subject.

Lexi clenched her jaw. "Cross Styx. Find a different gate. Ask Aphrodite or another god to send us. Anything that doesn't involve Cassandra. This isn't my home. It's not my place to ask her to leave. But I refuse to stay here as long as she's in the building."

"Consider her gone. You have my word." Icarus had no issue with kicking Cassandra out. He'd hoped Actaeon had a better reason than *she knows*

how to get into the underworld. A bit of insight or something.

Lexi gave him a tired smile. "Not on my account."

"Partly on your account, because you have a good point. Just as much because she shouldn't have been brought here to begin with." Icarus pointed a glare at Actaeon, who clenched his jaw.

"Sleep sounds like a good idea. Thank you again, for finding me." Lexi headed toward the stairs.

Cerberus followed.

"What are you going to do?" Actaeon asked when they were gone. "Toss her out on the street?"

Icarus grabbed his phone. "She was staying with Apollo. He can come get her."

"She's terrified."

If Cassandra was a random person on the street whom Hades occupied because it was convenient, Icarus would be sympathetic. He'd go above and beyond to keep her safe. Mortals deserved better than the bullshit that came with The Enlightenment and the gods' being in charge.

"She went into this situation eyes wide open." Icarus was furious that Actaeon didn't see this. Or didn't care. Sometimes the man had the emotional aptitude of a vibrator. "There's more at stake than her, and she willingly let Hades use her as a vessel. This isn't even a matter of her looking the other way. She knew she'd be used to kill Persephone. She *knew* Hades would kill hundreds of thousands to grow more powerful. And if none of that matters to you, let me appeal to your sense of self-sacrifice. She wants to kill Lexi."

"Which I won't let happen."

Un-fucking-believable. Icarus snapped off a laugh. "You're not even denying it."

"There's no point in pretending that's not the case." Actaeon's posture was deceptively relaxed. His arms dangled by his sides, and his joints were loose. He was prepared for a fight.

Icarus wasn't stupid enough to go hand to hand with him, but he refused to rein in his anger. He'd held a lot of things back, five-hundred years ago when they went their separate ways. Things that hurt too much to say at the time, because he'd been losing a lover. Now? He didn't have any reason to bite off his words. "Because you've never hidden from a problem before," he said sarcastically.

Actaeon's resistance was expected, but Icarus figured they'd trade a few logical words, and Cassandra would be on her way. With Actaeon pushing the issue, centuries of frustration bubbled to the surface of Icarus' mind.

Actaeon chuckled bitterly. "It's better than selling my mind to the highest bidder."

They were going that route? Back to petty fights about things that didn't matter? Fine.

"Is it?" Icarus should have anticipated Actaeon would pull up the same old retort. "We all deal in barter. I'd rather get currency up front, than be promised a random favor, to be fulfilled based on their whim and interpretation unless I draw up an extensive contract."

"I'm not going to let anything happen to Lexi. I love her."

Icarus nearly choked on his disbelief. "*Cerberus* loves Lexi. His adoration is palpable. You don't care about her any more than you did about Cassandra. *You* love the idea of your own martyrdom."

"You have no idea what's going on in my head." Actaeon clenched his fists. The silvery aura that usually rested around him flared to dancing, icy flames.

Icarus was glad he'd struck a nerve. "You're right. I can't see what's in your mind or in your heart." He questioned if Actaeon could see what was in his own heart. "You're a man of actions though, and your lack of them speaks volumes. You excel at falling for the people with the tragic stories and casting blame on everyone—but mostly yourself—for the world's misery. You love a good tortured soul. Morpheus, Cassandra, and now Lexi."

But never Icarus. His life wasn't quite miserable enough.

"You make me sound like a spoiled child."

"Sometimes you act like one. You keep going back to New York—"

"For Prometheus." Actaeon's words sliced through the air, implying the matter was closed.

But it wasn't. Not by a long shot. "For your own fucking ego, so that you can say, *But I tried to help him.* When Zeus sent him back to New York, you and the entire world saw that moment of clarity before Prometheus left. That same lucidity he had before Esper was born. Did you pursue him?"

"I—"

"Had Lexi. I get it." Icarus didn't agree with the logic, but it was easy to see. "Give me a minute, while I walk through this. A woman gets in the back of your cab. She's probably disoriented and obviously out of her element and—*holy shit*—Hades' daughter? Hades didn't have children. But here she is, dark as death, clear as day, and sexy as fuck. And she's not part of the *inner circle.* She's lost, confused, and needs help."

"She wouldn't have survived in the labyrinth alone." Was Actaeon's bite fading?

"She never had to go in there, and the way I hear it, the terrors that haunt your mind came closer to hurting her than anything else did. Besides, you and Cerberus were the ones who took a beating."

"So suddenly I'm a bad guy because I'm compelled to help people?"

Smarter people had twisted Icarus' words. "No. You're an insincere prick, because *helping people* is the cross you're trying to die on. And Lexi is your newest path there. *Tartarus,* she might even be your direct line to literal martyrdom."

"I don't have a death wish." Resignation mingled with the low hum of rage in Actaeon's voice.

Icarus hated having to twist this knife, but he was tired of the destruction Actaeon's martyrdom left in its wake. "You have a crucifixion wish. Literal or otherwise. You don't save people for them, you do it so you'll be known as the guy who did it. You want to be the MVP. You. Don't. Love. Lexi. You might learn to. She's close to falling for you, and she deserves better."

"Better, as in you? Is that what this is about? You're a better choice than me when it comes to Lexi?"

Icarus wouldn't mind making her list, but he had no interest in tearing her away from those she cared for and who cared about her. "I'm not that kind of selfish. But if you pursue her, you sure as fuck better make sure what you feel is real, rather than some misplaced sense of saviordom, before you make yourself a permanent part of her world."

"Fuck you."

Icarus shrugged. "It's not my decision. If she wants you in her life, and you feel comfortable staying, that's between the two of you. But I see through you, and you'd be better off if you learned some of the same insight."

"Call Apollo. I don't give a fuck. Get Cassandra out of here. Sacrifice Lexi, this woman you're so infatuated with, to Hades. I remember now why we don't speak, you arrogant, self-righteous prick." Actaeon strode from the room.

Icarus didn't want to do that. He didn't regret the words, but the delivery could have been less impassioned.

And if he was going to force a little soul-searching on Actaeon, he might need some himself, especially when it came to the reality of Lexi, versus the fantasy.

This was about the worst time for any of that, but he'd never been known for his great timing.

First, he needed to ask Cassandra to leave. Regret welled up inside at the idea of having to look her in the eye and tell her she couldn't stay. He'd never had a problem with her, but she was a risk now.

He hated the tough choices. Offer an old friend refuge and risk the death of the entire neighborhood in the process, or send her away to let a pissed-off god devour her mind? Use a new friend as a key to bind the same god away and make her a walking target in the process, or let Hades roam free?

Logically, the answers were obvious. That didn't mean the decisions were any easier to make.

CHAPTER TWENTY-TWO

Every inch of Lexi's body was heavy. Each step or breath or gesture took tremendous effort. Sitting on the edge of the bed in Icarus' guest room was a welcome relief, but untapped energy thrummed through her, making ants dance under her skin and along her nerves. "Is this how it starts?" she asked Cerberus. She meant it to be a joke, but the words came out strangled.

"How what starts?" He was a blurry visage to her, now that her earcuff was gone. The three-headed dog overlapped the man, like a bad double exposure.

It made her head ache if she studied him for too long in an attempt to distinguish one or the other, but as long as she accepted the sight as it was, she was fine with it. She loved him regardless.

Lexi was both grateful and regretful for the link that flowed between them. She didn't think she could put this feeling into words, but she didn't want him to experience it. "The not-sleeping thing you and Actaeon do."

If she added a couple more points of stress, would they smear together in big blur in her head, until she wasn't able to focus on any individual one? That would be easier than deciding which to give priority to.

"Not quite. Sit here. I'll be right back." He walked into the other room before she could find the strength to ask where he was going.

Cerberus returned with a washcloth. He took the spot next to her on the bed and pressed the warm, damp cloth to the side of her face. He was gentle as he wiped away the dried blood from where she'd ripped out her earring. He brushed the wound, and pain jolted through her.

She sucked in a sharp breath through her teeth.

He backed away from the injury. When he was finished, he tossed the rag into the adjoining bathroom. The sound of it hitting tile and falling into the bathtub echoed back to her. "You'll need to wash your hair to get the rest out, but at least you don't look like a B horror movie extra anymore."

"Something to be grateful for." Lexi managed a laugh. She'd take what she could get.

"Are you able to talk about anything on your mind?" Cerberus took her hand. The contact soothed parts of her, but the rest still hummed at high frequency. *"Out loud or not, I'm listening."*

"Verbally, please. I don't like it in my head right now," she said.

"Tell me. Anything you want."

He was so good to her. Had done and sacrificed so much on her behalf. She should say any of those things. Or offer sympathy for the mental torture he went through when Persephone escaped the underworld. Or change the subject to something non-threatening, like how much they both enjoyed the fifth Star Wars trilogy.

"Has Lorelei ever called in her favor?" she asked.

His shock raced through their connection. "No." The answer came without hesitation or deception. "Why? How do you know about that?"

"Actaeon told me the price for a siren-gate key." She nodded at the gem that hung on a leather cord around Cerberus' neck. "Was he wrong?"

"He wasn't. I owe Lorelei a favor, but she's never asked." He was telling the truth.

Why did she doubt him?

"Lexi? Tell me why you're asking."

"I…" She didn't want to relive the scene, and her vivid, lingering doubt wasn't something she could put into words. She took his other hand, gripping both to anchor herself. "I can show you."

Lexi'd watched the scene play out countless times, and it flowed easily through her head once she let it. Lorelei greeting Cerberus in her hut. Her demanding he kill Icarus. The contract that kept him from saying anything to Lexi.

She broke the connection between them with a sob, before the rest of her time in Lorelei's box could break free of the restraints she had on it. Silence settled in the room, while she struggled to bring her jagged breathing and racing pulse under control.

Cerberus' gentle touch on her forehead as he brushed away a strand of hair helped to ground her. "That never happened," he said. "I promise. And yes, she could make it part of the favor to not tell you, but I couldn't lie to you. Not ever. I could refuse to answer, but you'd see the truth. It's who you are."

He had so much faith in Lexi, and she didn't deserve it. She was still fumbling through life, barely a baby, compared to anyone in this world of gods and humans and servants. She'd doubted Cerberus, and on top of that, she was keeping secrets of her own. Guilt slid in to join the blobby mess that was her mind.

"Why does her favor override our link?" Lexi asked. "Why do you have to do what she asks, if I don't want you to?"

Cerberus sighed. "A favor isn't worth much if it can be overridden by another promise further down the road. Even if that promise is a servant's bond. No one would deal in favors if they could be tossed aside."

"Who makes these rules?"

He shrugged. "They've been there as long as I can remember. Maybe the Titans did. Perhaps it happened even earlier than that."

"Oh." She didn't like that, but it wasn't high on her *pursue it and find an answer now* list.

"There's more, isn't there?" His question didn't hold any expectation.

If she got this confession out of the way now, it wouldn't hang over her anymore. It wasn't even the big deal she'd turned it into. A random thing—insignificant, next to Hades' trying to destroy her and the gods. Why did it sit in her gut with such a heavy pit, then?

"You need to keep your head in the game for what we're about to do. If you talk about it now, it will help," Cerberus said.

And there was that. She couldn't focus, with so much looming over her. "Though Aphrodite didn't have much to offer about Hades, she did have some very specific thoughts around Icarus," she said.

"Like what?"

"She's got some strong beliefs when it comes to fated love."

"Who's he..." Cerberus looked at Lexi with shock. "You?"

Lexi nodded. "She implied he was the third and final one." That was supposed to make the situation better, but it came out as a weak excuse.

"There's obviously chemistry between the two of you." The emotion didn't flow as freely from Cerberus as it had moments ago. He didn't shut her out completely, but there was a wall between them.

Disappointment gnawed the lining of her stomach. "There's more to it than what Aphrodite said. I guess she and I are the only ones who see it.

There's a red string that runs from me to both you and Actaeon. It's faint"—*fuck*, it was barely visible right now, and that devoured her—"but now that I know what it is, I always see it."

"And it's there with Icarus, too."

"Yes."

"But it's faint?" Cerberus asked.

Icarus is your mind, and you value that above all else. Aphrodite's words taunted Lexi.

"I didn't see it with him the first time we met. I don't know why not. But I did in the bar. It's distinct and vibrant. It might as well be a real red string. Aphrodite said… It doesn't matter. I'm not letting her or fate make up my mind for me. She acts like if I choose to ignore it, I'll be miserable forever. I barely know the guy." Lexi bit off the rambling thought when she realized Cerberus had gone mostly blank—both his expression and his emotions.

A sliver of hurt poked through his defenses, though. "You knew about it before you talked to Aphrodite."

"I suspected." Lexi could gloss over the revelation, but she didn't want to pretend anymore. "The night after I met him, we shared a dream. It was… intense. Nothing happened. We just talked. But he was in my head. Similar to what he did when he found me in Lorelei's prison."

Cerberus was silent. She waited for any other indicator of what he was thinking.

She didn't like this idea of anyone besides her and the people she was with having a say in who she loved. Defensiveness rose inside. She didn't have a right to cast this on Cerberus, but she couldn't smother the feeling. "I didn't tie an ethereal string between myself and anyone else, and I never said I intended to do anything about it."

"I wish you'd told me." Cerberus' voice was flat.

Lexi deflated. "I was trying to figure out how."

"You were trying to figure out if you could ignore it until it went away."

"Is that such a bad thing?"

Cerberus stood. The loss of contact with him was another layer of pain in this conversation. "It is if you're in denial. Things are happening between the two of you anyway."

Lexi wanted to say the same things she had to Aphrodite. That this was a phase. A crush. A passing fancy. She didn't know if any of that was true. She hadn't spent enough time with Icarus to say the opposite either—that this was budding love. So she kept her mouth shut.

"This is why he can talk to you in your dreams." Cerberus spoke matter-of-factly.

"You know how I feel about fate. I'm not with you because of a stupid red cord, and I refuse to let it dictate how I feel about Icarus. I didn't mean to hurt you." She added the last bit weakly.

"But you did."

"I didn't—" Didn't what? Mean to like this new man? Know how to tell Cerberus?

He frowned and dropped the emotional wall. The feeling of hurt flowed fast, hitting her hard. "You didn't believe me, is what you didn't do. You felt me when I said the words. When I promised I was okay with you loving other people in addition to me. The last few days have been a mess. Barely enough of a chance to think, but there's always time for me to listen to you. You made a conscious decision to keep me out of that part of your head. You didn't trust me with the information, despite everything that's transpired between us."

His words dug deeper than any of Lorelei's stupid fucking torture scenes. Lexi didn't have an argument, but one forced its way past her lips anyway. "I didn't want to break anything between the three of us—you, me, and Actaeon—if Icarus doesn't mean anything."

"Can you open yourself up to me completely and say with no hesitation this is only lust?"

She shook her head. "I don't know what it is."

"You would have preferred to wait until it became full-blown love, and then dumped the news on me? You only had to tell me. All I ask from you when it comes to our relationship is that you not keep secrets from me."

She didn't care for the accusation. "I've spent my entire life hiding. Being lied to. As a pawn in a game I never wanted to play. I love you and I trust you and I know when you're telling the truth, but those habits that kept me alive are hard to break. I didn't do this to hurt you."

Cerberus' frown deepened, and then he let the wall down. Understanding flowed between them. There was hurt, but she couldn't force him to turn off his reactions any more than he could her.

"This is new to me." Lexi didn't want either of them to walk away from this conversation hurt. "To all of us. I'm trying to learn, but there are going to be some bumps. I've learned from this."

Cerberus knelt in front of her and rested a finger under her chin. "If something happens with Icarus, I'm okay with it. You *feel* me when I say that. The sincerity is there. If you're not okay with the situation, don't pursue it. I love you either way."

She let his sincerity and assurance seep into her.

He rose to kiss her on the forehead. "I'm fumbling too. We'll figure things out as they come up."

She managed a grateful smile. "Thank you."

"Actaeon is going to be more annoyed that it's Icarus, than because there's a third suitor."

The statement tugged at irritation. Actaeon hadn't earned the right. After bringing Cassandra back here, he was barely a friend. He certainly wasn't more, regardless of what fate said.

"But he doesn't have the right to judge you for you who you love any more than anyone does," Cerberus said.

"You don't care for Actaeon."

"He's growing on me. And I don't resent you for your feelings."

She recognized the difference. Did she respect Actaeon's opinion above Icarus'? Not right now.

But she felt stronger when Actaeon was around. The world wasn't such an intimidating place.

If she was using Actaeon as a crutch, instead of learning to cope on her own, that was an entirely different problem, and not one she liked having.

An eardrum-shattering *boom* roared through the room, and the building shook from the concussion. A familiar aura coated Lexi's tongue, carried on the dust kicked up by the explosion.

The sick feeling in her stomach soured with dread.

Cerberus looked at her, eyes wide with terror that matched her own. *"Hades is here."*

CHAPTER TWENTY-THREE

Actaeon was fuming over Icarus' words. *A martyr?* The thought was ridiculous.

One moment the space on the other side of the plate glass window was empty, and the next Apollo appeared on the street, looking like a bad movie effect.

He entered the shop and fixed a glare on Actaeon. "I asked you to stay away," Apollo said.

Actaeon had. Cassandra came after him.

After I sought her out twice. And then I brought her here, instead of turning her away.

He didn't know why he thought it was a good idea. It made more sense at the time. "I'm sorry."

"You… what?" Apollo sounded as surprised as he looked.

"Sorry to keep you waiting." Cassandra's sweet greeting floated through the room, as she and Icarus emerged from the basement.

"How are you doing?" Apollo turned his attention to Cassandra.

She wore a pleasant smile, as though she hadn't alternated between pleading for her life and letting Hades use her as a vessel to threaten them. "I'm fine."

She paused next to Actaeon and kissed him on the cheek. "I meant everything I said on the beach. I hope to see you again."

Her lack of distress or any strong emotion was disconcerting. Wait. Did that mean she'd seen him survive? Good, because he wasn't looking to martyr himself.

"We should go." Apollo offered his arm, and Cassandra looped her hand around his elbow.

They strolled out the front door.

The air crackled across Actaeon's skin, and the potent scent of ozone filled his nostrils.

"*Watch out*," he shouted at the same time Icarus did.

They both raced toward the door.

Actaeon felt like the world around him was moving in slow motion.

Apollo shoved Cassandra away from him and jumped in the other direction.

Icarus and Actaeon burst through the front door.

A spike of white flame struck the middle of the road, sending debris flying everywhere and shaking the buildings.

The aftershock shattered all nearby windows, including those in the shop.

Actaeon's ears were ringing, as the world returned to its normal speed.

Hades stood in the fresh crater. A two-headed dog, almost as tall as Hades, was next to him. Orthus was Cerberus' brother. That explained who Actaeon saw on the ferry.

"Stay inside," Cerberus said from behind Actaeon.

Actaeon suspected Lexi wouldn't listen, but this was a no-hesitation situation. He couldn't check on her *and* attack Hades. His bow appeared in his hands, and he fired at Hades as quickly as he was capable. These wouldn't be killing blows, but they'd do damage. Death could come after.

Apollo followed-suit. His bow was similar to Actaeon's but golden, and he was a couple meters farther back. His opposing angle to Actaeon meant Hades couldn't see them at the same time.

Good advantage.

"Stop." Hades sounded annoyed. He grunted as arrows hit him from both sides.

Good. Their shots were having an impact.

"I said *stop*." Hades flung white spears of flame toward Actaeon, who dodged.

The attack tore new gaps in the street, scattering more rubble.

There were people in this town. They shouldn't get hurt. Actaeon didn't know how to stop or relocate this, though.

He exchanged glances with Apollo. Actaeon might not like his uncle, but as with Heracles, they'd trained together when Actaeon was younger. Actaeon knew how to hunt with Apollo, and this was the ultimate prey.

Actaeon twitched his fingers against his bow's grip.

Apollo gave the briefest nod.

Actaeon fired three small arrows in rapid succession, holding Hades' attention.

Apollo summoned a more powerful arrow and send the flaming head into Hades' back.

Hades stumbled and whirled.

Actaeon ditched his bow for his dagger and sprinted toward Hades, focusing on a more intimate and up-close attack. He didn't notice Orthus charging him until he was within slicing distance. It was too late to change his path.

Cerberus leaped between them, snarling and snapping his jaws, and knocked Orthus aside, clearing the way for Actaeon.

Actaeon drove his blade into Hades' side.

Hades backhanded him. The impact jarred Actaeon's thoughts and propelled him back. Hades' follow-up fireball to the chest threw him several feet away.

Realization spread through Actaeon. Cassandra's attack at the cafe wasn't Apollo's magic. It was from Hades, made to look like Apollo.

And where was she? He dared a glance around while he sprung to his feet. She stood at the edge of the mayhem, staring blankly at the fight.

Fucking disturbing.

Actaeon's chest burned, and he struggled to draw in air. None of that mattered. Trusting Apollo to draw Hades' attention, he darted forward and took another swing. This one connected with flesh, meeting resistance as he sliced.

Hades faltered and forced Actaeon back with another fireball.

Actaeon gasped through the agony, trying to breathe but not getting much oxygen for his effort. He could survive without the stuff, but not stay mobile.

"This isn't how you greet an old friend." Hades' voice was strained. "I'm here for Cassandra and Alexandra, not to fight."

"Which is why you made your entrance on a pillar of fire." Actaeon used the pause to assess the situation, knowing every other combatant did the same.

Cerberus had Orthus pinned, all three heads snarling as he struggled to keep his brother from jumping back into the main fray.

Hades smiled and looked past Actaeon. "It was simple showmanship. Alexandra, my dear, I was wrong about you. We need to talk."

Actaeon wouldn't risk following Hades gaze. He circled, keeping Hades in his sight, so he could see Lexi.

She stood in front of the shop, staring down Hades. "You can talk," she said. "I'm not listening."

How could Actaeon *not* love that defiance? Icarus was an idiot sometimes.

"What if I say I'm sorry for trying to kill you?" Though Hades spoke to her, he'd turned his attention back to the fight.

Apollo twitched, Hades fired, and Apollo leaped back while he shot another arrow.

Their attacks connected with their targets at the same time. Actaeon used the opportunity to duck, roll, and come up behind Hades.

Hades caught him with a backhand before he could strike.

Actaeon was prepared for the blow and sliced. He didn't make the contact he wanted, but Hades' hiss of pain told him he'd done something.

Actaeon recovered in a blink. His body screamed in protest with each step. This was worse than the last fight with Hades. It wasn't just an energy drain; Actaeon was taking severe physical damage as well. He didn't know how much longer he could keep this up.

And why the fuck was Lexi still on the street, watching everything?

Faking his own death when he plunged into the ocean, to escape his father's labyrinth and oppression, was the first time Icarus felt true terror. There had only been a handful of moments since.

Watching Lexi distract Hades, seeing how badly injured Actaeon was, and wondering if Cerberus was the kind of guy who would kill his brother if it came down to it had Icarus' hands shaking.

He needed this to work, but he wasn't confident it would. He'd taken an old sword that hung at the back of his shop. It was a souvenir piece of junk from the city's centennial celebration a few decades ago. It wasn't even sharp enough to slice soft butter.

Icarus was infusing it with a combination of magic and electricity. The prison wasn't ready for Hades, or he'd use that. This might buy them time.

It might not, but he didn't see any other options. His friends and everyone in this neighborhood would be slaughtered if something didn't change in the next few minutes.

Hades' words to Lexi disturbed Icarus. It was a drastic shift from the mantra of, *I'm going to kill you.*

Icarus didn't want to let her step onto the street, but she refused to stop. And he had to admit she was an effective distraction.

But if Hades threw one of those fireballs in her direction, would she survive?

She'd told Icarus she had to. Otherwise, who would make him invisible when the time came?

He needed to focus on his work. Ignore the taste of ash and ozone in the air. Push aside his concern for everyone else, and complete his task.

Icarus closed his eyes and did something no hero did unless they were desperate or losing their mind—and he was both.

He prayed. "Athena, I don't know if you're listening, but please, lend me your strength."

Nothing changed.

Then his body tingled with the rush of foreign power, flowing through him and mingling with his own. He collected everything he could grasp, blended it with the electricity in the air, and passed his hand along the blade of the sword.

One single-use, magically imbued weapon, coming up.

He gripped the hilt so tight his knuckles ached. He'd trained in the basics of sword fighting, but he wasn't a fighter. Was he better off giving the sword to Actaeon, or using it himself?

This blade wasn't meant to endure. One thrust, and it would be spent.

Actaeon and Apollo were keeping Hades occupied. The openings they created for each other were apparent, but Icarus didn't know they were coming until they were there. If he got in the wrong person's way, they were all fucked.

His one advantage was Hades either didn't know Icarus was there or didn't care.

Icarus braced himself and strode forward. He paused in the shop window.

Apollo flicked a gaze over him. "I know she's a first and only child for you. But a lot of us have been talking, Hades, and we think your obsession with your daughter is unhealthy."

Hades rolled his eyes and glanced at Apollo long enough to shoot a spear of flame at him.

Actaeon rolled away from the shop, loosing arrows and holding Hades attention.

Lexi brushed Icarus' hand. He looked down, but he couldn't see himself.

It worked. Neat trick.

He forced hesitation aside and charged at Hades, sword extended and pointed at the god's back.

Orthus slammed into Icarus, knocking his breath away. The sword clattered to the ground, and Orthus used one head to toss it away.

How was Icarus seen? He must have cast a reflection somewhere. *Fuck.*

Orthus growled and snapped his jaws at Icarus. Icarus had strength, and these weren't advanced fighting techniques, but he couldn't do any more than hold both Orthus' heads at bay.

Cerberus growled when he plowed into Orthus. Cerberus clamped down on both of Orthus' necks before his brother could react, and tore.

Orthus died with a gargling whimper. Blood ran along the street, filling nearby pits.

Icarus gasped and struggled to his feet.

Lexi strode past. Her aura glowed more brightly than the sun, weaving pink and purple around her in flowing snakes of energy.

She picked up the sword, and it vanished when she dropped her arm to her side.

"You want to talk? Let's talk." She strode into the center of the chaos.

Calling Hades' bluff was a bold move, and terror on her behalf clenched around Icarus' lungs.

Everyone stopped. It was as if someone had hit *Pause* on the scene. The eerie quiet made Icarus want to clean his ears, to make sure they still worked.

Hades smirked. "Lorelei told me what she saw in the horrific confines of your past."

"A handful of unfortunate moments in time. Hardly the types of thing that scar a person." Lexi's voice shook.

"You're scared. That's reasonable." Hades reached for her. "I swear to you, on your mother's grave, I want to talk. Explore our options. Nothing more."

Creepy. Oh shit. Lorelei heard the same thing Icarus did, during the memory with Conner and Aphrodite. She'd heard what the goddess said to Lexi's dad. Hades knew Lexi was—

Lexi lunged and drove her sword arm up, aiming for Hades throat.

He moved to the side, but she was close enough that, when the blade appeared, several inches of it were buried in his neck.

"This was your last chance." His threat carried on the wind, rather than being spoken. "Next time, I'll kill you."

Hades and Cassandra vanished.

Everyone fell to the ground, on their knees or collapsed, breathing heavily.

Actaeon, Cerberus, and Apollo had to be in pain. That was Hades at nearly full strength. Whatever happened to him in Las Vegas—whatever Heracles and Actaeon did—didn't have the impact they thought.

Hades was injured more severely this time, but with the scores he'd killed recently, he might only need a few hours to recover.

They had to find a place he wouldn't look for them, and Icarus needed to build the prison.

Please, Creation, don't let him come looking for us before I'm done.

CHAPTER TWENTY-FOUR

Lexi's legs gave out, and she fell on her ass in the middle of the street. She couldn't stop shaking.

Cerberus' grief, along with the growing acceptance of what he'd done spilled through her, clenching like a fist around her heart.

She couldn't see past the onslaught of emotion clogging her thoughts. A hand on her shoulder dragged her from inside her head.

Apollo was crouched in front of her. "You're a credit to the post-Enlightenment generation. What do you need from me?"

Lexi couldn't find her voice.

"A place to hide," Icarus said. He and Actaeon had reached her as well.

She couldn't focus on the conversation. Too much pressed in on her. Actaeon offered her a hand and helped her stand. She gave him a grateful smile and joined Cerberus. Haze was settling into her thoughts, muffling the overload. Part of her mind screamed there was still danger, but her emotions couldn't keep up. It was like watching a movie through a blurry filter.

She knelt next to Cerberus, not caring that blood soaked her jeans. He was lying on the ground in his dog form, whimpering.

Lexi pulled one head into her lap and stroked his ears. "I'm so sorry." She wanted to say it over and over again until the words accomplished something. They never would. She rubbed one of his necks instead.

"I have a place you can go," Apollo said. "I can't guarantee it will hide you for long, but it will buy you a little time."

"We only need time to finish the prison for Hades." That was Icarus. Why were they talking like nothing was wrong?

Because they didn't have a choice. The sorrow filling her didn't change the situation.

"It's a one-time trip for each of you, so bring whatever you need." Apollo spoke with urgency. "Coming and going will increase the odds of Hades' finding you. Especially Alexandra."

Lexi hated that the gods called her that. Her preferred name wasn't a secret. The irritation prickled under her skin in a way it never had before. "It's *Lexi*."

"I apologize. Lexi." Apollo sounded surprised. "I need to ask something in return. I don't have a right, because this is already a fair trade, but I'm going to, anyway."

"All right." Lexi forced the response out before someone else could tell him *no*. He'd fought with them. He was helping them. He deserved to be heard.

"Bring Cassandra back?"

Lexi clenched her jaw until the ache distracted her from what lay inside. "Ultimately it's her decision, but I'll try." She didn't know why, but it felt like the right thing to do.

"Give me five minutes, and I'll be ready," Icarus said, before heading inside.

Cerberus stumbled to his feet and padded to Apollo. "I need to bury my brother. Will I be able to join them later?" It was odd to hear Cerberus speak like this. His voice was an illusion when he was in dog form. Lexi caught ripples of both the illusion and the mental projection, plus a third echo through their connection. It added to the sensation that she was clawing her way through the world around her.

Apollo nodded, and a small stone attached to a leather cord appeared in his hand. He hooked it around Cerberus' neck. "You're familiar with how it works. Everyone will be waiting for you."

"Do you want company, or to be left alone?" Lexi asked.

"I need to do this myself. But what we talked about earlier? I'm not upset about Icarus or the cord, and there's nothing to forgive. I love you, and I'll see you soon." He stepped back to Orthus' body, and they both vanished.

Icarus returned a moment later, a pack slung over one shoulder. "I'm ready."

Their surroundings were replaced with an apartment. The view implied they were high up, if not on the top floor, and the vast open floorplan said *penthouse suite*.

Icarus raised his brows. "Is this... a Sunshine Seasons Resort?"

"Of course it is," Apollo said. "This floor is shielded, and reserved for myself and guests. No one will know you're here. If Hades guesses that I'm hiding you, he can go knocking at every single resort. He'll find you if he searches enough of them, but there are two-hundred-forty-seven, so cross your fingers that he starts at the other end of the list."

That was almost encouraging. Numbness seeped into Lexi. "Thank you."

Apollo gripped her fingers and kissed her knuckles. "Godspeed." He vanished.

She wanted to laugh at the ridiculous statement.

The place was more like a sweeping home than a hotel room. The living room was sparsely decorated with a futon, leaving a large throw rug mostly visible. Wicker furniture decorated the balcony. Compared to Artemis' house, the two places were night and day.

Another wave of irrational laughter bubbled in Lexi's chest at her pun. She was losing her mind. She must be.

Actaeon and Icarus were silent. She swore tension flowed between them, but she had so much of her own that she wasn't certain.

"Should we tour the place?" Actaeon asked. He gave Icarus a look she couldn't interpret.

Icarus nodded.

Actaeon hung back as they wandered through the suite. The kitchen was stainless steel with stone counters. There were two bedrooms on this floor, and a set of stairs lead to a loft with three more rooms. Each space had a similar setup with a bed, nightstand, chair, and an adjoining bathroom with a shower.

It was both simple and opulent. Impressive combination.

Actaeon was struggling to keep up, leaning against nearby walls whenever they paused. He looked battered, and his face was pinched. How did she miss that before?

"You need to rest, to heal," Icarus said.

"I'm fine."

Lexi wasn't in the mood for false bravado. "We have to face Hades again. If you're beat-up and lying about it, you're a risk to everyone."

Actaeon clenched his jaw, then pushed away from the wall. "I'm going to shower and lie down. I won't need long." He headed into the nearest room.

When he was gone, an unfamiliar awkwardness settled over Lexi. A different thing to feel. *Yay.* She didn't know how to act around Icarus.

He nudged her shoulder with his. "You sleeping anytime soon?"

"Maybe never again." She forced a chuckle.

He brushed his fingertips over her injured ear. Instead of pain, a spark of calm seeped into her. He dropped the strap of his bag into his hand and reached inside. "I collected clothes for all of us." He handed her a folded stack. "Wash the blood off and find me in the kitchen. I'd like your help."

Help. She could do that. Anything to occupy her mind.

Lexi was tempted to take her time in the shower. Having access to hot water that didn't run out had spoiled her during the last few weeks. She let the stream wash over her and tried to relax into the heat.

As her mind drifted, too many thoughts assaulted her at once. Some of the images were from her time with Lorelei, but those didn't haunt her the way she expected.

More of what she felt came from Cerberus, wherever he was. Lexi's heart ached for him.

And something was wrong with Actaeon, beyond physical pain. Was she grateful or disappointed she didn't share any sort of mental link with him?

It would be nice if she could help either one of them. Once again, she was powerless. Icarus needed her assistance. That was something.

After talking to Cerberus, she felt a little silly, making such a big deal out of a stupid ethereal string. If she wasn't going to let fate control her life, that meant not acting out of spite either.

She washed away what water and soap could cleanse, and shut off the faucet. After she dried off, she dressed. Her second set of brand-new clothes in less than twenty-four hours. It almost felt like when she was younger, and a good day involved more than having a roof to sleep under that kept the elements out.

She joined Icarus, who had spread a large number of items across the stone island in the kitchen. She recognized wires and circuit boards but couldn't put names to most of his collection.

What he'd done with the sword, as well as the jukebox in the bar, the volume on the TV, came back to her. "What is it you do?" she asked.

He looked up, startled, then smiled. "As in, what's my superpower?"

"I guess so." Her short laugh felt natural, which was calming.

"I mix the magical and electrical. I see energy as it flows through the air, and I bend it to my will." He shook his head. "I'm not doing a very good job of explaining."

She got it, though. "You're like Neo."

He furrowed his brow, studying her. "Did you just make a Matrix reference?"

"Dad—my stepdad—was a fan of the classics. You might say he raised me well."

Icarus smiled. "That explains so much. Maybe not *that* much, but enough. Are you ready to help?"

"I am, but I can't do what you do. Understanding and being able to mimic are two different things."

"I need you to be a sounding board. I'm not always… I have a bad habit of missing pieces when I create. I have no idea if this will work, but I think you can help me fill in those holes. You don't have to go above and beyond or do anything different than being yourself. Listen to me, tell me what you're thinking, and we'll take it from there." As he spoke, he worked with some of the wires.

"You make it sound easy." Nothing was that simple.

"I'm hoping it is." He fiddled with a small board, using his finger to melt solder. A tiny drop hung suspended in the air, then floated and landed on the point he'd made with copper and circuit.

"You've built this prison before, though."

He sighed and rested his palms on the counter, leaning his weight in. "I did. And it had flaws. I figured one of them out, but I need to make sure there are no others."

He wasn't lying, but he was holding something back. She'd push, but this wasn't the time to start another argument. "In that case, talk to me."

"What was your favorite?" he asked. "Out of everything your dad introduced you to." He was the first person she'd met in this sub-world who didn't refer to him as her stepdad.

"That's like asking a parent to pick a favorite child."

"Every parent has a favorite."

She was surprised at the flippant response. "Who was it for your parents?"

"Not me." His tone went flat.

She shouldn't push, but now she was curious. "How many siblings do you have?"

"One." He gave a tiny shake of his head, and a flat smile appeared. "Tell me this instead. If you could watch or read or listen to one right now, what would it be?"

Dad would want her to say *Star Wars*. "I'd re-read *The Billionaire's Accidental Email Baby*." She paused, waiting for his laugh.

Icarus didn't flinch. "I have a copy of that book back home."

"Now you're fucking with me." Except she knew he wasn't.

"It's not mine. Esper stumbled on a stash of romance novels at a yard sale, and was too embarrassed to admit to her dads that she was reading them, so I keep them for her. I've read it, though."

"And?" Lexi asked.

It was fascinating, watching him work. He didn't look at his hands, and he dedicated as much focus to the conversation as to what he was building. His concentration and skill were sexy.

He fitted two pieces of board together. "I wouldn't pick it over the fifth trilogy, but I've read it more than once. I liked *The Stepbrother's Intentional Mafia Baby* better."

It felt good to smile and relax. Which seemed wrong.

He studied her. "What's up?"

"I feel guilty, having fun, with so much going on."

"You enjoy the moments as they come. Trust me, even though you have centuries ahead of you, if you ignore something because you don't think it's the right time to feel it, you'll regret it."

His words tugged at a thought she'd had in the shower, about not fighting whatever was between them. Letting things happen as they would, instead. It was time to stop holding back. "You know something you're not telling me. What is it?" she asked.

"I could say the same to you."

She looked at her hand and followed the red cord to where it tied around his finger. "All right. I'll spill. There's a red cord that binds me to Cerberus, and one to Actaeon."

He rolled his eyes. "Yeah. We had that conversation."

"There's another that ties me to you. And it's much more distinct."

"*Oh.*" He met her gaze. "That's why you freaked out in the bar."

"Yes." She expected him to be mad or irritated or defensive.

Instead, he watched her with curiosity. "Why are you telling me now? It's not just because you want to swap a secret for a secret."

She liked that—how he plucked information from her and filled in the blanks. "I won't let fate tell me how to live my life. I pushed Cerberus away because it scared me, and I can't give it that kind of power over me again."

"And Actaeon?" Icarus asks.

She didn't know. Things with Actaeon were... She couldn't describe them, and after what he did with Cassandra, she didn't know if she could trust him. "Maybe all true love is predestined, or it becomes a self-fulfilling prophecy once someone pushes the issue. Perhaps I have a choice, and perhaps I don't. I fell for Cerberus before I knew fate was involved. It doesn't matter what a magic piece of string or a goddess of love says; I'm going to enjoy my life and make the decisions that feel right to me."

"Where does that leave us?" Icarus stopped what he was doing and moved to her side of the island. He was close enough to touch, but didn't reach out.

"I don't know. I'm thinking in the figuring-things-out stage."

"If I kiss you again, will you push me away?"

"No." Heat raced through her veins. This wasn't the time or place, but what he said about not passing up opportunities rang true. "In fact, I'll be disappointed if you don't. But I'll understand if you feel we've lost the moment."

He searched her face, and her heart hammered in her ears as she waited for his response.

CHAPTER TWENTY-FIVE

Icarus cupped Lexi's face and kissed her. She gasped against his mouth and stumbled until her back hit the wall, not wanting to break contact. Unbridled need filled her. It wasn't like with Cerberus or Actaeon. This was hands trying to be everywhere at once. His lips on her neck, sucking and moving down at the same time. Her hands roaming his chest, wanting to feel everything.

"What if this is just an outlet for stress?" She hated the breathless question.

"This isn't *just* anything." He glided a palm up to squeeze her breast, then pinched her nipple. "And there's nothing wrong with releasing some tension."

Her chuckle faded into a moan. "*Goddess.* I like the way you think."

He kneaded and teased, sending fissures of pleasure through her. Each touch pushed another thought into the background, until the only thing that mattered was being closer. Feeling more. She thrust her hips, grinding against him.

"I've been fantasizing about you since we met." He nipped her good ear.

Lexi sighed and leaned into him. "I know. I've been in your dreams. Your head is a wicked place."

"Takes one to know one." Icarus trailed a finger down and over her stomach, pausing to undo her jeans before slipping under her panties.

He parted her folds and dipped between. When he brushed her clit, she bucked against his hand. He traced circles around the tender nub, teasing with a hint of contact before pulling away again.

As the playful touch brought her closer to climax, clouds filled her head. Not the haze she'd been stuck in before—this was exhilarating and intoxicating. Orgasm spilled through her, clenching over every inch of her body with intensity. She floated along the wave until the rush ebbed.

"You're stunning when you come." Icarus brushed his lips over hers.

The only response she could find was to sink into his kiss. This was fun, but desire still clawed her senses, demanding more. She hooked her thumbs in her jeans, shoved them to the ground along with her panties, and kicked the clothes aside.

He dragged his fingers down her back, and she swore her skin sparked everywhere he touched. "Your wish is my command," he murmured against her mouth, before cupping her ass and lifting her.

She wrapped her legs around his waist. Her back hit the wall harder, and she giggled at the gasp the impact knocked from her. This was… fun. Not meaningless, but not fraught with expectation, either. It rode somewhere in a wonderful middle ground.

Lexi reached between them, to drag down his zipper. She refused to think about how the physics worked. Icarus held her up without visible effort, and that was enough for her. She worked him free, drawing a long groan that she felt all the way in her toes.

He thrust inside, filling her up. The sensation was amazing. The pace started slow, but built to a rapid hammering as he slammed into her.

Closing her eyes, she sank into the moment. The slap on her skin each time he pounded against her. The texture of the wall biting into her back. His grunts, loud and unrestrained. And the tasted of his kisses when he crushed his mouth to hers again.

It was distinct and ran together at the same time. Nothing existed but them. The world stopped spinning as he fucked all of her senses at once. She was vaguely aware of her cries when she came again and the way they mingled with his voice.

He came inside her, not slowing until he was spent.

They sank to the floor, a tangle of limbs and breathless panting. She rested her head against his chest. His pounding heart beat in time with hers.

She didn't know how long they sat there. Her butt was getting cold and her pulse returned to normal. He tipped her chin up for another kiss, a smirk decorating his face.

"Was it that good?" she asked.

His smile grew. "You're incredible. And I know what's missing from the prison."

"Does that mean I can brag that sex with me is inspirational?"

He kissed her on the nose, then helped her to her feet as he stood. "You're my fucking muse. You can tell people whatever you'd like about that."

"*Muse*? I'm pretty sure for everything in my lineage, I'm not a muse," she teased.

"You're my muse. That's all there is to it."

Actaeon couldn't get Icarus' accusations out of his head. None of it was true, but it still burrowed under his skin, burning hotter than the rapidly healing wounds Hades left behind. Bits of the argument mingled with Lexi's words, her frustration, when she discovered Cassandra was nearby.

Icarus was wrong though. Actaeon didn't reach out to her, didn't bring her back to the shop, because he had some twisted desire to suffer on behalf of those who were suffering.

Cassandra had answers.

Other people have answers too. Athena promised me access to the library. I didn't even make it to the third person on my list.

Why was Cassandra at the top of it?

Because Actaeon owed her.

No. That wasn't an answer. Besides, Apollo said the same thing.

But Actaeon was responsible for Cassandra being where she was. He went after Zeus when she'd told him it would mean her death. He left her in the underworld—

And even if I were to blame for her reactions to that, Apollo was taking care of her. And I'm not responsible for her actions.

No, but if Actaeon drove her to them…

He didn't have answers, and the two halves of his brain arguing were giving him a headache.

Is Icarus right?

No.

He's not? Then why did I go after Cassandra?

Actaeon hated this. That part of him agreed with Icarus. And if Icarus was right, was Actaeon only pursing Lexi because she needed saving?

No.

How can I be so sure? Especially if Icarus was right.

Lexi'd had a tough life. She was exactly what Icarus said—a powerful immortal living outside the inner circle, and struggling through this world.

A knock interrupted his mental sparring match. These rooms of Apollo were essentially isolation chambers—cutting the person inside off from all sounds and smells of the rest of the hotel.

Apparently, they were warded to let knocks through, though.

So much for a peaceful rest. The interruption was welcome at this point. He crossed the room, unlocked the door, and summoned a half-smile when he saw Lexi.

He didn't flinch at the smell of sex that clung to her skin. He'd gotten used to it, since she and Cerberus had moved in. But this wasn't Cerberus' scent, and smelling Icarus on her sent twin pangs of jealousy racing through Actaeon's veins.

He took a step back, needing to keep his thoughts relatively clear, and gestured to one of the chairs in the room. "Have a seat."

"I'm only here to let you know we're almost ready. We'll explain everything you need to know when you join us." Her tone was cool, despite the flush of heat sending pink climbing up her neck and into her cheeks.

"Is that it?"

"What else do you want me to say?"

Actaeon wanted her to say why she'd fucked Icarus. He wanted to know where he and Lexi stood. He wanted her to tell him if she was still pissed off about Cassandra. "The only thing I need to hear is what's on your mind."

She shook her head. Her lips were drawn in a thin line. "You don't need that. You didn't listen last time and my opinion hasn't changed."

I'm sorry. The apology died in the back of his throat. If he said it, would she believe him?

"Nothing?" Sarcasm leaked into her question. "You don't have a witty retort for me? A smooth line to convince me I'm safe opening up to you? No snarky comeback about how I smell like sex?"

A wince slipped out without his permission.

Her smirk created tight lines around her mouth and eyes. "At least you're not trying to shame me for who I fuck."

"That's your business."

Lexi gave a bitter laugh. "So first of all, you're lying. And second? If you cared, *actually* gave a shit about us working out the way you claim—sharing a home and a life—you'd be willing to admit that who I sleep with isn't just my business. Does it matter to a random stranger on the street? No. Fuck them. Should it matter to another guy I'm involved with? I think so."

"That's not what I meant." He didn't like being on the defensive. Worse, he hated not having answers.

"Oh?" She raised her eyebrows. "Go ahead, then. Spin me a tale about what you *do* mean. Make it as good as the one about Cassandra. When you swore she'd be gone from our lives, and lied so well you even believed it yourself. Do you ever listen to the words you say?"

The instinct was to bite back. To tell her she was being selfish and unreasonable, and to point out she was too young to have any idea what she was talking about. He didn't feel that way, though. He understood why she was hurt.

Icarus' argument made sense.

"I'm sorry." The words tasted good. Right. "I see what a mistake it was to seek out Cassandra. Not only because of what happened with Hades, but more importantly, because it hurt you. Because I broke my promise. I'm sorry."

"That's nice." Her barking laugh wasn't the response he expected.

"You know I'm telling the truth."

Her shoulders slumped, and she leaned against the wall, arms crossed. "That's the problem with you. I can see *you* believe you're telling the truth. For all I know, tomorrow, or an hour from now, you'll figure out that you didn't mean it."

Her words dug deep, but after what he'd done, it was reasonable. "Where do we go from here?"

"I don't have that answer. There are sides to you that I adore. I want to discover more, but…" Lexi sighed. I'm not willing to put up with your volatile sense of saviordom. Why did you go after Cassandra?"

Actaeon frowned at the same word Icarus had used. "I convinced myself what happened to her was my fault." Saying it aloud was different than fighting over it in his head. Hearing the words, they sounded like a weak excuse.

"It wasn't. It isn't." Exhaustion mingled with Lexi's frustration. "She made her choices, the same way all of us do, and you're not responsible for that. A lot of people die and get dumped, and don't threaten the fabric of existence because of it."

Lexi was pretty wise for someone so young.

"I see that now," Actaeon admitted.

She shook her head. "There you go again—believing your own words. I want to do the same. I want to try again, but… wow, I can't believe I'm saying this… my heart isn't the only thing on the line when it comes to you. If you can't figure out what your problem is, people will die. Also, I won't let you string me along for decades while you make those discoveries."

"I'll ask again, where do you want to go from here?" Actaeon wasn't pushing the issue to be a pest, or because he felt he was owed an answer. This was a point to offer closure. The idea of losing Lexi squeezed the air from his lungs. "I want to explore our relationship right, but if you're not interested…"

"I don't know, and now's not the greatest time to stop and figure it out."

"I understand." He wished he didn't. It would be easier if he could just plow ahead and convince her to get over whatever this hesitation was. That wasn't the right answer, though.

"But I can't tell you *no*." She jammed her hands in her pockets. "I'm not willing to cut things short with you yet. After this is over, and Hades is dealt with, you're going to buy me dinner—someplace nicer than you ever took Cassandra—and we'll have an actual conversation. Not a *do we stay together for eternity* conversation. One of those things where we talk like two people who need to get to know each other."

He smiled. "I'd like that. Dinner it is."

She turned away and grabbed the doorknob. "Come find us in the living room when you're reading."

"One other thing." Actaeon had one answer. While he'd talked to her, it knocked itself loose.

Lexi didn't open the door, but she didn't face him either.

"Icarus has accused me on more than one occasion of needing some to die for in order to feel fulfilled."

Lexi snorted.

Actaeon didn't blame her, and he wasn't surprised she and Icarus were of the same mind on the matter. "He's right. I've looked for that for a long time."

"I see." The coolness was back in her voice.

"That's not you."

"Gee. Thanks."

"Because you're not helpless." Actaeon saw it clearly when he looked at her. "You're not lost or adrift or in need of saving. You're so strong. I don't know what's going on between us, but I promise you, I'm not sticking around because I need someone to die for." The words tasted real and sweet. "I'm here because I want to see what happens when we live."

She glanced over her shoulder, and a soft smile played on her face. "Same. We're in the living room." She left, closing the door behind her.

Creation, that felt good. Actaeon wasn't looking forward to the fight with Hades, but this gave him something new to anticipate after.

Icarus couldn't shake the silly grin that mirrored Lexi's. He'd finished the prison, riding the high of their shared moment.

There was only one step left. The one he'd rather put off for eternity. He sent her to fetch Actaeon while he prepped the bracelet.

When he finished, she still hadn't returned. He hoped Actaeon wasn't being an ass, whatever they were talking about.

Cerberus appeared in the middle of the living room.

Good timing. "How'd it go?" Icarus kept his question sympathetic.

"I'm sorry." Cerberus' frown deepened.

That didn't sound good. A chill raced down Icarus' spine. "For what?"

Cerberus strode toward him, closing the distance quickly and quietly. It reminded Icarus of a hunter stalking his prey. He couldn't shake the feeling he was about to be an entirely new kind of fucked.

Cerberus twisted his hand, caught Icarus' wrists in a single sweep, and pinned him to the wall. Icarus had more power than the hellhound, but it wasn't manifested in strength. His struggling only made his muscles ache.

A knife appeared in Cerberus' free hand, and he pressed the tip to Icarus' throat.

"You can't kill me with a regular blade." Icarus should be asking what this was about, but fear short-circuited his thoughts.

Cerberus pressed the tip harder, drawing blood.

Fuck, that hurt. Icarus bit the inside of his cheek, to keep from screaming at the burning agony that spread from his neck to his feet.

"I'm not stupid." Cerberus' voice was mechanical. It was too much like Cassandra's had been, but there was no trace of another aura mixed with his. "*This* knife will kill you."

Fuck, fuck, fuck, fuck, fuck.

Lexi didn't feel like she had a resolution when she left Actaeon's room, but the conversation sat better with her than any other they'd had recently. It was going to be quite a ride finding out what came next.

As she walked down the hall, she felt Cerberus return, but his thoughts were closed off.

Her stomach dropped into her shoes when she walked into the kitchen and found Cerberus with a blade to Icarus' throat.

"Stop." She forced every ounce of command into the word. This wasn't the time to worry about pushing him to do something he didn't like.

"No." Cerberus didn't twitch. His voice was cold.

Did he actually refuse her? "Why?" That wasn't what she should have asked.

"I have to do this."

"No. You don't." Icarus sounded surprisingly calm for someone who was on the verge of losing his ability to speak. "I'm an inventor. Frequently a shitty one. I'm not a threat to anyone."

None of this made sense. If commands didn't work, she could beg. "Please stop, Cerberus."

"What the fuck are you doing, asking?" Panic slipped into Icarus' voice. "He's your servant. Order him to stop."

Cerberus growled. "Don't talk to her like that."

"Why not? What is this? Are you upset that we had sex? What?" Icarus sounded like he was on the verge of babbling.

Overlapping thought and emotion, neither of them hers, assaulted Lexi. Icarus was right about one thing—she shouldn't have to ask. She hated pushing the bond with Cerberus. Commanding him to do something felt like a breach of trust, but so were his current actions. "*Stop*. I command it."

Cerberus' hand shook. "I can't. I'm—" He pressed the weapon in with more force.

Icarus screamed, and the agony rocked Lexi to the core.

"*You don't understand,*" Cerberus said in her head.

"*There's nothing to understand. This doesn't need to happen. I'll order, beg, plead—whatever it takes, to make you back away.*"

He shoved her out of his mind. "I'm sorry. I can't."

"So you're going to break the bond?" Lexi was about to be cruel, but this was hardly the time to consider feelings. Panic and betrayal were setting in. "This means your death, too. No one will take you if you sever another servant bond."

"I'm not interested in swearing loyalty to anyone but you," Cerberus said. "And I'm not severing the connection. I'll beg you not to as well, but I can't sto…" He violently shook his head and moved the knife to Icarus' gut so quickly, Lexi only saw a blur.

She threw a wall between him and Icarus, and the blade clinked against Plexiglas. She didn't know where the inspiration came from, but there was no time to think. She summoned the illusion of shackles and bodiless hands, to bind Cerberus' wrists behind his back.

The dagger clattered to the floor.

Icarus grabbed it and put several feet between them. "This is a siren blade."

Oh fuck. An irrational sob rose in Lexi's throat, and she swallowed it. Lorelei's vision rushed back, vivid and painful.

Cerberus struggled against his restraints. "These aren't real."

"They'll hold you." Lexi didn't know where she found the strength to keep her voice from quaking. "Tell me what's going on."

"I can't. This isn't a matter of *I don't want to. I'm incapable.*" The last bit bounced in her skull.

Lexi strode toward him, rested her hands on his face, and held his gaze. She couldn't ignore the treachery and didn't try to hide her reaction. "Show me," she commanded.

Images of him talking to Lorelei flashed in her mind, like a whispered dream. The conversation wasn't identical to the one Lexi saw in the prison, but it was close. This time, it was real, though. Lexi forced her way into the memory, digging further back. Cerberus was saying *goodbye* to his brother, and Lorelei visited him at the grave.

She said he wasn't allowed to tell Lexi about this. That he was bound by his promise of a favor, regardless of his master's demands. He'd made the promise to Lorelei first, and it overrode his bond with Lexi.

"I had to. I *have* to. I don't have a choice." Cerberus was muttering to himself.

It was true. Lexi wanted there to be more to this. A greater reason. Jealousy, or that Cerberus thought this was for the greater good. It hurt more that all it took for him to turn against her was someone calling in a favor.

He didn't have a choice. But she did. "If I can't order you to stop, I command you to not do it in my presence."

"I don't think that's going to work." Cerberus frowned.

But it would. Somehow she knew she'd found a loophole. It tore her apart to build all these confinements into their relationship. "If you find it's not working, I order you from my sight until I say you can return or until you can be in the same room as Icarus without killing him."

She pushed past her doubt and let the shackles fall away.

Cerberus' hand twitched, and Icarus backed up.

"Leave." Saying the single word devoured Lexi.

"I'll be in the other room. Send Actaeon when it's time to leave." Cerberus' hurt was the perfect companion to her tired, angry heart.

When he was gone, she sank to the floor. She was spending a lot of time down here. She was grateful Icarus didn't speak. Lexi had wanted to spend more time getting to know him. She didn't expect that to come at the cost of not being able to let him out of her sight.

CHAPTER TWENTY-SIX

Actaeon sat on the edge of the bed, collecting his thoughts. Physically, he'd recovered. It was amazing what a little soul-searching could do for the psyche.

He was still furious at Icarus, but his friend's point was sinking in. Actaeon wasn't going to admit that to anyone, though.

He flexed and stretched. Everything was functioning fine.

He should go find Lexi and Icarus.

He discovered them in the kitchen, both wearing scowls, and neither speaking. Icarus spun a metal bracelet on the counter like a top. It was identical to the one he'd given Cerberus in the abandoned building.

Lexi traced the pattern of the stone countertop.

"Did I miss something?" Actaeon asked. *Besides the sex?*

"Yes." Lexi cut off the word.

That was informative. "Did the pup ever come back?" He hoped she'd see the nickname as playful, and not an insult.

Icarus nodded behind Actaeon. "He's in one of the rooms. It was the best way to keep him from killing me."

"Why?" Jealousy wasn't Cerberus' thing.

Lexi sighed and scrubbed her face. "Because Lorelei called in her favor. She didn't like that I *stole her favorite toys*, and Hades gave me to her. In return she offered Cerberus up as an assassin."

Wow. "Wouldn't have guessed that in a million years."

"I should have," Lexi muttered.

And Actaeon should have left the door open a crack while he slept, so he wasn't playing catch-up. "What now?"

"We gamble on taking the time we need to talk through all the skeletons in our closets—as well as figuring out how to invalidate the favor—and hope Hades isn't as refreshed as you when we get there. Or we admit we're out of time, say *fuck it*, and go do this."

"Do *what* exactly?" Actaeon asked. "We need details beyond *trap Hades.*"

"Go get Cerberus, and we'll explain." Lexi sounded tired and looked worse.

And Actaeon had no idea how to help.

He located Cerberus in an upstairs room. The hellhound sat cross-legged, eyes closed, and breathing even as if he was meditating.

"I was sent to fetch you," Actaeon said.

"Probably smart."

"If we go in there, will you have to kill him?" Actaeon could stop Cerberus, if it came down to that. He'd rather not deal with the fallout—Lexi's reaction and the loss of someone he was learning to call *friend*—but he'd act if needed.

Cerberus shook his head. "I don't know. Now's as good a time as any, to see if Lexi's loophole works."

Fucking barter contracts.

He and Cerberus returned to the main room of the house. They stayed at the edge of the living room, with Lexi and Icarus on the far side.

Icarus held up the bracelet. "The plan is painfully simple, but that doesn't mean it's going to be easy. The two of you beat on Hades until he's weak. Preferably at least as worn down as he was on the street. Then Lexi puts this on." He handed her the jewelry.

"And then he's imprisoned." Lexi dropped the titanium circle into her pants pocket.

This was such a bad idea. Every point in the plan held an infinite number of opportunities for failure. "No one else can do this?" Actaeon knew the answer, but he needed to hear it one more time.

"Don't make us have this conversation again." Icarus sounded exhausted.

If Actaeon was the only one going into things well rested, that was bad.

"How do we get to the underworld?" Cerberus asked. "Call Apollo? Someone else?"

"Lexi will take us." Icarus nodded in her direction.

She would?

Her jaw dropped. "I will?"

Icarus turned to her and took her hands. "I give you my word that I'll explain when this is over. I'll answer every question you have. For now"—he tugged her with him as he crossed the room, and placed her and Actaeon between him and Cerberus—"join hands, boys and girl, and let's take a field trip."

"How?" Lexi asked.

Icarus screwed his face up. "You don't have any ruby slippers, but I say you Dorothy it."

"I don't get that reference."

Cerberus gave a strained laugh. "Assuming he's not talking about flying monkeys taking us, click your heels together three times and say, *there's no place like home.*"

"*But*"—Icarus' shout was jarring—"picture the underworld when you do it."

Lexi looked at everyone. When her gaze fell on Actaeon, he shrugged. "I'm just the muscle."

She smiled. "And I'm grateful for that." She closed her eyes, clicked her heels together, and moved her lips.

Actaeon's body fell away, and he tumbled into nothingness as the world vanished.

And then they were in front of Persephone's house. Though it had only been a few weeks, the yard was overgrown, and the paint was peeling from the wood.

It was a sad thing to see. Lexi's gasp said she felt the same.

"You are good, my child." Hades' voice came from behind.

They whirled, to find him standing next to Cassandra.

"You brought the inventor. *Lorelei.*" Hades roared, and it shook the world. "Your favor remains unfulfilled."

"She didn't account for every scenario." Defiance replaced the exhaustion that had been in Lexi's voice moments earlier. "If you want my opinion—and I figure you must, since you keep trying to talk to me—she's an arrogant bitch and not a great business partner."

Actaeon liked the venom in her words. Pissing off Hades, and probably Lorelei, didn't seem like the wisest decision, but it held a great deal of satisfaction.

"You're really bringing this fight to my doorstep?" Hades asked.

Actaeon had his bow drawn, and Cerberus was in hellhound form.

"Where I'm strongest?" Everything rattled with Hades' question.

Actaeon let an arrow fly. It disintegrated before it reached Hades.

Well, fuck.

"I'm not worried about it," Icarus said.

Actaeon was.

Hades grinned. "As those wacky kids used to say, *come at me.*"

That was so two-thousand-late. Actaeon fired a volley of shots, but none reached their target. He glared at Icarus. "This is a shitty plan."

Icarus tilted his head next to Lexi's and whispered something.

She gave him a puzzled look.

"Do you trust me?" Icarus asked.

"Yes."

Would Actaeon get the same immediate, certain response, if he asked her that question? Did he deserve it? It didn't matter right now.

"Do it," Icarus said.

Lexi's lips moved again, but whatever she muttered didn't reach Actaeon's ears.

He kept firing at Hades, and one shot connected with the god's shoulder. That was more like it. Actaeon smiled, and Cerberus charged in.

Actaeon and Cerberus continued the assault, but Hades didn't budge. The longer Actaeon fought, the more it drained him. Cerberus was slowing as well.

Hades wore a scowl, but he wasn't staggering or fumbling the way he had on earth.

This was a bad idea. Why did they bring this fight to him, again?

Actaeon reached inside and summoned a massive ball of energy. The arrow knocked Hades off balance, and Cerberus lunged, pushing the advantage. Actaeon swapped bow for dagger and buried the blade under Hades' ribs.

Hades elbowed Actaeon in the jaw. Even without a fireball, the pain seared through Actaeon's skull and sent him flying.

They weren't doing enough damage. Actaeon only had so many tricks up his sleeve, and they all involved *attack harder*.

Hades appeared in front of him, gripped his throat, and raised him off the ground.

Actaeon kicked, but something kept his feet from swinging. He clawed and gasped for air.

Cerberus sank the teeth of one jaw into Hades' arm, his second head went for his side, and the third clamped onto the god's thigh.

Hades dropped Actaeon but drew a fingernail across his skin in the process, leaving a wide gash in his neck.

Actaeon pressed against the wound, and blood poured over his hand, thick and slick. It had been a long time since someone did this kind of damage to him.

Hades flung Cerberus aside like a ragdoll, then kicked Actaeon in the gut.

Actaeon struggled to climb to his feet but dropped back to his knees. Pain rose inside, and darkness clawed at the edges of his vision.

CHAPTER TWENTY-SEVEN

Lexi felt every blow Actaeon and Cerberus took. She was doing what Icarus told her—hoping, wishing, and every positive *-ing* there was—that Actaeon and Cerberus would win.

"This is bullshit," she said to Icarus. "Thoughts and prayers never saved anyone."

"Because no one else is you. If you don't have faith in yourself, Zee, no one else will."

She liked the nickname coming from Icarus. His words didn't make a lot of practical sense, though. She couldn't just turn off her self-doubt.

He stepped behind her. It was an oddly intimate gesture, given the circumstances. "You said you trusted me." Desperation ran through his voice.

"I do."

"I know you can do this. If your confidence isn't enough, borrow mine."

"Do what?" She couldn't figure out what he wanted from her. But if he thought she could do whatever it was, she'd try. She shoved as much doubt as she could to the back of her mind and let the desire to help Actaeon and Cerberus flow through her.

Music drifted to her ears. It was beautiful and terrifying. *Lorelei.*

The illusion in front of her fell away. Actaeon and Cerberus weren't as injured as they believed. There were no cuts or bruises. Hades didn't stand so straight, and he favored his right shoulder.

Lexi was seeing through the siren's illusion. That shouldn't be possible, but she was doing it.

Where the fuck was the Lorelei? Lexi searched the area, trying to see past shadows. The atmosphere in this place crushed in around her. Hades' power churned in her gut and tried to fill her with panic.

She fought the sensations. If she squinted, she could see an outline a few feet back from Hades. It was Lorelei. The siren's eyes were closed, and her neck strained with her song.

Actaeon landed at Lexi's feet and didn't move for several seconds. He pushed to his knees, arms wobbling. Blood ran down his neck, but it was a siren illusion.

Lexi crouched next to him and touched his cheek. "It's not real." She kept her voice low, not wanting Hades to hear about her discovery.

"It hurts like fuck." Actaeon sounded exhausted. He found his footing and charged back into the fray.

Lexi needed to do something else. She'd injured Lorelei in the prison. Could she do the same here?

Icarus took her wrist. "It's worth a shot." He handed her the siren dagger Cerberus had brandished. .

How did he know what she was thinking?

Lexi made the dagger invisible. She didn't dare do the same to herself. Hades might not be paying much attention to her, but he'd notice if she blinked out of sight.

"Draw his attention away from me." She sent the mental request to Cerberus.

He wove around Hades' legs and darted away from Lexi. Actaeon followed his lead.

Lexi hoped Lorelei stayed distracted. She crept toward the siren, stepped behind her, and raised the dagger.

Memories spilled into her thoughts. The prison. Slicing Lorelei with an imaginary weapon. The blood that coated her hands.

Bile rose in Lexi's throat, and she hesitated. She hadn't killed the siren then. What made her think she could do it now?

I have to.

Could she take a life? Death wasn't Lexi's to deal.

"I shouldn't have asked that of you. Let it be my burden." Icarus stood next to her.

She hadn't said the words aloud, but she wasn't surprised he answered her. He took the knife and sliced Lorelei's throat in a single swipe.

The air shattered, shards of energy and illusion crashing down around them. It was similar to when Persephone died, and Hades was released.

Lorelei collapsed, and her illusion of injuries vanished.

Hades roared. "Irritating child."

Before he could turn, Actaeon and Cerberus were attacking again. They'd shaken off the non-existent pain.

The only person who remained unaffected was Cassandra. She stood in the same spot. Watching. Unmoving and unspeaking.

Actaeon stabbed Hades, and the god faltered.

Cassandra screamed, as though she was being dragged across hot coals.

Lexi felt compelled to help her. Was it guilt? *Fuck*, Lexi didn't need this. Cassandra-Hades' words from Icarus' shop echoed in her head. Could Lexi actually paint a demon trap on the ground, using a tangible illusion?

"It's worth a shot," Icarus said.

Lexi should be freaked out he was picking up on her thoughts. Instead, she was grateful. It felt as though half her inspiration came from him. "I don't know anything about a binding circle." She'd seen them, when Cerberus was trapped in one and then when Hades created one around Lexi. But observing and recreating were two different things.

"I think it's more about the intent than characters or language."

I think didn't reassure Lexi. The bracelet suddenly felt heavy in her pocket. She traced its outline while she pictured a circle.

Cassandra screamed a string of gibberish.

Actaeon and Cerberus fought Hades. He was taking damage now, but it wasn't enough.

Lexi couldn't focus enough to create an illusion, let alone a tangible one.

"Yes, you can. You don't have a choice." Icarus' voice was firm.

She clung to his faith in her and pictured a six-pointed start on the ground.

Hades glanced at his feet and laughed. "You're yanking my chain with this. You must be."

Make it real. The command shouted from Lexi's head at the same time Icarus spoke the words aloud.

Hades' glow vanished. *"What?"* His yell pushed the edges of Lexi's focus.

She poured more into the illusion. If he kept fighting her, she wouldn't be able to hold him. She reached for the bracelet.

Icarus covered her hand. "He's not weak enough yet."

Actaeon stabbed Hades again, and the god fell to his knees.

Lexi fingered the jewelry.

"Not yet." Icarus was insistent.

Cerberus tore a chunk from Hades' throat.

"Wait for it," Icarus said.

Lexi wanted to shout at him to shut the fuck up. She fumbled, and the bracelet fell to the ground. "Shit. Fuck. Damn it." She lunged to retrieve it and lost her focus.

Her circle vanished. Hades stood, his wounds healing almost as quickly as they'd been delivered.

Cassandra darted past Lexi and grabbed the jewelry, as Lexi reestablished the circle.

Icarus reached for Cassandra, but she snapped the bracelet on before he could get to her.

No. Nonononono.

Actaeon plunged his dagger into Hades' chest as Cerberus went for his throat again.

Cassandra screamed as though she was being torn to shreds, and vanished.

Hades exploded in a cloud of energy. The atmosphere wobbled against Lexi's skin, and a nauseating wave passed through her.

"Shit." Icarus grabbed her hand and yanked her toward the others.

Lexi needed answers. "What's going on?"

Everything around them exploded, the way it had in Lorelei's prison. Lexi and Icarus weren't in the underworld anymore. They stood on a sidewalk, in front of the house Lexi grew up in. Not the labyrinth version, but the real thing.

People milled about in other yards, and a little girl was watching Lexi. "Are you all right? Where did you come from?"

Lexi wanted to answer, but the voices were back, screaming in her head.

Where were Actaeon and Cerberus?

Aphrodite appeared on the sidewalk next to the girl. "Oh you sweet child." She looked at Lexi. "What have you done?"

And then Zeus arrived. His face was twisted with ugly anger.

"Honey, leave the gods alone." A woman's voice came from inside the house. She sounded terrified.

"You two, with me. Now." Zeus spoke through clenched teeth.

Aphrodite stepped between him and Lexi. "No."

Zeus growled. Lighting and thunder crackled through the sky. "This isn't up for debate."

"Then I'm coming with them." Aphrodite seemed unfazed.

"I don't care. Fine. Whatever. *Now.*"

Lexi's world changed again. She hadn't adjusted to the last one yet. Her limbs were heavy, and her brain couldn't keep up. The voices in her head screamed so loudly, it was difficult to hear the gods. So many voices. What did they want with her?

She fell to her knees and vomited.

Her world went black.

CHAPTER TWENTY-EIGHT

Icarus lifted Lexi from where she'd collapsed, and set her on Zeus' couch. If he wasn't so concerned, he'd be amused she threw up on Zeus' rug. But it had been a long time since he'd seen Zeus so furious, and the anger probably had little to do with a vomit-covered rug he could clean with the flick of his wrist.

Aphrodite handed Icarus a cool, damp washcloth she'd produced from thin air. He dabbed Lexi's forehead and wiped her face clean. He could go into her head and see if she was all right, but it felt like a violation. He felt bad about what he'd picked up on in the underworld without her permission. They'd need to figure out the link, but now wasn't the time. Especially with Zeus watching.

Did Zeus know about Lexi? Icarus had a feeling he didn't. Aphrodite did, though. She was the one who told Lexi's dad that Lexi wasn't a hero. Lexi was a goddess.

It was going to be a lot of fun explaining this to her. The only reason he didn't do it before the fight with Hades was because the information would be distracting.

Icarus wasn't looking forward to telling her he didn't know where Actaeon and Cerberus were.

Lexi groaned, and her eyelids fluttered. She wobbled as she sat, then turned a scowl on Zeus. "What?"

"That's my question. What the fuck did you do?" Zeus' voice shook the room.

It was nothing, compared to Hades' making the entirety of the underworld tremble with a single word.

Icarus rolled his eyes at the theatrics. Now that he thought about it, the whole *shout and make glass rattle* stopped being terrifying about two-thousand years ago.

Lexi didn't flinch. "You tell me. As in, actually tell me, instead of spinning a bullshit story about how Hades can't die. What *did* we do?"

"You idiotic child. You destroyed him."

It was true, then. They'd done it. The combination of Lexi cutting off his power just as he was bound, and Actaeon striking at the same moment. Icarus never would have imagined this as an outcome. Cassandra was probably gone too. Actaeon and Cerberus were all right though, weren't they?

"What happened to *Hades can't be killed*?" Icarus asked flippantly.

"Where are Actaeon and Cerberus?" Lexi stood. She wavered on her feet, and Icarus wrapped an arm around her waist.

Zeus' face was red. "Don't ignore me when I'm speaking to you."

"Shut up, old man," Aphrodite said.

Icarus swallowed a snort of laughter.

Zeus turned his fury on Aphrodite. "Hades wasn't just the god of death, he *was* the underworld. Locking him away meant the underworld stayed intact. Killing him destroyed it all. Tartarus, the Elysium Fields—it's all gone. The dead no longer have a home."

Creation. That was bad. "Why didn't you mention that sooner?" Icarus demanded.

Zeus glared at him. "I don't owe you anything. Or the girl. It was a simple request—build a new prison and trap Hades inside—and you fucked it up."

"Where are Cerberus and Actaeon?" Lexi stalked forward until her nose almost touched Zeus'.

Zeus looked like his fury might crack his face. The rage morphed into a sneer. "I don't know. They weren't with you, and I can't feel them. You tell me."

"I don't know either." Lexi frowned and stepped back. She looked at her hand, and then at Aphrodite. "Can I follow these?"

Aphrodite shook her head. "You can try, but I can't see where the threads lead. I don't feel Cerberus or Actaeon either."

"Do you care what you've done?" Zeus asked.

Lexi turned back to him. "I do. A lot more than you do, you fucking dickwaffle. If it mattered more, you would have told us up front." She studied him. "But you were stronger while he was here. If he was locked away, you'd rule it all, with him intact to keep the dead in their homes."

"How dare you—"

"Shut up." Lexi pressed her palm to her forehead. "My head is screaming, you're not helping, and I'm considering puking again."

Icarus loved this side of her. He'd never seen anyone dismiss Zeus this way. Not even Actaeon.

"You should be cowering," Zeus said.

"If you wanted to kill me, you would have. You want to shout and intimidate and bend me to your will, like you do with everyone." Lexi sounded bored.

"I'll deal with this on my own. Get out of my sight." Zeus waved his hand, and his office disappeared.

Icarus, Lexi, and Aphrodite were back in the goddess's temple.

Aphrodite brushed Lexi's cheek. "How are you?"

"I need to know where they are." Lexi frowned. "I'm sorry to be a broken record but… it's quiet in my head. It's not right. Where did they go?"

"I would tell you if I knew." Aphrodite was apologetic. She looked at Icarus. "Take care of each other."

Icarus nodded and took Lexi's hand. "We need to talk."

Lexi started to follow, then paused and looked at Aphrodite. "Answer something else for me."

"Of course, child." Aphrodite's voice was sugar.

"When I was a teenager, the night I lost my virginity to Conner, why did you take my memory and not his?"

Aphrodite's jaw worked up and down. "I don't... What?"

"If you were worried about the other gods knowing about me, why not take the memory from him? He was far more likely to tell."

Aphrodite's smile looked strained. "I guess I didn't think of it at the time."

Lexi clenched her jaw. *You're lying*, echoed in Icarus' head.

"Get some rest." Aphrodite vanished.

Lexi growled.

Icarus didn't blame her. "I don't have that answer, but I have others. Let's go home."

"I don't have a home." She looked lost.

The words broke his heart. "You do. Anywhere I live is your home. Cerberus and Actaeon feel the same."

"You can speak for them with that kind of certainty?"

"Yes. And they're out there. You'd feel it if they were dead, so they're somewhere."

She wasn't convinced. He could tell without looking at her. But when he started walking again, she fell into step beside him.

They rounded the corner to his street, and he faltered. Potholes filled road, and debris lay everywhere. Barriers and steel plates had been put in place, but they didn't hide the damage.

When they reached his shop, a new level of destruction greeted them. They'd left so quickly after the fight with Hades, he hadn't dealt with his broken windows.

Lexi's gasp mirrored the dull throb in his chest.

They stepped inside. Shelves were broken, and shattered electronics littered the ground. Graffiti decorated one wall. *Go home, Hades' whore.* The message dripped in bright red, and the thicker spots of paint were still damp.

There was a dark-haired Barbie nailed to the wall next to the message.

"I'm sorry." Lexi's voice was tiny.

Icarus clucked and shook his head. She was hurt more by the damage than he was. "It's not your fault. I didn't think..." This was his neighborhood. He'd taken care of these people for decades. This was their *thanks*.

"I know," she said softly. "But they were scared, and it's been a bad week for them."

"You're defending these people, and you don't even know them."

"Do I need to?"

"No." He smiled. "I love that it matters to you. They're as much my family as anyone, but they're no one to you. They've never treated you anything other than poorly, and you still want what's best for them."

"Until they prove they don't deserve it." Lexi's shoulders drooped. "I should have offered Cassandra the same courtesy. She sacrificed herself for us."

Icarus didn't know if saving them was the reason Cassandra had done it, but there was no point in unpacking something they'd never have an answer to. "Come on." He and Lexi picked their way through the carnage. "This is just the shop. Things, all of them replaceable. No one can get into the upstairs or the basement without my permission."

He led her downstairs. "Above us is for guests. I live downstairs."

He guided her along the edge of the workshop, toward his private space. The kitchenette was small—enough room for a microwave, a hotplate, and a small fridge. He didn't need much else.

They reached his room. Shelves of knickknacks lined the walls. These were the things that held sentimental value. Pieces he'd collected over the millennia. A handmade quilt—a gift from George—covered the bed.

He lay on the bed and tugged Lexi down next to him. Her arm rested against his. It was comfortable and right.

"Want to see a magic trick?" he asked. They needed something to lift the mood, and it was an easy gimmick, but he hoped it would make her smile.

"Almost always."

Icarus snapped his fingers, and the star-filled night replaced the ceiling.

"Is it real?" Awe filled Lexi's voice.

"It's what's above the building right now."

"I used to wonder why none of the gods ever did magic, if they could do so much."

"Zeus can summon lightning, and Apollo wields a bow made of sunlight," Icarus said.

"But that's not like magic; it's everyday life for them. They don't treat it like it's special."

He understood what she meant. "No, they don't."

She sat and pulled her knees to her chest. "So many are dead. People. Heroes. Apollo will never find what he wanted from Cassandra—forgiveness or something else. Cerberus can never make right with happened with Orthus…"

"And that's life."

"You sound so clinical." Lexi glanced over her shoulder.

"I hurt at the thought. Every time someone passes, when untapped potential is snuffed out, I grieve. If I could give each person a neat little bow on the end of their life, let them tie up all the loose ends and leave this world without regrets, I would. I don't have that power."

"I don't suppose anyone does."

He made himself comfortable next to her, and rubbed her back. "Maybe you'll be the one to figure out how."

"Do you think Actaeon and Cerberus left?" Lexi asked.

The rapid change in topics didn't faze him. It was as if he felt the gears change in her head. "Disagreements happen. But no. I don't think they chose to be away from you."

"Why not?"

"Because I wouldn't. I *won't*. Not willingly."

"But we're not... I don't..."

"It's not love?" Icarus supplied the words for her.

"Not right now."

He felt the same. There were things he adored about Lexi. And the sex was incredible. Inspirational even. "The potential is there, and I'm all about that. We aren't in love yet, but I worship you." He never thought he'd say something like that. She was a deity he could make that promise to, though.

She laughed nervously. "Worship. Really?" Her question was flat.

"You don't remember what Aphrodite said to your dad the night you left your hometown." Now that he had his chance to tell her, he was hesitating. It was going to be a big burden, but she could bear the weight.

"It's not that I forgot. I couldn't hear."

"You did hear, because I did when I was watching from inside your head."

She faced him. "Are you going to tell me?"

"There's a reason you've blocked it out, even after living it thousands of times in a memory. Once I tell you, you won't be able to unhear it."

"Tell me. No. Wait." She chewed her bottom lip. "Considering some of Aphrodite's secrets… It's not that there's another guy out there somewhere, who I'm fated to love, is it?"

Icarus shook his head.

Lexi took a deep breath. "Okay. Tell me."

"Persephone wasn't born mortal. Only she and Aphrodite ever knew. She was a goddess before she married Hades."

"So…" She was hesitant to put the pieces together. "I'm not a hero."

"No. You're a goddess."

She laughed, then her expression went blank, and then she laughed again. "You're serious."

"Completely and totally. It's why you were able to make the contract with Cerberus. I don't know if it's got anything to do with what's happening between you and me, but it's also the reason you could take us to the underworld. Why your blessing helped them fight. I suspect there's a lot more that will manifest once you start pushing yourself."

She flopped onto her back and pointed at the ceiling. "Teach me how to do that?"

"I can try." He felt the excitement rushing through her. It matched his own, mingled with it, and amplified it. "You realize I'm going to poke and prod you to find out how powerful you are."

She smirked. "Is that a euphemism for sex?"

"It could be, depending on the mood." He dipped his head for a kiss and swallowed her giggle.

Energy sparked between them, but it wasn't the alluring electricity he'd felt in the past. He jerked back with a gasp, as the heat singed his mouth. "What the fuck?"

"I don't feel good." Lexi's voice was strained.

The lights flickered. A rush of ethereal energy raced past and through Icarus, burning his skin and soul.

It flooded into Lexi, who arched her back. Her mouth opened in silent scream.

And then she collapsed back on the bed, eyes closed and chest heaving.

"Zee?" Icarus took her hand and rubbed his thumb over her knuckles.

An unfamiliar fear grew inside, stronger than when they'd fought Hades. "Lexi?"

Her breathing slowed, and she didn't move.

This wasn't right. Something ethereal was inside her. Icarus forced himself to relax and slide into a meditative state. He nudged the edges of her mind.

Another spark jolted him, kicking him out. His eyes flew open.

This was so bad. "*Alexandra*. Lexi? Zee? Talk to me. Please?

THE END